Shirley Rousseau Murphy

A JOE GREY MYSTERY

This is a work of fiction. Names, characters, places, and incidents are products of the author's imagination or are used fictitiously and are not to be construed as real. Any resemblance to actual events, locales, organizations, or persons, living or dead, is entirely coincidental.

AVON BOOKS
An Imprint of HarperCollins*Publishers*
10 East 53rd Street
New York, New York 10022-5299

ISBN: 0-06-105989-7
www.avonbooks.com

First Avon Books paperback printing: November 2001
First HarperCollins hardcover printing: January 2001

Printed in the U.S.A.

10 9 8 7 6 5 4 3

Acclaim for
Cat Spitting Mad

"The pace never falters . . . Will have fans wanting to down the sometimes scary, madcap tale in one gulp."
Booklist

and the Joe Grey Series

"Excellent reading, whether you believe or not. Not to be missed!"
Armchair Detective

"Joe Grey and his ladyfriend Dulcie aren't just your ordinary feline detectives. Murphy's raised the stakes of the feline sleuth genre."
Kirkus Reviews

"Cat–chy . . . fast-paced."
Publishers Weekly

"Delightful."
Library Journal

"Murphy's love for animals, and her intimate knowledge of their unique qualities and personality quirks, shines clearly throughout."
The Library Cat Newsletter

"Shirley Rousseau Murphy demonstrates that she has the feline touch."
Bookbrowser.com

"If a cat is part of your life, but you haven't discovered Joe Grey and Dulcie yet, it's time you did."
Monterey Herald

Books by
Shirley Rousseau Murphy

CAT IN THE DARK
CAT TO THE DOGS
CAT ON THE EDGE
CAT RAISE THE DEAD
CAT UNDER FIRE
CAT SPITTING MAD
CAT LAUGHING LAST

And in Hardcover

CAT SEEING DOUBLE

For the cats who know more than we dream.
And for every human who knows that some cats live a secret life, but who can never catch them at it.

For Pat. For E.L.T., Lucy, and Toby.

With special thanks to
Terry Palmisano, senior wildlife biologist,
California Department of Fish and Game,
for answering all my questions with patience and good humor.
Any departure from fact is mine alone.

The sleek, supple . . . cat lowered itself slightly, cocked the short, rounded ears on its smallish, intelligent-looking face, and with a flowing ripple seemed to almost float up into the tree. Fifteen vertical feet up it landed with a fluid grace. . . .

The puma . . . reaching over nine thousand miles, from the tip of South America into isolated pockets of southern Alaska . . . is an intelligent, highly adaptable predator that, along with the wolves and the bears, adds an excitement to the U.S. wildlands that simply would not be there in their absence.

—Tom Brakefield,
Kingdom of Might: The World's Big Cats

CAT
SPITTING
MAD

1

It was the tortoiseshell kit who found the bodies, blundering onto the murder scene as she barged into every disaster, all four paws reaching for trouble. She was prowling high up the hills in the pine forest when she heard the screams and came running, frightened and curious—and was nearly trampled by the killer's horse as the rider raced away. Churning hooves sent rocks flying. The kit ran from him, tumbling and dodging.

But when the rider had vanished into the gray foggy woods, the curious kit returned to the path, grimacing at the smell of blood.

Two women lay sprawled across the bridle trail. Both were blond, both wore pants and boots. Neither moved. Their throats had been slashed; their blood was soaking into the earth. Backing away, the kit looked and looked, her terror cold and complete, her heart pounding.

She spun and ran again, a small black-and-brown streak bursting away alone through the darkening evening, scared nearly out of her fur.

This was late Saturday afternoon. The kit had vanished from Dulcie's house on the previous Wednesday, her fluffy tortoiseshell pantaloons waggling as she slid under the plastic flap of Dulcie's cat door and trotted away through the garden beneath a light rain, escaping for what the two older cats thought would be a little ramble of a few hours before supper. Dulcie and Joe, curled up by the fire, hadn't bothered to follow her—they were tired of chasing after the kit.

"She'll have to take care of herself," Dulcie said, rolling over to gaze into the fire. But as the sky darkened not only with evening but with rain, Dulcie glanced worriedly toward the kitchen and her cat door.

Wilma, Dulcie's human housemate, passing through the room, looked down at the cats, frowning, her silver hair bright in the lamplight. "She'll be all right. It isn't raining hard."

"Not yet, it isn't," Dulcie said dourly. "It's going to pour. I can smell it." A human could never sort out such subtleties as a change in the scent of the rain. She loved Wilma, but one had to make allowances.

"She won't go up into the hills tonight," Wilma said. "Not with a roast in the oven. Not that little glutton."

"Growing kitten," Joe Grey said, rolling onto his back. "Torn between insatiable wanderlust and insatiable appetite." But he, too, glanced toward the cat door.

In the firelight, Joe's sleek gray coat gleamed like polished pewter. His white nose and chest and paws shone brighter than the porcelain coffee cup Wilma was carrying to the kitchen. His yellow eyes remained fixed on the cat door.

Wilma sat down on the couch beside them, stroking Dulcie. "You two never want to admit that you worry about her. I could go look for her—circle a few blocks before dinner."

Dulcie shrugged. "You want to crawl under bushes and run the rooftops?"

"Not really." Wilma tucked a strand of her long white hair into her coral barrette. "She'll be back any minute," she said doubtfully.

"Too bad if she misses supper," Dulcie said crossly. "The roast lamb smells lovely."

Wilma stroked Dulcie's tabby ears, the two exchanging a look of perfect understanding.

Ever since Joe and Dulcie discovered they could speak the human language, read the morning paper, and converse with their respective housemates, Dulcie and Wilma had had a far easier relationship than did Joe Grey and his bachelor human. Joe and Clyde were always at odds. Two stubborn males in one household. All that testosterone, Dulcie thought, translated into hardheaded opinions and hot tempers.

The advent of the two cats' sudden metamorphosis from ordinary cats (well, almost—they had after all always been unusually good-looking and bright, she thought smugly) into speaking, sentient felines had disrupted all their lives, cats and humans. Joe's relationship with Clyde, which had already been filled with good-humored conflict, had become maddening and stressful for Clyde. Their arguments were so fierce they made her laugh—a rolling-over, helpless cat laugh. Were all bachelors so stubborn?

And speak of the devil, here came Clyde barging in

through the back door dripping wet, no umbrella, wiping his feet on the throw rug, then pulling off his shoes. His dark, cropped hair was dripping, his windbreaker soaking. Dropping his jacket in the laundry, he came on through to the fire, turning to warm his backside. He had a hole in his left sock. Violent red socks, Dulcie saw, smiling. Clyde was never one for subtleties. As Wilma went to get him a drink, Clyde sprawled in the easy chair, scowling.

"What's with you?" Joe gave him a penetrating, yellow-eyed gaze. "You look like you could chew fenders."

Clyde snorted. "The rumormongers. Having a field day."

"About Max Harper?"

Clyde nodded. The gossip about his good friend, Molena Point's chief of police, had left Clyde decidedly bad-tempered. The talk, in fact seemed to affect Clyde more than it did Harper. To imply, as some villagers were doing, that Harper was having an affair with one of the three women he rode with—or maybe with all three—was beyond ridiculous. Twenty-two-year-old Ruthie Marner was a looker, all right, as was Ruthie's mother. And Crystal Ryder was not only a looker but definitely on the make.

But Harper rode with them for reasons that had nothing to do with lust or romance. The cats couldn't remember the villagers—most of whom loved and respected Harper—ever before spreading or even tolerating such gossip.

Clyde accepted his glass from Wilma, swallowing

half the whiskey-and-water in an angry gulp. "A bunch of damned troublemakers."

"Agreed," Wilma said, sitting down on the end of the velvet couch nearest the fire. "But the gossip has to die. Nothing to keep it going."

Clyde glanced around the room. "Where's the kit?"

"Out," Dulcie said, worrying.

"That little stray's twenty times worse than you two."

"She's not a stray anymore," Dulcie said. "She's just young."

"And wild," Clyde said.

Dulcie leaped off the couch to roam the house, staring up at the dark windows. Rain pounded against the glass. The kit was off on another scatterbrained adventure, was likely up in the hills despite the fact that now, more than ever before, the hills were not safe for the little tortoiseshell.

Returning unhappily to the living room, she got no sympathy. "Cool it," Clyde said. "That kit's been on her own nearly since she was weaned. She'll take care of herself. If Wilma and I fussed about you and Joe every time *you* went off . . ."

"You do fuss every time we go off," Dulcie snapped, her green eyes filled with distress. "You fuss all the time. You and Wilma both. Particularly now, since . . ."

"Since the cougar," Clyde said.

"Since the cougar," Dulcie muttered.

Wilma grabbed her raincoat from the hall closet. "Dinner won't be ready for a while. I'll just take a look."

But as she knelt to pull on rubber boots, Dulcie reared up to pat her cheek. "In the dark and rain, you won't find her." And she headed for her cat door, pushing out into the wet, cold night—and Joe Grey was out the plastic door behind her.

He stood a moment on the covered back porch, his sleek gray coat blending with the night, his white paws and the white strip down his face bright, his yellow eyes gleaming. Then down the steps, the rain so heavy he could see little more than the dark mass of Dulcie just ahead, and an occasional oak tree or smeared cottage light. Already his ears and back were soaked. His empty stomach rumbled. The scent of roast lamb followed the cats through the rain like a long arm reaching out from the house, seeking to pull them back inside.

Along the village streets, the cottages and shops were disembodied pools of light. They hurried uphill, their ears flat, their tails low, straight for the wild land where the cottages and shops ended, where the night was black indeed. Sloughing up through tall, wet grass, along the trail they and the kit usually followed, they could catch no scent of her, could smell only rain. They moved warily, watching, listening.

It was hard to imagine that a mountain lion roamed their hills, that a cougar would abandon the wild, rugged mountains of the coastal range to venture anywhere near the village, but this young male cougar had been prowling close, around the outlying houses. Nor was this the first big cat to be so bold. Wilma had, on slow days as reference librarian, gone through back issues of the Molena Point *Gazette*, finding several such cases, one where a cougar came directly into the village at four in the morning, leaving a lasting impression with the officer on foot patrol. Wilma worried about the cats, and cautioned them, but she couldn't lock them up, not Joe Grey and Dulcie, nor the wild-spirited kit.

"Those big cats see every flick of movement," Dulcie said, pushing on through the wet grass.

"That kit's as dark as a piece of night, that mottled black and brown coat vanishes in the shadows. Anyway she'd hardly be worth the trouble, to a cougar—not even a mouthful."

Dulcie hissed at him and raced away through the rain.

The cougar had been on the Molena Point hills since Thanksgiving, prowling among the scattered small ranches, a big male with pawprints the size of Joe's head. He'd been spotted on Christmas Day, high up at the edge of the forest. Since Christmas two village dogs had disappeared, and four cats that Joe and Dulcie knew of; and huge pawprints had been found in village gardens.

Mountain lion. Cougar. Puma. Painter. The beast had half a dozen names. Late at night in the library, Dulcie had learned about him on the computer, indulging in a little clandestine research after the doors were locked and she had the reference room to herself.

She was, after all, the library cat. She might as well make use of her domain. Wilma had taught her the rudiments of the computer, and her paws were quick and clever. And of course no one among the staff would dream that, beyond her daytime PR activities of purring and head rubbing for the pleasure of the patrons, their little library cat followed her own agenda.

But what Dulcie had read about cougars hadn't thrilled her.

California had always had mountain lions. They'd been hunted nearly to extinction, then put on the protected list. Now, as their numbers increased, their range was growing smaller—more houses being built, more people moving into their territory. It took a lot of land to support a 120-pound carnivore.

The residents of Molena Point expected an occasional coyote to venture down from the coastal range; Joe and Dulcie were ever on the alert for the beast called God's dog. And there were sometimes bobcats and always bands of big, vicious racoons hunting in packs. But a mountain lion was quite another matter. When the two cats had first found the cougar's prints high up among the hills, a thrill of terror and of awe had filled them.

This was the wild king roaming their hunting grounds. His magnificent presence made them prowl belly to the earth, ears and tail lowered, their senses all at alarm, their little cat egos painfully chastened.

But it had been a strange year all around. Not only the appearance of the cougar, but the odd weather. Usually, fall in Molena Point was sun-drenched, the cerulean sky graced by puffy clouds, the night sky clear and starry or scarved by fog creeping in off the sea to burn away again in early dawn. But this fall had been wet and cold, a cruel wind knifing off the Pacific beneath thick gray clouds, pushing before it sheets of icy rain. Then people's pets began disappearing, and lion tracks appeared in the gardens.

A horrified householder had called police to report that the lion had entered his carport and had, in trying to corner his cat, slashed the tires of his black Lincoln Town Car, beneath which the cat had taken refuge: four flat tires, two badly scratched bumpers, a ruined paint job, lots of blood, and one dead Siamese.

And now the kit was headed alone into the black hills. And as the two cats moved higher, searching, they had only the brush of their whiskers against sodden grass and wet stone to lead them, and their own voices calling the kit, muffled in the downpour.

The kit had been staying in Dulcie and Wilma's house since her adopted human family, elderly newlyweds Pedric and Lucinda Greenlaw, left Molena Point for a jaunt in Pedric's travel trailer. The kit had refused to accompany the pair again. She loved Pedric and Lucinda and was thrilled to have a home with them, after being on her own tagging after a clowder of vagrant cats that didn't want her. But she couldn't bear any more travel. The old couple's drive up the coast to Half Moon Bay had made her painfully carsick, and on their weekend to Sacramento she threw up all the way.

The kit was special to Lucinda and Pedric, more special than any ordinary cat. Steeped so deeply in Irish folklore and Celtic history, they had quickly guessed her carefully guarded secrets, and they treasured her.

Brought to Wilma's house, the small furry houseguest had chosen for her daytime naps a hand-knitted sweater atop Wilma's cherry desk, beside the front window where she could watch the village street beyond the twisted oaks of Wilma's garden. The kit loved Wilma; she loved to pat her paw down Wilma's long hair and remove the clip that held her ponytail in place, to race away with it so the thin older woman would laughingly give chase. At Wilma's house, the kit dined on steak and chicken and on a lovely pumpkin custard that Wilma made fresh each day. Wilma said pumpkin was good for hairballs. The kit had nosed into every cupboard and drawer, investigated beneath every chair and chest and beneath the clawed bathtub, and then, having ransacked the house and found nothing more to discover, she had turned once more to the wider world beyond the cottage garden. The kit had grown up wild—who could stop her now?

Around midnight, on that Wednesday, the rain ceased. Joe and Dulcie found a nearly dry niche among some boulders, and napped lightly. It was perhaps an hour later that they heard a scream, a chilling cry that brought them straight up out of sleep, icing their little cat souls.

A woman's scream?

Or the cougar?

The two sounded very alike.

Another scream broke the night, from farther down the hills. One cry from high to the north, the other from the south, bloodcurdling wails answering each other.

"Bobcats," Joe Grey said.

"Are you sure?"

"Bobcats."

She looked at him doubtfully. The screams came again, closer this time, answering each other. Dulcie pushed close to Joe, and they spun away into the forest and up a tall pine among branches too thin to hold a larger predator.

There they waited until dawn, soaking wet and hungry. They did not hear the cries again, but Dulcie, shivering and miserable, spent the night agonizing over the little tattercoat, the curious little scamp whose impetuous headlong rushes led her into everything dangerous. By dawn, Dulcie was frazzled with worry.

The rainclouds were gone; a silver smear of light gleamed behind the eastern hills as the hidden sun began to creep up. The cats heard no sound beneath the dim, pearly sky, only the drip, dripping from the pine boughs. Backing down the forty-foot pine, the two cats went to hunt.

A wood rat and a pair of fat field mice filled them nicely, the warm meal lifting their spirits. With new strength and hope, they hurried north toward the old Pamillon estate, where the kit liked to ramble.

Entering among the crumbled walls and fallen, rotting trees and dark cellars, they prowled the portion of the mansion that still stood upright, but they found no sign of the kit.

The Pamillon estate had been, in the 1930s, an elegant Mediterranean mansion standing on twenty acres high above Molena Point, surrounded by fruit trees, grape arbors, and a fine stable. Now most of the buildings were rubble. Gigantic old oak trees crowded the fallen walls, their roots creeping into the exposed cellars. The flower gardens were gone to broom bushes and pampas grass and weeds, tangled between fallen timbers.

And the estate was just as enmeshed in tangles of a legal nature, in family battles so complicated that it had never been sold.

Some people said the last great-great-grandchildren were hanging on as the land increased in value. Some said the maze of gifts and trusts, of sales and trades among family members was so convoluted that no one could figure out clear title to the valuable acreage.

The kit had discovered the mansion weeks earlier. Newly come to that part of the hills, she had been as thrilled by the Pamillon estate as Magellan must have been setting anchor on the shore of the new land, as new wonders and new dangers shimmered before her.

Joe and Dulcie searched the hills for three days, taking occasional shelter in a tiny cave or high in the branches of an oak or pine, where they could leap from tree to tree if something larger wanted them for supper. They had never before given such serious thought to being eaten. Among the dense pine foliage they blended well enough, but on the hills, on the rain-matted grass, they were moving targets. And all the while they searched for the kit, running hungry and lean, the village was there far below them, snug and warm and beckoning, filled with the delicacies provided not only at home but in any number of outdoor restaurants.

It was late Thursday afternoon, as the two cats pushed on into new canyons and among ragged ridges, that they saw Clyde's yellow antique roadster climbing the winding roads, going slowly, the top down, Clyde peering up the hills, looking for them. Dutifully Joe raced down to where the road ended, causing Clyde to slam on the brakes.

Leaping onto the warm hood, he scowled through the windshield at Clyde. "The kit come home?" A delicious smell filled the car.

"Not a sign. I could help you look."

Joe lifted a paw. "We'll find her."

"I brought you some supper." Clyde handed over a small bag that smelled unmistakably of Jolly's fried chicken.

"Very nice. Where's the coleslaw and fries?"

"Ingrate."

Taking the white sack in his teeth, Joe had leaped away to join Dulcie. He hadn't told Clyde how despondent he and Dulcie were growing. And there was really nothing Clyde could do to help.

By Saturday evening the sky was heavy again, and the wind chill. If the kit was already home, slurping up supper and dozing warm and dry before the fire, Clyde would have come back; they'd see his car winding up the hills or hear the horn honking. One more day, they thought, and they'd give up and go home. And on sodden paws they moved higher into the lonely pine woods. They were well up the forested ridges, far beyond their usual hunting grounds, and the afternoon was graying into evening when they heard horses far below, maybe a mile to the north, and the faint voices of women.

Five minutes later, they heard screams. Terrified, angry, blood-chilling.

Joe was rigid, listening, his yellow eyes slitted and intent. He turned to look at Dulcie. "Human screams."

But the screams had stopped, and faintly they heard horses bolting away crashing into branches and sliding on the rocks.

Hurrying down out of the mountain, and racing north, it was maybe half an hour later when on the rising wind they caught a whiff of blood.

"Maybe the cougar made a kill," Dulcie whispered, "and frightened the horses, and the women screamed."

"If the cougar made a kill, we'd hear him crunching bone. It's too quiet." And Joe shouldered her aside.

But she slipped down the hill beside him, silent in the deepening evening, ready to run. They were just above a narrow bridle trail when a slithery sound stopped them, a swift, slurring rush behind them that made them dive for cover.

Crouched beneath a stone overhang, they were poised to run again, to make for the nearest tree.

A rustle among the dry bracken. They imagined the cougar slipping through the dead ferns and pines as intently as they would stalk a mouse—and something exploded out of the woods straight at them, bawling and mewling.

The kit thudded into Dulcie so hard that Dulcie sprawled. She pressed against Dulcie, meowing loud enough to alert every predator for twenty miles—"*Yow! Yow! Yow!*"—her ears flat, her tail down. She couldn't stop shivering.

Dulcie licked her face. "What is it? What happened

to you? Shh! Be still!" Staring into the woods, she tried to see what had chased the kit. Above them, Joe moved up into the forest, stalking stiff-legged, every hair on end.

"No! Down there," the kit said. "We have to go down there. It was terrible. I heard them scream and I smelled the blood and . . ."

Dulcie nudged her. "Slow down, Kit. Tell it slowly."

The kit couldn't be still. "The horses bolted nearly on top of me. I ran. I don't want to go back, but . . ."

"Start at the beginning," Dulcie said softly.

"I went back afterward, after that man was gone. I went back there just now and they're dead." The kit stared round-eyed at Dulcie. "Two women, one young and pretty. So much blood. They're all over blood."

"Show us," Joe said, slipping down beside them.

"I don't want . . ."

"Show us, Kit," Joe Grey said, towering over her.

The kit dropped her head obediently, this kit who was never obedient, and padded slowly down the hills where the black pines reached in a long and darkly forested peninsula. Slipping along through the edge of the forest, the two cats stayed close beside her. Down three steep, slick shelves of stone, dropping down among the dry ferns and loose shale, then onto the bridle trail and that was walled, all along, by the forest. The night was filled with the smell of blood and with the stink of death, mixed with the scent of the kit's fear.

2

The night was alive with the tiny noises of other creatures, with little rustlings and scurryings and alarm-cries where small nocturnal browsers fed on the forest's vegetation, prey to nocturnal hunters and to each other. The kit led Joe and Dulcie down through the forest over the jagged ridges toward the sharp, metallic smell of blood—but then the kit drew back.

Warily, the two older cats approached the bridle trail and the two dark heaps that lay there. The smell of death forced their lips in a deep flehmen; that stink would soon bring predators crouching unseen in the night.

But no four-legged predator had done this terrible deed.

Where was the person who had stabbed and torn his fellow humans? Was he hidden in the forest, watching? Might he be listening, so that if they spoke, he would know their secret?

Tasting the damp wind, they sniffed and tested before they approached the two dead humans. When at last they slipped closer, they were skittish, ready to bolt away.

They looked and looked at the two women, at their poor, torn throats, at their pooled blood drying on their clothes and seeping into the earth.

The cats knew them.

"Ruthie Marner," Dulcie whispered. The younger woman was so white, and her long blond hair caked with blood. Dulcie crouched, touching her nose to Ruthie's icy arm, and drew back shivering. Blood covered the woman's torn white blouse and blue sweater. She had a deep chest wound, as well as the wide slash across her throat. So much clotted blood that it was hard to be sure how the wounds might have been made.

Helen Marner's wounds were much the same. Her blond hair, styled in a short bob, was matted with dirt where she had fallen. She was well dressed, much like her daughter, in tan tights, paddock boots, a tweed jacket over a white turtleneck shirt, her clothes stained dark with blood. A hard hat lay upside down against a pine tree like a sacrificial bowl.

No horse was in sight. The horses would have left the fallen riders, would have bolted in panic, the moment they could break free.

Dulcie backed away, her tail and ears down. She'd seen murders before, but the deaths of these two handsome women made her tremble as if her nerves were cross-wired.

The cats could see no weapon, no glint of metal near the bodies. They did not want to pad across the footprints and hoofprints, to destroy the tenuous map of what had taken place here.

But something more terrible, even, than the sight of the double murder held both cats staring.

A jacket lay on the ground beside the bodies, trampled by the horses' hooves, a creamy fleece jacket with a strand of red hair caught in the hood, a jacket the cats knew well. They sniffed at it to make sure.

"Dillon." Dulcie's paws had begun to sweat. "Dillon Thurwell's jacket."

Dillon always wore that jacket when she rode, and she'd been riding every day with the Marners. Dulcie looked helplessly at Joe. "Where is she? Where is Dillon?"

Joe looked back at her, his yellow eyes shocked and bleak.

"And Harper," he said. "Where's Max Harper? It's Saturday, Harper always rides with them on Saturday." He backed away from the bodies, his angled gray-and-white face drawn into puzzled lines.

Police Captain Harper had taught Dillon to ride. These last two months, the foursome had been seen often riding together, as Dillon and Ruthie trained for some kind of marathon.

Leaping up the stone ledge, Dulcie stood tall on her hind paws, staring around her into the night, looking for another rider.

Nothing stirred. There was no smallest whisper of sound—every insect and toad had gone silent. High above her in the forest she could see the kit, peering out from among the rocks.

Trotting up to join her, Dulcie began to quarter the

woods, as Joe searched below, both cats scenting for any trace of Dillon.

Circling ever wider, rearing up to sniff along a clump of young pines, Dulcie caught a hint of the child, well to the north of the bodies. "Here. She was here—she rode here. I can smell her, and smell a horse."

But Joe was assessing the hoofprints that raced away from the scene tearing up the trail.

"Four horses." He looked up solemnly at Dulcie. "One with small, narrow hooves. That would be Ruthie's mustang. And a big horse, heavy—wide hooves. The other two sets seem ordinary."

Dulcie looked at Joe. "The big horse—big hooves, so deep in the earth. Like Max Harper's gelding."

"But Harper couldn't have been with them. They wouldn't have been harmed if Harper was with them." Joe's yellow eyes blazed, the muscles across his gray shoulders were drawn tight. "Four horses. The Marners. Dillon. And the killer. Not Max Harper."

The prints of the big horse showed a scar running diagonally across the right front shoe, as if the metal had been cut by a hard strike, maybe from a stone.

Warily the kit came down out of the rocks to press, shivering, between Joe and Dulcie. She was usually such a bold, nervy little morsel. Now her eyes were wide and solemn.

Helen and Ruthie Marner had lived in Molena Point for perhaps a year. Joe's housemate, Clyde, had replaced the brake linings on Mrs. Marner's vintage model Cadillac. Clyde ran the most exclusive automotive shop in Molena Point, and he was as skilled and caring with the villagers' imported and antique cars as a master jeweler with his clients' diamonds.

Clyde hadn't liked Helen Marner much; he called her stuck-up. It had amused him that Max Harper encouraged Helen's friendship, but they all knew why. Harper had refused to ride with Dillon alone and put himself in a position that might attract slander.

Harper had gotten to know Dillon during a grisly murder investigation at Casa Capri, an upscale retirement home. Joe and Dulcie had begun their own investigation before anyone else suspected foul play. But Dillon had come into the act soon after—before anyone had a reason to call the police. She, too, had sensed something wrong. And her stubborn redhead's temperament had kept her prying, despite what any grown-up said. Of course she'd been right, just as Joe and Dulcie had been, all along.

Max Harper had been very impressed with Dillon—had, during the surprising investigation, grown to respect and admire the child.

When Dillon told Harper that she longed to learn to ride, the captain had volunteered some lessons, if Dillon's parents agreed and providing someone else came along. An ever resourceful child, Dillon had recruited the Marners, as well as Clyde Damen's girlfriend, Charlie, as an occasional backup.

"And now they're dead," Joe said, looking down the night-dark hills, his ears and whiskers back, his yellow eyes blazing.

"Maybe," Dulcie said softly, "maybe Dillon got away."

"On that little, aged mare? Not hardly. Escape a

killer on a big, heavy horse, a rider bent on stopping her?" He turned to look at Dulcie. "If Dillon saw him murder Helen and Ruthie, he'd have to silence her."

She sighed and turned away.

He crowded close to her and licked her face and ear. "Maybe she did escape, Dulcie. She's a spunky, clever kid."

That was what he liked about Dillon. Thinking of Dillon hurt made him sick clear down to his tomcat belly.

The cats could see no bike tracks along the trail, and the path was too narrow for a car. Staying on the bracken, studying the dirt and the surround, they could find no boot or shoe prints leading in to indicate someone had followed the riders on foot. Joe imagined a stranger on horseback pulling Helen Marner from her horse, grabbing Ruthie's horse, and pulling her off, knifing them as Dillon escaped, whipping Redwing to a dead run.

Why? Why had someone done this? What had they gained?

"Robbery?" he said softly. "How much money would people carry, out for a Saturday ride? And their horses weren't valuable, just common saddle horses." He knew that from hearing Harper and Clyde talking.

He wanted to shout Dillon's name, bawl her name into the night until the child came running out of the bushes, safe.

He tried again to catch the smell of the killer but could detect nothing beyond the stink of human death, and the sweeter perfumes of horse and of the pine woods.

To look upon a human person brutally separated from life by another human never ceased to sicken the tomcat. This kind of death had no relationship to his own killing of a rabbit or squirrel for his supper.

Dulcie had left him; he could hear her up in the forest padding through the pine needles, and he caught a glimpse of her sniffing along, following Dillon's scent. Calling the kit, he leaped up the hill, watching for the predators that would soon come, drawn by the smell of blood.

He didn't like to leave the bodies alone, to be ravaged by hunting beasts—both out of respect for the sanctity of human creatures and because evidence would be destroyed. But the highest urgency was to find Dillon.

The sky had cleared above them, enough so he could see through the treetops a sliver of rising moon, its thin light seeping in hoary patterns between the black pine limbs.

"I saw more," the kit said softly.

Joe paused, his paw lifted. "What did you see? Did you see the person who killed them?"

"I heard the screams. I ran to see. Two horses bolted right at me and swerved away down the mountain. No riders, reins flying. Then a girl came racing, leaning over her horse, and a man riding after her, trying to catch her. He grabbed at her horse. They were deep in the trees. I couldn't see what happened. They disappeared over the hill. The man was swearing."

"What did he look like?"

"He looked like Police Captain Harper."

"What do you mean, he looked like Captain Harper?"

"He was tall and thin and had a cowboy hat like Captain Harper, pulled down, and a thin face and a jacket like the captain wears. A denim jacket. I could smell the girl's fear. I ran and ran; I didn't go back until just now, when I found you. I came back in the dark when I heard you. I don't . . ."

"Listen," Joe said. Voices came from far down the hills, calling, calling, moving up toward them. "Ruthie! Ruthie Marner! Dillon! Helen! Helen Marner! Dillon! Dillon Thurwell!"

And below them, all across the bare slopes, lights came rising up and they could hear horses—a snort, the rattle of a bit, a hoof striking stone. Up the hills they came, their torches sweeping the slopes and shining down into the ravines. And down beyond the horses and hikers, cars moved along a winding road shining spotlights among the far, scattered houses. The red bubble of a police car rose up over the crest, then two more red-lit units searching for the Marners and for Dillon—searching too late for the Marners. Drawing slowly up the hills toward that grisly scene.

3

"Dillon! Dillon Thurwell! Ruthie! Ruthie Marner!" The night hills rang with shouts, and swam with careening lights that faded and smeared where scarves of fog crept up the little valleys. "Dillon! Dillon Thurwell!" Max Harper's voice cut through the others, tense and imperative. "Dillon! Answer me! Dillon, sing out! Whistle! *Dillon!*"

And up the hills above the searchers, Joe Grey stood on a rock beside the bleeding bodies, wanting to shout, too, wanting to halt the cries and bring the searchers swarming to where the murdered women lay, wanting to shout, *Here! They're here! Ruthie and Helen are here. Here, below the broken pine!*

Right.

He could do that.

Shout as loud as a cat *can* shout, bring the riders galloping to take one look at the murder scene and fan out again searching for the killer, their horses trashing every bit of the evidence in their urgent haste—to say nothing of trampling three fleeing cats.

He had to draw the searchers without alarming them into tearing up the surround.

Slipping behind the rock where he wouldn't be seen, rearing tall behind the boulder to nearly thirty inches of sleek gray fur, Joe Grey yowled.

Opened wide and let it out, yowled-howled-caterwauled-bellowed-ululated and belly-coughed like a banshee screaming its rage and venom into the black, cold night.

Every light swung up. Torchlight illuminated the cats' boulder as if its edges were on fire. Captain Harper pushed Bucky fast up the hill, the tall, thin officer pulling his rifle from the scabbard as the big buckskin ran sliding on the rocks. A rifle!

Joe knew that the men of Molena Point PD carried rifles in their squad cars, along with a short, handy shotgun and an array of far more amazing equipment. He'd never thought about an officer carrying a rifle on horseback. He guessed that in the wild mountains to which these foothills led, in the rugged coastal range, a rifle might come in handy—there had been times, up in these hills, when he'd wished a cat could use a firearm.

"There!" Harper shouted. "By the boulders—under the broken pine!"

Every beam centered on the rocks and on the angled tree behind them, and on the two bodies sprawled across the dust-pale bridle path. Lights scoured the boulder where the cats had been.

Crouching higher up the hill, they watched Harper's buckskin gelding top the rise at a gallop and, behind

Harper, riders flowing up like a stampede in a TV western, the pounding of their hooves shaking the earth. Crouched close together, the cats shivered with nervous excitement.

Harper held up a hand. The riders pulled up their horses in a ragged semicircle, some fifty feet below the bodies—a ring of mounted men and women, their flashlights and torches bathing the corpses in a brilliance as violent as if the light of final judgment shone down suddenly upon Helen and Ruthie Marner.

Around the grisly honor guard, the night was still.

A bit rattled. A horse snorted nervously, perhaps at the smell of blood.

Max Harper holstered his rifle and dismounted, swinging down from the saddle to approach the bodies alone. Leaving Bucky ground-tied, he stepped with care to avoid trampling any footprint or hoofprint. His long, thin face was white, the dry wrinkles deeply etched, his dark eyes flat and hard as he looked down on Helen and Ruthie, then looked away into the night, shining his light up into the forest.

When he did not see a third body among the rocks and trees, he clicked on his radio.

"Better have the ambulance up here. And the coroner." He called in his two detectives from the squad cars below, then knelt to check for vital signs, though there could be none. Dulcie and Joe swallowed, knowing the pain with which Harper must be viewing the scene.

Before he rose, he examined the ground directly around the bodies; the cats knew he'd be committing to memory every mark or disturbance, studying every footprint and hoofprint, every detail of the position of the bodies, memorizing the way the blood was pooled, seeing each tiniest fragment of evidence—though all such facts would be duly recorded by his detectives in extensive notes and photographs.

Joe didn't like leaving their prints at the scene—he could only hope they looked like the tracks of a squirrel or fox, though surely Harper knew the difference. Crouching, Harper studied the earth for a long time, then, rising, he looked away again into the night, shaking his head as if dismissing that wild cry that had summoned him. Maybe he thought it *had* come from some small, wild beast drawn there by the smell of blood, stopping to yowl a hunting cry, leaving its prints, fleeing at the approach of the searchers.

It was as good a scenario as any. They didn't need Harper to be unduly aware of cats at the scene; they knew that too painfully from past encounters.

Harper, shining his torch across the ground in ever-widening arcs, turned at last, singling out Officer Wendell.

"Call Murdoc Ranch, Wendell. See if the Marner horses have come home. See if they've seen Dillon—or if Dillon's mare is there." And again he swung his torch up into the black forest, searching for a red-headed little girl whom Max Harper cared for just as he would love his own child. His light swam over the boulder beneath which the cats crouched. But if he saw them at all, they'd be no more than mottled brown leaves and rotted gray branches, their eyes tight closed,

Joe's white markings concealed behind the kit and Dulcie.

And soon, below them, the familiar routine began. Officers emerged from their squad cars on the narrow road a quarter mile below. Detective Ray and Detective Davis hurried up the hill, the two women loaded with cameras and equipment bags, Davis to shoot roll after roll of film of the victims and the surround while Ray made notes and drew a diagram of body positions. Borrowing Bucky, Davis took many pictures from horseback, to gain the higher angle. The cats thought the team would likely work all night, sifting the earth, bagging and labeling minute bits of evidence, making casts of footprints and hoofprints.

Kathleen Ray was young, maybe thirty-five, a small, slim woman with long dark hair and huge green eyes, a woman who looked more like a model for petite swimwear than a cop. Juana Davis was pushing fifty, a stocky, solid woman with short dark hair and brown Latin eyes. Harper stood watching them, going over the scene, the muscles of his jaw tight.

For the first time in many days, the cats felt safe from predators, with the entire Molena Point PD and half the village milling around the hills and forest.

Soon another squad car arrived and four officers double-timed up the hill to organize teams of searchers. Two smaller parties, of skilled climbers, headed up toward the steep mountains.

When Davis had finished photographing, Max Harper laid out for her what he knew of Dillon and the Marners' activities that afternoon. As the detective taped Harper's flat, clipped voice, his words stirred a strange fear in Joe Grey.

"Helen and Ruthie met Dillon and me at my place about ten this morning; they rode over from the Murdoc Ranch, where they board their horses. We headed south along the lower trail toward Hellhag Hill. Rode on beyond Hellhag maybe five miles, turned back around eleven, and stopped at Café Mundo for lunch. Loosened the saddles, rubbed down our horses and watered them. Had a leisurely meal."

Café Mundo was located just above Valley Road, adjacent to one of the many bridle trails that bisected the Molena Point hills. It was famous for its fine Mexican dishes. The proprietor, having horses himself, liked to cater to the local horsemen, advertising a water trough and plenty of hitching racks. Café Mundo was always first to help sponsor overnight trail rides, charity calf roping, and rodeos.

"If Dillon's not still on horseback," Harper told Davis, "if she's fallen, Redwing will come home. I sent Charlie down to see, maybe half an hour ago. She knows the horses, knows how to put Redwing up. They were—Dillon was going to spend the night with Ruthie, going to stable Redwing with the Marner horses until morning. She . . ." Harper's voice missed a beat. "She's a strong, resourceful little girl."

He cleared his throat. "When we finished lunch, Helen and Ruthie and Dillon left. That was about one-thirty. They headed up in this direction, were planning on another two hours, up into the foothills and back. Dillon and Ruthie are—were training for an endurance competition." Harper fidgeted nervously. "Where the hell is the coroner?"

Joe watched him with interest. Harper had only called for the coroner maybe fifteen minutes earlier. It would take Dr. Bern a little while to get up the hills. They'd never seen the captain wound so tight.

But he couldn't blame Harper. If the captain had remained with the riders, this wouldn't have happened. Besides Harper's intimidating presence, even on horseback he would have been armed, very likely carrying the Smith & Wesson .38 automatic in its shoulder holster—if for no other reason than against predators. No one said what kind of predators. Every cop had enemies.

It had been the habit of the foursome, lately, to take an all-day ride on Saturday, as the girls worked on their endurance skills. Charlie Getz had ridden with them until Crystal Ryder came on the scene. Crystal had been too much for Charlie. Too bubbly, too much flirting—too much all over Max Harper. With both Helen Marner and Crystal attempting to take over Harper as private property, the skirmishes had been more than Charlie could endure.

From what Harper had told Clyde, the women's ongoing battle didn't thrill him either. He put up with them, to have ample chaperones for Dillon.

Max Harper hadn't dated since his wife, Millie, died several years earlier. His friendship with Helen had caused some talk in the village. But when Crystal moved to Molena Point and began to pay attention to Harper, there'd been a lot more gossip. Crystal was far more glamorous than Helen, and her persistence was amazing. She was, in Joe's opinion, pushy, wore too much makeup, and was always "onstage." Not Harper's type of woman.

Joe was no prude. And maybe his view of these matters was different from that of the human male. But he considered sleazy women totally boring—as tiresome as a perfumed Persian decked out in pink claw polish and a rhinestone collar.

Joe enjoyed a roll in the hay as well as the next guy, but he preferred his ladies with sharper claws and more fire.

"Interesting," Joe said, "that Crystal didn't ride with the group this afternoon—and that Harper didn't mention her."

Dulcie looked at him, wide-eyed. "What are you thinking?"

"Not sure. Just strange."

"Well, whatever's on your mind, we need to tell Harper which way that man chased Dillon. The kit said there, to the north."

"This is one time, Dulcie, the secret snitch is not going to tip the chief. Not with every cop and half the village swarming, and no phones except in the squad cars."

"But we have to! Dillon could be . . . You did it before. You called Harper from a squad car while the officers had their backs turned."

"Not this time," Joe said, his eyes blazing so fiercely that Dulcie drew back. "Anyway, there's no need." They watched Harper swing into the saddle and head Bucky away to the north, shining his torch along the trail, following those racing hoofprints. And soon the silhouette of horse and rider, backlit by the torch, melted into the night.

Dulcie stared after him, praying that Dillon had escaped, that she was out there on the dark hills hiding, and Harper would find her.

Glancing at Joe, she started to follow. But Joe, leaping away beside her, hit her with his shoulders and nipped at her until she slowed. "Don't, Dulcie. Leave him alone. What could you do? You couldn't keep up forever—alone in the night, you're cougar bait. If Dillon's out there, he'll find her."

She sat down in the pine needles, looking at him forlornly.

"Is nothing safe?" she said. "Is no simplest thing people do beyond danger? It was such a harmless pleasure for Dillon, having a horse to ride."

The two cats looked solemnly at each other, and padded back through the woods to join the sleeping kit; and to watch, below them, as Detective Davis began to lift plaster casts in their little frame boxes, where the creamy liquid had hardened into bootprints and hoofprints. As Davis worked, the mist blew thicker over the hills, veiling the moon, casting moon-shadows across the coroner's thin face, where he stood watching the forensics team, making Dr. Bern look paler than ever. Beside Dulcie, the dozing kit woke, yawning a wide pink gape. Joe, angry at the world, it seemed, didn't wait for her to wake fully; he fixed her with a steady yellow gleam that shocked her right up out of her dreams.

"What were you doing, Kit, all that time after he killed them and you saw him chasing Dillon? Didn't you know something should be done? That Dillon needed help? Why didn't you race down to find us?"

"You weren't *there* to find. You were up here on the hills."

"But you didn't *know* that," Joe said impatiently. "What *were* you doing?"

"I ran after the man and the girl, I followed them, I didn't *know* what to do. Their scent led down the hills, and when I couldn't see the horses, I could hear them. I ran and ran. So many smells. I wanted to see if she got away, and then I couldn't smell her anymore and that was near the ruins so I thought she might hide there and I went in to look."

"Well?"

Dulcie said more gently, "Did you smell Dillon there? In the ruins?"

"So many smells. Foxes and raccoons. A coyote. I could smell *him,* and I hurried away under the rubble where he couldn't come. I smelled all the night hunters. There is water in the cellars. The big hunters come there to drink."

"We know that," Joe said impatiently.

"Don't you remember," Dulcie said, "we told you not to go there? *Did you smell Dillon?*"

"I smelled the cougar."

For a moment, the kit would not look at Dulcie. Then, "I couldn't smell the little girl in all the other smells. And then I lost the man-smell. But I smelled the lion and I was afraid. I hid," she said softly. "I hid and I didn't know what to do.

"Then when I thought he was gone I slipped away and came back here again and looked at the dead bodies, and I was going to go home and *tell* you but then I saw you. I saw you, you were here," she said, crowding against Dulcie.

Dulcie licked the kit's mottled face. The little black-and-brown patchwork creature with the round yellow eyes was the strangest young cat she'd ever known.

The kit lifted a dark paw to Dulcie, the fur between her claws so long and thick that it made Dulcie smile. The kit, with her furry paws and the long fur sticking out of her ears, resembled too closely some wild feline cousin—wild looks that exactly matched her unruly temperament.

Tenderly, Dulcie washed the kit's mottled face. "We will search," she said. "Just as Harper is searching. But where were you, Kit, for three days? Didn't you think we worried? We looked and looked for you. You could have said, 'I want a ramble, I need to go off alone.' You could have told us you were going."

"Would you have let me go?"

Dulcie only looked at her.

Joe studied the kit, his yellow eyes nearly black, his white paws, white apron, and the white patch down his nose bright in the night. "What is that smell on you, Kit?"

"What smell?"

"Musty. Deep musty earth. I don't remember a smell like that in the ruins, even in the cellars—not *that* kind of smell."

The kit looked innocently at Joe.

Joe fixed her with a hard gaze.

And Dulcie moved close to the kit, standing tall over

her, her own neck bowed like a tom, her tail lashing. "*Where,* Kit? *Where* were you?"

"I went down," the kit said softly. "The deep, deep place below the cellars." And she moved away from them, suddenly preoccupied with patting at the dry leaves.

"Pay attention!" Joe snapped. "What deep place!"

"Down under the ruin," said the kit, flattening her furry ears and turning her face away.

"Deep down?" Dulcie said softly. "Why, Kit?" But she knew why. The tattercoat kit was keenly drawn to strange, frightening fissures. She was as obsessed with the cellars of the old Pamillon estate, and with the yawning cave-ins that dropped away even beneath the cellars, as she had been with the deep and mysterious caverns that she claimed lay below Hellhag Hill.

"I went down and down." The kit's round yellow eyes filled with a wild delight. "Down and down under the cellars. Down and down where my clowder wanted to go. Down and down under water dripping, down long cracks into the earth, down and down until I heard voices, until . . ."

"You did not," Joe snapped. "You didn't hear voices. You didn't go below any cellar. You're making it up—inventing silly tales."

"Deep down," said the kit. "Down and down and I heard voices."

"It was echoes," Joe hissed. "Echoes from water dripping or from sliding stone. You're lucky to be up in the world again, you silly kitten, and not buried under some earthslide in one of those old cellars."

The kit looked at Joe Grey. She looked at Dulcie.

"Down and down," she said stubbornly, "to that other place beneath the granite sky."

And Dulcie, despite herself, despite her better judgment, believed the kit. "What was it like?" she whispered.

"You didn't go there," Joe repeated, baring his teeth at the two of them.

"Terrible," said the kit. "It is terrible. I ran up again, but then I lost my way. I had to go back and start over, I had to follow my own scent."

Dulcie said softly, "Were the others from your clowder there?"

"I was all alone. I don't know where they went when they left Hellhag Hill. I don't like that place, I was afraid. But . . ."

"Then why did you go?" Joe growled, pacing and glaring at the kit. Half his attention was on her—his anger centered on her—and half his attention on the torchlit scene below them where the coroner and detectives were doing their grisly work.

But Dulcie, pressing against the kit, could feel the kitten's heart pounding at thoughts of another world—even if it was her imagination—just as Dulcie's own heart was pounding.

"She's making up stories," Joe said, his eyes slitted, his ears flat to his head, his scowl deep and irritable. He didn't want to think about that other place, if there was such a place. Didn't want to imagine other worlds, didn't want to dwell on his and Dulcie's ancestry. If their dual cat-and-human natures had risen from some strain of beings among the ancient Celts, who had come, then, to this continent, he didn't care to know more about it.

Joe wanted only to *be*. To live only in the moment, fully alive and effective, in this life that he had been dealt.

And Dulcie loved him for that. Joe was his own cat, he felt no need to peer into the lives of his ancestors like some voyeuring genealogist longing for a time before his own.

Joe spoke the human language, he read the morning paper—with a sharply caustic slant on the news. Dulcie considered him smarter than half the humans in the world. But Joe Grey valued what he had here and now, he wanted nothing more. Any additional mysteries about himself would be an unnecessary weight upon his tomcat shoulders.

With tender understanding, Dulcie licked his ear, ignoring her own wild dreams of other worlds and even more amazing talents. And she snuggled the kit close, too, wondering about the skills that this small cat might show them.

She was washing the kit's splotchy black-and-brown face when they saw Clyde striding up the hill between the swinging spotlights. Immediately Joe and Dulcie ducked, dragging the kit lower behind the boulders.

"Why?" whispered the kit. "Is he not your human, Joe Grey? Why are you hiding from him?"

Joe gave her a slant-eyed look. "He hates finding us at a murder scene. All he does is shout. It's bad for his blood pressure." He watched from between the boulders until Clyde turned away again, to where Officer

Ray was cataloging the scene. Standing outside the cordoned-off area, Clyde said, "Is Harper out looking for her?"

Kathleen Ray nodded. "The captain, and five search parties."

"I'll swing by Harper's place, see if the mare came home. No word from Charlie? Is she down there?"

"No word. She said she'd be there. The captain asked her to see to the mare."

Clyde turned, heading down the hill.

"Move it, Kit," Joe whispered. "Stay close."

Racing down ahead of Clyde, staying in the heavy grass and dodging torchlight, the three cats covered the quarter mile, scorched between cars parked along the narrow dirt road, and leaped into the seat of Clyde's antique roadster.

Before Clyde was halfway down the hill, they had slipped up behind the seat and beneath the car's folded top. Stretching out nose to tail, warm beneath the layers of leather, they were ready to roll.

Clyde wouldn't have a clue—unless he saw their muddy pawprints. But in the dark, with only the dash lights, he likely wouldn't see the mud on the seat—not until morning.

The kit, warm and comfortable between them, rumbled with purrs—until Dulcie poked her with a soft paw. "Hush, Kit. Here he comes, he'll hear you."

But the kit had fallen sound asleep.

4

A week before Ruthie and Helen Marner were killed, a hundred miles north in San Francisco, someone else was considering the Pamillon estate, thinking of the overgrown grounds exactly as Dillon Thurwell might have done, as a place to hide, to escape a killer.

To Kate Osborne, an invitation to view the Pamillon mansion was a welcome excuse to get out of the city and away from the danger that, perhaps, she only imagined.

Whatever the truth, the stories in the papers had fired her fear until she couldn't sleep at night, until she had put a bolt on the inside of both the front and the bedroom doors, until she was afraid to walk, except in the middle of the day, or even to take the bus or cable car. She was losing all sense of proportion, and that terrified her.

She had vowed, before ever she fled the city, to make herself visit the Cat Museum, to lay to rest that part of her fears. She would not leave until she had made that short trip up Russian Hill.

Last year, when she'd moved up from Molena Point to the North Beach apartment, she'd been eager to see the museum. Pictures of the gallery had so intrigued her, the lovely Mediterranean buildings tucked among their sprawling gardens, beneath the old, magnificent oaks. She'd been so eager to study the museum's amazing collection of cat paintings and cat sculpture. How strange that she'd lived in the city when she was younger and had known about the museum, but had never bothered to go there.

Well, she hadn't known, then, all the facts about herself. Anyway, she'd been so busy with art school. Her museum visits, then, had been school related, to the San Francisco Museum and the de Young.

Yet the art collection at the Cat Museum included work by Gauguin, Dubuffet, Picasso—fine pieces, housed in that lovely complex at the top of Russian Hill.

It was only now, after going through a divorce and returning to the city—and after learning the shocking truth about herself—that she had a really urgent reason to visit there. Yet she'd procrastinated for over a year, unable to find the courage, unable to face any more secrets. Each time she'd tried to make that short journey, she'd become all nerves, and turned back.

So they keep real cats, too. Of course they do. Everyone says those lovely cats wandering the gardens add a delightful charm to the famous collection.

Well, but what kind *of cats?*

That doesn't matter. No one will guess the truth—not even the cats themselves. And what if they did?

What do you think they'd do? Come on, Kate. You're such a coward. Can't you get on with it?

And on Saturday morning she woke knowing she would do it. Now. Today. Put down her fear. No more hedging. The morning was beautifully foggy, the way she loved the city, the wet mist swirling outside her second-floor windows, the muffled sounds of the city calling to her like a secret benediction. Quickly she showered and dressed, letting herself think only of the perfect morning and the beauty of the museum, nothing more. Debating whether to have breakfast at the kitchen table, enjoying her view of the fogbound city, or go on to her favorite warm, cozy coffee shop two blocks up Stockton and treat herself to their delicious Swedish pancakes and espresso and homemade sausage.

Hardly a choice. Pulling on her tan windbreaker over jeans and a sweatshirt, fixing the jacket's hood over her short, pale hair, she hurried down the one flight and into the damp breeze that had begun to swirl the fog. Only once, striding along Stockton, did her thoughts skitter warily again, forcing her to take herself in hand.

Slipping in through the glass door of the Iron Pony, she settled in her favorite booth, where she could look out at Coit Tower, fog-shrouded and lonely.

From the kitchen, Ramon saw her, and brought her a cup of freshly brewed espresso, greeting her in Spanish and laughing. She returned his "*¿Buenos días. Cómo está?*" laughing in return. Ramon's English was impeccable, but, he'd told her solemnly, he spoke only

Spanish when a patron angered him. He'd told her he had a violent temper, that he found it imperative sometimes to hide a sudden anger behind the barrier of language to avoid calling some customer names that would get him, Ramon, fired. If he pretended not to understand the insults, he need not confront them.

A strange young man. Maybe twenty-five years old. Very quiet. And except when he'd been insulted, which she'd never witnessed, a content young man, she thought, seeming totally pleased with the world. Maybe he shifted as quickly as a cat from cool satisfaction to raking claws.

Did she have to drag in the simile of a cat? She sipped her espresso crossly. Couldn't she think of some other description?

She had the notion that Ramon's alabaster-pale skin offered a clue to the quick temper he described, that such bloodless-looking skin and slight build were signs of a person capable of deep rage. She had no notion where she'd gotten such an idea. Of course it was silly. Ramon's obsidian hair and black Latin eyes simply made him look paler—as did the birthmark that splotched his left cheek, the rust-colored deformity spreading from his eye to the corner of his mouth as dark as dried blood, in the shape of the map of India.

She had never dared ask him, in the months she'd been coming here, if it was indeed a birthmark or was perhaps a burn scar—though the skin looked smooth.

She enjoyed chatting with Ramon; she didn't have many friends in San Francisco except her boss, Hanni, and Hanni's uncle, Dallas Garza, a detective with San Francisco PD. She hadn't tried hard to make other friends, because of her situation. She felt uneasy with other people—as if they might be able to tell what she really was. Her casual acquaintance with Ramon allowed her to walk out of the coffee shop and that was the end of it, no social obligation, no secrets shared, nothing more expected.

"The pancakes and sausage as usual, señora?"

"Yes, and orange juice if you please, Ramon, it's such a beautiful morning."

He seemed to understand that a beautiful morning called for orange juice. "The fog is going quickly—like a watercolor washing away. Look how the sun makes jewels."

Together they watched diamonds of dazzle spark at them from the sidewalk where the sun sliced down through the vanishing fog. Ramon had a good eye; he was a student at the art institute where she herself had gone ten years before. It was so good to be back in San Francisco. Nowhere in the world, she thought, were the subtle city colors as splendid as on these hills. When soon the sun rose, every hill, with its crowding houses, would be alive with swift-running cloud shadows, the whole world seeming to shift and move. The city stirred such a fierce joy in her, made her want to race through the streets, turning flips and laughing.

Ramon brought her breakfast and the morning *Chronicle*, frowning at the story that slashed across the bottom of the front page. The lead and first details were so gruesome that all the fear rose in her again, sour as bile. Why had he brought this paper to her? She wanted to wad it up and run out of the café.

"This terrible thing," Ramon said, setting the paper

down beside her plate. "How can this be, that a man could do such a bloody deed? For why would a man do this?"

She did not look up at him. She thought she was going to be sick. She imagined far too vividly the poor dead cat hanging limp and twisted from a lamp pole, its throat constricted by a cord tied in a hangman's noose.

"That man should be hanged," Ramon said. "*Muerto. Debe murir.*"

She looked up at him, and swallowed. Ramon wanted only to share with her his rage, share with another his own indignation.

For the last week, all over the city someone had been killing cats, hanging the poor beasts by a twisted noose, choking out their gentle, terrified lives. There had been nineteen incidents, in Haight, Nob Hill, Russian Hill, North Beach, the Presidio. Shoving her plate away, she felt her hands clench and stiffen with what she would like to do to the cat killer.

She did not want to read the accompanying article; she hated that Ramon had brought this ugly thing for her to see. She was about to toss the paper away when she saw the upper headline.

DEATH ROW ESCAPEES STILL AT LARGE

SACRAMENTO—Ronnie Cush, James Hartner and Lee Wark, the three death row inmates who broke out of San Quentin ten days ago, are still at large. None has been apprehended. This is the first escape from the maximum detention wing in the history of the prison.

The breakout occurred when prisoners overpowered a guard. All staff in that section have been replaced. Prison officials believe that Hartner may have sought family in Seattle. There is no clue to where Ronnie Cush might be headed. Lee Wark may have returned to San Francisco, where he had numerous contacts. Any witness to the escapees' whereabouts will be kept in strictest confidence by police and prison authorities.

Kate looked helplessly at her breakfast. She wanted to pitch the plate away. Ramon still stood watching her, so intent she wanted to scream. Why was he staring? As she looked up angrily, he turned quickly back to the kitchen.

But he couldn't understand how upset she would be, how the articles would terrify her. He could have no concept of how powerfully the cat story would hurt her. And no idea, of course, that the prison break was, for her, perhaps even more alarming.

She was ice cold inside. She felt absolutely certain that Lee Wark had returned—to the very city where she had come to hide from him.

Ramon returned with the coffeepot and stood beside her table, speaking softly.

"Dark the cat walks," Ramon said, watching her. She looked up at him, startled. "Dark the cat walks, his pacing shadow small." Ramon's Latin eyes gleamed. "Dark the cat walks. His shadow explodes tall. Fearsome wide and tall."

The shock of his words turned her rigid. Before she could speak, abruptly Ramon left her.

She sat very still, trying to collect her emotions. Her hands were shaking.

Why had he said that? What could he mean?

Dropping the paper on the floor, she threw down some money and hurried out to the street, wanted out of there, wanted out of the city.

What was Ramon telling me? Then, *Wark can't know I'm here.*

Can't he, Kate? Remember, before, how easily he discovered your secret?

If it is Wark who's killing cats, she thought, shivering, *Ramon's right. He ought to be* muerto. Debe murir.

Hurrying back to her apartment, she locked herself in, sliding the new dead bolt on the front door, checking the window locks. She made some cocoa and curled up with a book, a tame, quiet read that wouldn't upset her, couldn't stir any sense of threat—a soothing story that offered nothing to abrade her raw nerves.

She couldn't stop thinking about Wark.

Wasn't the Cat Museum the first place the cat killer would go?

Had he already been there, stalking the grounds? Did the museum staff not know? Or *had* museum cats been killed, and the museum had kept that out of the papers?

Had some of the poor, dead cats that were found around the city come in fact from the Cat Museum?

What kind of cats, Kate? What kind of cats is he killing?

Was Wark saving the Cat Museum for last? Last and

best, in Wark's sick mind—before the cops got too close and he had to flee?

Was she imagining all this—the connection between Wark and this maniac?

She didn't think so. A sick, sadistic killer was loose in San Francisco. Lee Wark reveled in that brand of cruelty. Lee Wark had escaped from prison only thirty miles north of the city.

Coincidence? She had the terrible feeling that if she were to visit the Cat Museum, no matter when she went there, Lee Wark would be stalking those gardens.

5

As Charlie Getz turned her van up the quarter-mile lane that led to Max Harper's small ranch, the yellow light of the security lamps was mighty welcome. The dark roads were behind her, where perhaps a killer lurked, the hills pitch black, the sky black and starless.

Heading the van down the lighted fence line toward the white frame house and stable, she prayed for the safety of the Marners and Dillon as she'd been praying all night.

The idea of three riders missing was so bizarre—the implication of a child missing made bile come in her throat. Heading eagerly for the stable yard, she knew she was driving too fast.

Slowing the old van, she studied the dark pools of night beneath the overhanging oaks, looking for the mare. She could see, up on the hills behind the ranch, flashes of torchlight jiggling and careening, and could see lights higher up the foothills, disappearing into the pine forest. Parking before the house, she cut the engine and headlights and sat listening to the far, faint shouts of the searchers.

After the wash of light up the lane, the yard was too dark. Harper didn't like lights glaring in his windows; his yard lights were operable from remotes in his car and truck, and from inside the house and stable.

Now, in the tangle of black shapes around her, nothing shifted or moved.

She'd never been afraid at night, not in Molena Point, not when she'd lived in San Francisco. Tonight her fear made her weak.

Slipping out of the van, she switched on her torch and started across the yard toward the stable, swinging her beam wide, causing the shadows to run and dance—probably only tree trunks, maybe a wheelbarrow.

Then, beneath a far oak, a shadow shifted and turned.

She aimed her light toward it like a gun—wished it was a gun.

Her beam caught the whites of frightened eyes, the line of the mare's head and pricked ears. Redwing stood pressed against the fence, her eyes wide with fear.

Gently Charlie approached her, aiming her torch away. The mare stood stiffly, holding one leg up. The reins were broken, trailing in the dirt. Harper's nice Stübben saddle hung down Redwing's side, the stirrup dragging, the girth loose where a buckle had broken. When she reached for Redwing, the mare threw her head and snorted, rearing to wheel away. Charlie grabbed the broken rein, moving with her, letting her plunge, then easing into her. Laying her hand on the mare's neck, she felt Redwing trembling. At the same instant, loud barking erupted from the barn where the two big half-Dane dogs had been shut in their box stall for the night. The sound of their voices eased Charlie—as if their bellowing would drive away danger. And the furor seemed to calm Redwing, too. The mare knew the dogs, she played with them in the pasture; she seemed easier at their familiar presence.

Removing the saddle, placing it on the fence rail, she led the mare out to see if she could walk.

The mare limped badly.

Leading Redwing to the barn, Charlie flipped on the lights, found a halter, and carefully removed the bridle, touching it as little as possible. Maybe that was silly, but if someone had grabbed the reins and pulled Dillon off, there could be fingerprints.

Harper would laugh at her. Maybe she read too many detective stories. Hanging the bridle on its hook, she put the mare in the cross-ties and went out to the yard to fetch the saddle, supporting it by two fingers under the pad.

Maybe, when the saddle slipped, Dillon had fallen; maybe she was lying, hurt, up on the dark hills, confused or unconscious.

But why would she be alone, without Helen and Ruthie?

Ignoring the whining dogs, she wiped down the mare, cleaned her skinned knee, and daubed on some salve. Putting her in her stall, she fetched a flake of hay for her and filled her water bucket. The dogs continued to bark and to scrabble at their stall door. Too bad the year-old pups weren't trained to track; they could be of use tonight. But those two mutts, as much as she loved them, would only get in the way.

When she had the mare bedded, she removed one of the two leashes hanging from the nail beside the dogs' stall and, by opening their door only a crack, managed with a lot of shouting and strong-arming and ignored commands, to let Hestig out and leave Selig confined.

Leashing Hestig, she tied him to a ring at the side of the stable alleyway. He stood whining, watching her soulfully. She felt easier with the big pup near. The Great Dane part of him gave him a voice like a train horn, and he had the size and presence to intimidate any stranger.

She and Clyde together had started training the two strays in obedience, but it was slow going. Dog training wasn't Clyde's talent. The pups had ended up at Harper's, and she and Max had been working with them in the evenings, taking advantage of the wide, flat acreage to teach them the basic commands. They were learning. But tonight, with the unusual routine, and having listened to the shouting from the hills, they were too excited to pay much attention.

She remained still a moment, stroking Hestig. In the long, quiet evenings, she hadn't meant for her relationship with Max Harper to turn personal, hadn't meant to become so attracted to him—and the trouble was, it *hadn't* turned personal. She didn't think Max felt anything for her but friendship.

Harper was Clyde's best friend. It wouldn't be like him to hurt Clyde. And he was a cop, his feelings all buttoned up and in control—or at least hidden, she thought wryly.

Except, what about Crystal Ryder?

That one had thrown herself at the captain and gotten a response. But then, the woman was gorgeous, with that tawny blond hair and big brown doe eyes and deep dimples and a figure that, to quote Clyde, was stacked like a brick outhouse. How could Max resist?

While she, Charlie, was just a skinny, gawky redhead with no sex appeal and more freckles than brains.

Crystal Ryder was the first woman Max had looked at since his wife died.

How can I be thinking about such inanities, about my personal problems, when Dillon's lost and hurt?

Shutting the mare's stall door, she unsnapped Hestig's leash from the wall and, with the pup at heel, she circled the stable yard, shining her light deep beneath the trees and up into the hay shed, keeping an eye on the lane, hoping to see a squad car turning in.

But the dirt drive remained empty—empty and lonely. And the winding road beyond the lights was unrelieved in its dense and endless blackness. Feeling vulnerable, she pulled Hestig close to her, and headed for the darkened house.

Using the key Max had given her this evening, and pushing open the back door, she felt Hestig cower against her, so her heart did a double skip.

Quietly she told him to watch. To his credit, the big honey-colored dog came to attention with a surprised growl. Laying her hand on his shoulder, she reached inside and flipped the switch, illuminating the big country kitchen.

No one was there, no one standing against the oak cabinets or lurking beneath the table. Beyond the two inner doorways, the dining room and hall were dense with shadow. She stepped inside, keeping Hestig close, reached for the phone on the kitchen table, and dialed Harper's cell phone.

"Yes?" he said softly.

"I'm in your kitchen. Redwing came home. No sign of Dillon."

"We haven't found her."

"The mare slipped her saddle, it was hanging down, a girth buckle broken, the reins broken."

"Does it look like the mare fell?"

"She's lame on her left front knee. An abrasion, blood and dirt. Yes, like she stumbled. I doctored it. You haven't found Helen and Ruthie either?"

"We found Ruthie and Helen." Max's voice was flat. "They're dead, Charlie."

"Dead?" Her breath caught. "How? What happened? Where is Dillon?"

"Someone was up there in the hills. Someone met them on the trail. Their throats were cut. We haven't found Dillon," he repeated.

Every drop of strength had drained away. She sat down at the table, pulling Hestig close.

"Both Ruthie and Helen were slashed across the throat," Harper said, as if perhaps she hadn't heard, or understood. Hadn't wanted to hear.

She stared into the shadows of the hall, holding the dog close, filled with the sickening picture of the mother and that lovely young woman lying up there on the dark hills alone.

"Dillon," she said again. "Where is Dillon? The mare . . . The mare came home alone."

"I told you, Charlie. We haven't found her. Did you unsaddle the mare?"

"Yes, of course."

"How much did you handle the tack?"

"I . . . As little as possible."

"Why, Charlie? How did you know I'd want prints?"

"I just—with three riders missing, I just—thought it might be wise. I don't know. Just seemed a good idea. Where—where are you?"

"In the hills north of you. I'll send an officer down. Are you alone?"

"I have Hestig with me."

"Be wary. Stay in the kitchen. Squad car will be there pronto."

She hung up, staring at the two dark doorways, wondering if the killer had *brought* Redwing home—maybe ridden her home—then come into the house.

But why would he do that? After he killed Helen and Ruthie, he'd surely run, try to get away. Shivering, she looked more carefully around the kitchen.

Nothing seemed out of place, not even a dirty dish in the sink. Max kept his house, and even the feed room and tackroom, in the same orderly manner in which he ran the police station, every piece of equipment clean and ready, in its place where it could be quickly found.

She knew Max's house; she knew where he kept his gun-cleaning equipment, and where a .38 Chief's Special was cushioned beneath the shoe rack in his closet.

But she would have to go down the dark hall to reach the closet, passing the dark bathroom and bedrooms. She remained at the table, stroking Hestig, feeling cowardly and anxious, waiting for the squad car.

The kitchen still showed a woman's warmth, Millie's cookbooks still on the shelf above her little desk, her dried flowers in a vase, the flowered chair cushions. Millie had been a cop, and a good one. But she'd liked having a cozy home. All this, the flowers, the little pretty touches, he had kept, legacy from a cherished and cherishing wife. Millie had been dead for nearly two years before Charlie ever knew Max, before Charlie ever moved to Molena Point.

These last weeks, as she and Max worked with the pups, Max had told her more than he realized about Millie. He'd told her a lot about Clyde, too, as he recalled their high school days, their summers riding bulls on the rodeo circuit. And Harper had told her a lot about himself and the way he looked at life. She hadn't known he could be so talkative.

And all the evenings she had spent up here, with the excuse of training the pups, she'd kept turning down dinner with Clyde, turning down dates, a simple movie, a walk on the beach.

She *had* gone with Clyde to the jazz concert, though she wanted to be up here with Max. And she'd agreed to see the outdoor theater's production of *A Midsummer Night's Dream,* but only to ease her conscience—then had sat on the hard bench during the performance, thinking about Max.

She was such a fool.

And how could she think about all this tonight?

But she couldn't think steadily about what had happened to the Marners. About what could be happening to Dillon. She was terrified to think about Dillon. Staring at the black windows, she realized that Dillon could be here on the ranch, could have slipped from the saddle out there beyond the lights.

She rose, nearly toppling her chair, snatching up the torch. Commanding Hestig to heel in a voice that brought him lurching to her side, she headed out to the yard, was sweeping her meager torchlight between the oaks, jumpy at every imagined sound, when headlights came down the road and turned onto the lane.

It was not the squad car she'd expected, but Clyde's roadster, flashing down the lane butter-yellow, stirring in her a picture of the night Clyde had escorted her to the opening of her first art exhibit—not a one-man show, but her work prominently featured among that of five local artists. What a lovely evening, and how caring Clyde had been, dressing up for her, polishing the antique car until it gleamed, timing their arrival to pull up grandly before a crowded gallery, handing her out as if she were a movie star.

Behind Clyde's bright antique convertible, a black-and-white turned in from the road. Clyde was coming up the steps as it parked. The instant she released Hestig, the big pup rushed at Clyde, leaping and whining. Officer Wendell got out of his unit and stood in the yard, asking if she was all right, then went in to search the house. Wendell seemed even more rigid than usual, less friendly. He was always a quiet man. Thin and sour, not a lot of laughs. Maybe the murder had sickened him—or maybe just a sour mood. Wendell had taken a severe demotion recently, after getting into some kind of trouble over a woman. Charlie didn't know what had happened. She knew that Max wasn't easy on his men.

Clyde put his arm around her and drew her into the house. "Any coffee?" He looked tired. His dark hair stood in peaks, his T-shirt hung limp with sweat. His voice was hoarse the way it got when he was upset or out of sorts.

She poured the last of Harper's breakfast coffee into a mug and stuck it in the microwave. "Redwing came home." She pointed out toward the fence where she'd found the mare huddled. She'd never thought of a horse being huddled, but Redwing had been.

Another squad car arrived. Detective Davis and Lieutenant Brennan got out. Both had cameras. Usually, Davis did the photography. Davis waved her out, nodding toward the stable, her short, dark hair catching the light.

As Charlie hurried out, Lieutenant Brennan began to photograph the stable yard, his strobe light picking out every ripple in the soft earth, every hoofprint. Charlie showed him where she had led the mare to the stable and then crossed from the stable beside the pup. Brennan nodded curtly. She guessed murder of a woman and young girl was not business as usual to these officers.

She hadn't known the Marners well. Helen was divorced; she and her daughter had been in the village maybe a year, having moved up from LA about the same time that Charlie herself moved down from San Francisco to stay with her aunt Wilma.

Stepping into the stable alleyway, she pointed out to Juana Davis which saddle and bridle belonged to the mare, answered Davis's questions about where she'd found the mare and in what condition, where she had moved within the stable, how she had handled the tack. Her footprints showed clearly where she had crossed the alleyway from the mare's stall to the feed room and to the dogs' stall.

"Nice stable," Davis said. "You spend much time here?"

"Yes, since we started training the pups. Not before that." She didn't let her expression change, would not let herself bristle or take offense.

But cops could be like that. Blunt and nosy.

The stable *was* cozy—two rows of four box stalls running parallel, separated by a covered alleyway, and with a sliding door at each end. It had originally been a two-stall barn, which Harper had enlarged.

When Davis, making careful notes, had all the information she needed from Charlie, Charlie headed back to the house. She could see in through the bay window; Clyde was standing at the sink, filling the coffeepot. She paused a moment in the yard to watch him—his dark, rumpled hair, his sweaty T-shirt across his heavy shoulders, his jaw set into lines of anger and resolve. She could imagine him up on the mountain searching for the riders, then looking at the torn bodies, and suddenly she wanted to hold him, to ease his distress and her own. Suddenly she felt a great tenderness for Clyde. Quietly she went in, shutting the screen door behind her.

6

One instant the kit was there beside Joe and Dulcie, under the folded convertible top, and the next minute she was gone, vanished in the night. The minute Clyde parked in the stable yard, the three cats had leaped out and slipped beneath the car—except that then the kit wasn't with them.

"Why does she do that?" Dulcie hissed. "She has to be exhausted, wandering the hills for three days. Has to be hungry—but now she's off again, with cars and riders everywhere. She makes me crazy. What possesses her?"

"She won't be found if she doesn't want to be. Let her go, Dulcie."

"I haven't any choice," she said crossly. But Joe was right. Looking for the kit, in the black night, would be like trying to catch a hummingbird in a cyclone.

They watched from beneath the car as Lieutenant Brennan photographed the yard. They watched Charlie cross from the house to the stable behind Detective Davis, and return some ten minutes later. They could see, in through the bay window, part of the kitchen where Clyde stood doing something at the sink, and soon they could smell coffee brewing, a cozy aroma filling them with visions of home and hearth fires. They remained under the Chevy roadster for perhaps an hour watching Brennan at work, watching Charlie and Clyde sitting at the kitchen table, drinking coffee. When they heard a horse coming down the lane, they slipped out to see Captain Harper, on a very tired Bucky, the gelding eating up the road with his distinctive running walk, even though his head hung. Dismounting in the yard, Harper paused for a moment to speak with Brennan.

"The Eagle Scouts and several more riding groups will be out at first light. Three groups of hikers will work along the sea cliffs, and we have kayakers out. A Civil Air Patrol unit is standing by to make a series of passes over the hills and take photographs. Not much chance she'll be seen from the air, but with telephoto lenses and observation with binoculars, they might turn up something."

As Harper moved away, leading Bucky to the stable, Joe and Dulcie slipped through the shadows into the alleyway behind him, and into the feed room, to vanish among the bins of grain. They could see through to the stable yard. Beside the fence, Detective Kathleen Ray knelt beneath powerful lights, sifting sand where the mare had stood, looking for any small bits of evidence, a lost button, even a few threads from the killer's clothes.

In the alleyway, they watched Detective Davis dust the mare's bridle and saddle and broken girth for prints. When Harper loosened Bucky's cinch and eased the saddle off, the gelding sighed deeply. Gently Harper sponged Bucky and rubbed him down, his brown eyes distant and hard, the lines of his thin face etched deep. The cats could guess what he was thinking—that Dillon's disappearance was his fault, that it was his fault Dillon had ever begun to ride.

Dillon's mother had never let her have riding lessons, until Max Harper said he'd teach her, until Harper took a liking to the child and said she could ride Redwing. The Thurwells had thought Dillon would be safe with the chief of police—and Harper *had* taken good care of her. Harper had told Clyde once that Dillon was the spunkiest little girl he knew. Told Clyde that if he and Redwing could help get Dillon through her teen years without mishap, that was all he asked.

Harper was cleaning Bucky's feet, lifting Bucky's left front hoof, when he paused, frowning.

"Davis, give me more light. Shine your torch here."

The gelding stood patiently, resting his left front hoof in Harper's hand, leaning his head on Harper's shoulder. Harper looked up at Davis. "We'll need shots of this."

"Looks like a stone cut, right across the metal." She adjusted her camera. Her lights flashed and flashed again, taking half a dozen shots.

Setting Bucky's foot down, Harper shone his torch along the line of Bucky's hoofprints leading out into the yard. "Same prints as at the scene." His face was set like a rock. "Photograph them, Juana. Every few feet, back down the alleyway, across the yard, up the lane. Pick out individual trails of prints, going and coming.

Get them going down the road, where I left this afternoon, and coming back, as far as you can see them."

Davis knelt, looking. "Exact same scar. I got plenty of shots at the scene."

"Shots where I rode?"

"Shots where Bucky never set foot." Rising, she began the tedious, close-up photographing, while Harper put Bucky in his stall, fed and watered him, and headed for the house, avoiding the lines of hoofprints.

Two shadows followed him, flashing across the porch into the darkness beneath a metal chair, Joe's eyes blazing with anger.

Moving inside, Harper picked up the phone, dialing quickly.

"Turrey, you awake?" Through the screen door, his voice was clear and decisive. He listened, and laughed. "I know it's not light yet. I need you now. Get a cup of coffee and get over here. We need to pull Bucky's shoes to be entered as evidence, and reshoe him. No, I can't pull his shoes. They're evidence. I need someone not connected. I have to tell you, Turrey, somewhere down the line you'll likely have to testify in court."

Turrey must have reacted sharply to that announcement. The cats could hear the faint, sharp crackle of his voice at the other end of the line, and Harper smiled.

"That's all right, the judge doesn't care if you're not a professional speaker."

"I don't understand," Dulcie whispered. "Those big heavy hoofprints at the scene, they did have a scar. But they weren't Bucky's. They were there before Harper arrived."

But Joe was watching the threesome in the kitchen.

Clyde and Harper sat at the table, where Harper was opening a cold can of beans and a box of crackers. Outside, Detective Ray had stopped sifting sand, retrieved a box from her car, and came carrying it into the kitchen. "Here are the Polaroid shots, Captain. And the first plaster casts."

Harper wolfed down cold beans and crackers as he studied the casts and the photos.

"Same scar, deep in the outside curve."

Kathleen Ray looked hard at the captain. "That one, Captain, is from Bucky. This one, with the leaf at the edge of the cast? That was underneath the bodies. Underneath Helen Marner's shoulder. The casts are of the same horseshoe. Or one is a good copy."

Harper just looked at her.

"And this shot was made way up the hill, in a place you didn't go. I know where you rode. You didn't go up there, didn't go near that part of the hill."

"Appears to be Bucky's shoe," Harper said tiredly. Joe and Dulcie looked at each other. Charlie, standing at the stove, scrambling eggs and cooking bacon, was white faced and grim, her freckles as dark as paint splatters. Harper looked up at her. "Charlie, I don't have time to eat."

She stared at the cold beans and crackers. "You are eating. I bet you haven't had a hot meal since yesterday."

Harper nodded to Detective Ray. "Turn your tape recorder on, Kathleen. You can take my statement."

Charlie turned away. Clyde looked at Harper a long time, his eyes filled with helplessness. He looked around him once as if half expecting help to materialize from the woodwork; then he rose and left the house, passing within three feet of Joe and Dulcie. He was too preoccupied to see them.

The two cats, sitting in the shadows beneath the porch chair and peering in through the screen door, listened to Harper recount his movements of the previous afternoon, giving Detective Ray place and time for every smallest action, laying it out in far more detail than he had for Detective Davis—as if Harper were the suspect. And as the facts and Harper's vulnerability were revealed, the cats' fears deepened into a raw, claw-tingling indignation. Joe Grey sat glowering, working himself into a deep rage.

Any pleasure he had ever taken in teasing the police captain vanished now. Any smug tricks and sly innuendos, as Joe secretly collected and passed on information, were forgotten. At this moment, Joe's admiration for Max Harper ruled him.

Someone, some lowlife, was out to get Max Harper, to ruin him big time.

Harper, with no witness to his movements during the time of the murder, would have only his uncorroborated statements, as told to the two detectives. As the cats crouched listening, deeply alarmed, above them the sky began to pale and the dawn wind to stir sharper; and up the hills, the lights of the searchers moved ever higher into the wild, rocky forest.

And farther north, at the edge of the forest within the Pamillon estate, the cougar prowled, stepping soundlessly on thick pads among the fallen walls of the mansion, the big male seeming, in the first gray haze of dawn, no more than a shifting shadow. He was a powerful beast, sauntering casually across the rubble as if he owned this land. In his own wild way, he did own it—had made it part of his territory.

The front walls of the big Mediterranean mansion had fallen away, leaving the first and second floors open like a two-story stage set on which the king of beasts was, at this moment, the only player.

Pausing at the threshold to the open parlor, he scented out keenly, his ears sharply forward, his eyes narrowed and intent. Softly panting, he lifted his gaze up past the broken stair to the second-floor nursery, where something drew his attention.

Moving silently into the parlor, he prowled among the rotting, vine-covered furniture, his yellow eyes fixed on the ragged edge of the floor above. He crouched.

In one liquid and powerful leap he gained the broken ceiling and stood in the upstairs nursery.

Moving without sound among the remnants of chests and beds, he sniffed at the fallen bricks beside the fireplace. He licked the leg of a rocking chair, tasting blood.

He pawed, for some moments, at the bloody debris around the chair, then dug beside the fireplace at a pile of broken timbers. Something was there, *had* been there, something had bled there.

But the sharp stink of wet ashes within the fireplace warped all lesser scents. The smell stung his nose, made him grimace. He could scent nothing alive now, nothing edible. He dug again at the timbers, stopping when he raked his paw on a nail and his own blood flowed. Snarling, he backed away.

Padding to the edge of the broken floor, he looked back once, then dropped down again to the parlor, his movements as smooth as water flowing, and sauntered away into the garden. He was, in the rising dawn, the color of spun honey.

Deep beneath the timbers, the kit listened to the cougar depart. Her little body was iced with terror. From the moment the big beast gained the nursery and began to paw and dig, she had been frozen with fear. Even concealed inside the woodbox, beneath the fallen wall, she was petrified. Why had she come here? Why had she left the safety of the ranch yard to go adventuring on such a night?

The lid of the box did not close fully. Crouching in the black interior, she had seen the cougar looking in. She had prayed so hard she thought her heart would stop, prayed that her black and brown coat was invisible. That the stink of ashes would conceal her scent. They were old, wet ashes, packed deep.

The kit did not know or care that the fires of the nursery hearth, laid down forty years before, had, over generations, been augmented by the fires of hoboes and then of occasional flower children, then of the present-day homeless wandering the Molena Point foothills, seeking shelter on cold nights. But indeed, the accumulated charcoal and lime, sour water and rot and mildew hid many scents from the lion.

The kit cared about none of that. She cared only that she was still alive and uneaten. But when, warily, she slipped out and padded across the nursery to hide herself at its edge, looking down, she forgot even her debilitating fear.

He was down there.

The kit, standing on the edge of the broken floor, peered shyly over, watching the golden king.

The cougar, out in the air again, forgot the elusive and confusing scents from the nursery and centered on the fresh trail of a doe, looking up the hill searching for any faintest movement, for the twitch of an ear, the gleam of dark eyes.

He was the color of the sun-struck desert. He was thirteen feet long from tail tip to nose, weighed a hundred and thirty pounds, and was still growing. Forced from the territory of his mother, the young male had come to claim a home range with water and sufficient game.

The Pamillon estate had water trapped in the old cellars, and there were plenty of deer and raccoons, and now, today, that strange, tantalizing whiff of human blood that he had earlier followed. And the vanishing scent of some small feline cousin, lost too quickly in the ashes.

But deer were his natural food, his game of choice. Moving uphill, away from the fallen walls, he padded along the well-used trail, stalking the doe, forgetting the small cat that stood above, so raptly watching him.

The sight of the lion made her shiver clear down to her soft little middle. Shiver with fear. Shiver with wonder, and envy. He was huge. He was magnificent. He was master of all the cat world. She had never dreamed of such a sight, so filled with powerful, arrogant grace. If she had any more lives yet to live, the kit thought, next time she would be a cougar. She would be lithe. Sleek. A golden lioness, amber bright. She was so overwhelmed by the wonders the lion stirred in her that it took a long time to remember that behind her in the nursery she had smelled the blood of a human child. It took her more time still to decide what to do about that.

7

From Harper's kitchen, the smell of coffee drifted out across the porch as the cats watched through the screen, Joe Grey fidgeting irritably, rocking from paw to paw, his ears back, every wary alarm in his feline body clanging, as he listened to Max Harper, at the kitchen table, giving his formal statement to Detective Ray.

Harper's long, Levi's-clad legs were stretched out, his thin, lined face was expressionless, his brown eyes shielded in that way he had—a cop's closed face—so you could read nothing of what he was thinking.

From the time he had left the Marners and Dillon at the restaurant, until he arrived at the station three and a half hours later, an hour after he was due to go on watch, he had been in contact with no one. As far as Harper knew, no one had seen him.

"I left Café Mundo at about one twenty-five, maybe five minutes after Dillon and the Marners. I rode home along Coyote Trail, around the foot of the hills. That's the shortest way. The Marners and Dillon headed north up that steep bridle trail behind the Blackwell Ranch."

"And Crystal wasn't with you?"

"No, the horse she was leasing was to be shod today. I got home about two, unsaddled Bucky and cooled him off, sponged him and rubbed him down. Cleaned his tack and did some stable chores. Fed him, gave the dogs a run, and fed them. I had just come in the house to shower and change when the phone rang.

"It sounded like a woman. I couldn't be sure. Husky voice, like someone who has a cold. She wouldn't give her name. Said she thought I'd be interested in Stubby Baker because I was the one responsible for his going to prison. Kathleen, do you remember Baker?"

Officer Ray looked up at him. "Paroled out of San Quentin about three months ago. Mile-long list of scams."

Harper nodded. "She said Baker had come back to Molena Point to work a land scam involving the old Pamillon place. Said there was a problem with the title, one of those involved family things, and that Baker thought he could manipulate the records. Work through a fake title company, pretend to sell the land, and skip with the money. She said he had fake escrow seals, fake documents. Said he was working with someone from Santa Barbara, that the buyers were a group of older people down there, professionals wanting to start their own retirement complex.

"I'd seen Baker up around the Pamillon place, I'd ridden up there several times because of those cougar reports. And I knew Baker had been nosing around in the Department of Records. That, with her story, made me want to check him out.

"Baker's staying in a studio apartment over on Santa Fe. The informant said he was scheduled to meet with his partner at four that afternoon, at Baker's place. That they were getting ready to make the transaction. That the buyers were going to put a lot of money up front, that they had complete faith in Baker.

"The last scam he pulled here in Molena Point was so shoddy I can't envision anyone trusting him. But I caught a shower, dressed, and went over there. I thought if I could make his partner, get a description and run his plates, we might come up with enough to search the apartment, nip this before those folks got taken. I drove the old Plymouth."

Some months earlier, Harper had bought a nondescript 1992 Plymouth to use for occasional surveillance. Usually the detectives picked up a Rent-A-Wreck, a different car for every stakeout, so the local no-goods would find them harder to spot.

"I parked at the corner of Santa Fe and First behind some overgrown shrubs, sat with a newspaper in front of my face. Watched the apartment for over an hour. Not a sign of Baker. Only one person went up the outside stairs—the old woman from Two D. Baker's in Two B. No one came down, no one left any apartment I could see, and there's only the one entrance, there in front, except fire escapes. Even the garbage is carried out the front. I could see all of the second-floor balcony, could see Baker's door and window. Didn't see any movement inside, no twitch of the curtain, no light burning.

"Maybe Baker made me and had a quick change of plans. I left at ten to five, swung by my place to pick up my unit, got to the station at five."

Detective Ray pushed back her long, dark hair. "Did anyone see you, anyone you knew?"

"If they did, they didn't speak to me. I didn't notice anyone, just a few tourists."

"Did you know the woman who made the call? Recognize her voice?"

"As best I could tell, she wasn't anyone I've talked with in the past. No, I didn't recognize her." Harper frowned. "It wasn't that woman snitch who bugs me, at least not the way she usually sounds. That woman speaks so softly, with a touch of sarcasm . . ."

Outside the screened door, the soft-voiced snitch twitched her whiskers and smiled.

"This one—yes, probably disguised," Harper said. "Sounded older, rough and grainy. If it *was* a disguise, I bet it gave her a sore throat."

And both cats watched Harper with concern. This giving of a formal statement and all that implied had them more than frightened, left them feeling as lost as two abandoned strays in a strange city.

Max Harper was the one human who made their sleuthing worth the trouble, who, when they helped to solve a case, would see the perps successfully prosecuted—the one law enforcement type who made their sneaky feline efforts worth the trip.

And Harper was more than that to Joe Grey. Joe had a deep and caring respect for the police captain—for his hunting abilities, for his dry humor, which was almost as subtle as the humor of a cat, and for his general attitude of quiet power—all traits that the tomcat greatly admired.

But now, crouched in the dark beneath the deck chair, Joe imagined with painful clarity Max Harper facing Judge Wesley not as a witness for the prosecution but as a prisoner about to be prosecuted. The thought made his belly queasy and his paws sweat.

He might torment Max Harper, might be amused by Harper's irritable response to certain anonymous phone tips—amused by Harper's unease at never being able to identify the source of certain information. But he would gladly rip apart whoever had set up this scam.

And there was no doubt in either cat's mind that it was a scam. Some lowlife was out to ruin Harper, with the help of the American justice system.

During Harper's statement, Charlie had not left the room. When he was finished, she poured fresh coffee for him and Detective Ray, and dished up the breakfast she had kept warm. Harper was wolfing his scrambled eggs when the blacksmith arrived.

Thc cats followed Harper and Turrey to the stables, again streaking into the feed room. In the rising dawn, it was harder to stay out of sight.

Clyde's yellow car was gone from the yard. Whether he had left to give Harper privacy or was angry at Charlie for mothering Harper, the cats couldn't guess. Clyde and Harper had been friends ever since high school, and Clyde was the only non-law-enforcement type Harper hung out with. For Clyde to see his own girlfriend mooning over Harper—if he did see it, if he was even aware of Charlie's feelings—was enough to make anyone mad.

Well, Clyde had had plenty of girlfriends before Charlie; it wasn't like they'd been seeing each other forever. These human entanglements were so—*human*. Filled with subtleties and indirect meanings and hurt feelings. Awash in innuendos. Nothing like a good straightforward feline relationship.

From the shadows of the feed room, the cats watched as Turrey pulled Bucky's shoes, the small, leathered man easy and slow in his movements. As he pulled each shoe, he dropped it into an evidence bag that Detective Davis held open for him. Captain Harper stood aside. Already he had taken an arm's-length position, directing his people but handling nothing. He had approached Bucky only to bring the gelding from his stall and put him in the cross-ties, then stepped away.

The cats watched the blacksmith clean out the dirt from each hoof, and scrape it, too, into the evidence bags. Watched Turrey fashion a new pair of shoes for Bucky. Dulcie had a hard time not sneezing at the smell of burning hoof as Turrey tested the metal against Bucky's foot—the seared hoof smoldered as hot as Joe's anger at Max Harper's unknown enemy.

Of course Harper had been set up. What else? All Joe could think was, he'd like to get his teeth into whoever had hatched this little plot.

But while Joe wanted to slash the unidentified killer, Dulcie just looked sad, her pointed little face grim, her green eyes filled with misery.

Charlie seemed the last one to admit the truth. When Turrey left, and the cats followed Harper back to the house, Charlie said, "Maybe there was some mix-up. Maybe the photos and casts were made where you did ride, before the murder—maybe days before." She stood at the sink washing up the breakfast dishes, her face flushed either from the steam or from stifled tears.

"I haven't ridden up there in weeks," Harper told her. "And the evidence was *not* taken from where I rode last night."

"Maybe two separate shoes got scarred. Maybe some piece of dangerous metal is half-buried in the trail, and both horses tripped on it. If we could find it . . ."

Harper patted her shoulder. "Leave it, Charlie."

"But . . ."

"There's more here than you're seeing."

She looked at him, red-faced and miserable.

"I have good detectives, honest detectives," Harper said softly. "We'll get this sorted out. And we'll find Dillon."

But the cats looked at each other and shivered. Someone wanting to destroy Max Harper had killed two people and might have killed Dillon.

Still, if Dillon was alive, if they were holding her for some reason, the twelve-year-old would be a hard prisoner to deal with. Dillon wouldn't knuckle under easily.

Dulcie's voice was hardly a whisper. "What about this Stubby Baker? Harper said he's been in town only a few weeks. What if Baker *was* in his apartment? What if he saw Harper watching? What if he could testify to Harper's presence there on the street between four and five?"

"Oh, right. And an ex-con is going to step right up and testify for a cop he hates."

But he sat thinking. "What day was it that the kit had that encounter with Baker?"

"How do you know that was Baker?"

"She watched him through the window. Don't you remember? Saw his name on some letters."

Dulcie smiled. "I do now. The kit is not a great fan of this Baker."

A week before the murder, the kit ran afoul of Baker as she was licking up a nice bowl of custard in the alley behind Jolly's Deli.

Jolly's alley, to the kit, was a gourmet wonderland. The handsome, brick-paved lane, with its potted trees and benches, offered the village cats a nirvana of imported treats. And that particular afternoon she had been quite alone there, no bigger cats to chase her away. Had been up to her furry ears in cold boiled shrimp and a creamy custard when a tall, handsome man entered the alley.

He was dark-haired, slim, with dark, sparkling eyes, a movie star kind of human of such striking magnetism and appeal that the kit was drawn right to him. She sat up, watching him.

"Hello, kitty," he said with a soft smile.

In a rare fit of pleasure and trust she had run to him and reared up beside his leg—never touching him but curling up in an enticing begging dance, asking prettily to be petted.

The man kicked her. Sent her flying. She landed against a shop wall, hurting her shoulder. She had been shocked at his unkindness. Only in that second after he kicked her, when she landed staring up at him hissing, did she see the evil beneath his smiling mask. When, laughing, he drew back to kick her again.

That man's smell had burned into her memory. Within the dark side of her mysterious cat mind, she invented vast tortures reserved for this human, exquisite pain that she longed to visit upon him. Oh, she had told Joe and Dulcie in detail how, when he left the alley, she followed him, keeping to the shadows cast by steps and protruding bay windows. Followed him to an apartment building, where he climbed its open stairs from the sidewalk to a second-floor balcony tucked between tall peaked roofs and shaded by an overhanging tree. Swarming up into the branches, the kit peered past wooden shutters into a lovely apartment of white walls, tile floors, and soft leather that matched the way the man looked.

The mail on the coffee table told her his name was Baker. She watched this Baker and hated him. Tried to think of a way to hurt him. Her nose was inches from the glass when he swung around and saw her, and his eyes grew wide. The kit swarmed down the tree and ran.

"A mean-tempered dude," Joe Grey said. "With his record, and Harper having sent him up, you can bet he's connected."

"You may be right, but . . ."

"Baker's part of this mess, Dulcie, you can wager your sweet paws. And I mean to nail him."

8

A hundred miles north, in San Francisco, the morning after the Marners' murder, Sunday morning, Kate headed again for the Cat Museum, feeling upbeat and determined.

If she had known about the grisly deaths of Ruthie and Helen Marner, she might not have left her secure apartment.

She hadn't read the paper or turned on the TV or radio since last Saturday, when the headlines so upset her. She didn't care to know any more about Lee Wark or about the local rash of cat killings—but it was silly to put off doing something she wanted badly to do.

She was, after all, only two hours from home, from Molena Point and safety. She could run down there anytime. Hanni wanted her to go.

Anyway, Lee Wark was probably hundreds of miles from San Francisco. Why would he hide in the city, so close to San Quentin? Why would he stay in California at all, with every police department in the state looking for him? Wark had spent plenty of time in Latin America, likely that was where he'd gone. She had, for no sensible reason, let the newspaper's sensational muck-raking terrify her.

Heading up Stockton, walking fast in the fog-eating wind, resisting any smallest urge to turn back, she had gone five blocks and was beginning to feel better, was telling herself what a lovely outing this would be, how much she would enjoy the museum, was happily dodging people who were hurrying along in the other direction—to church, out to breakfast—when she noticed a man on the opposite side of the street keeping pace with her, his black topcoat whipping in the wind, the collar turned up and his black hat tipped low like the heavy in some forties' movie.

When she slowed, he slowed.

When she moved faster, he swung along just as quickly, his reflection leaping in the store windows.

He did not resemble Lee Wark; he was very straight rather than slouched, and broader of shoulder than Wark. His black topcoat looked of good quality, over the dark suit, his neatly clipped black beard and expensive hat implying a man of some substance. The very opposite of Wark. A man simply walking to church or to an early appointment, or to work in some business that was open on Sunday, maybe one of the shops near Fisherman's Wharf.

She turned up Russian Hill, disgusted with herself, angry because her heart was tripping too fast; she was letting fear eat at her. Behind her, the man continued on up Stockton, never looking her way. She felt really stupid.

Yet something about him, despite the broad shoulders and beard and nice clothes, left her sick with fear.

Had she caught a glimpse of his eyes beneath the dark brim? Lee Wark's cold gray eyes? She couldn't help it, she was overwhelmed again with that terrible panic.

Maybe she *should* drive down to the village with Hanni, for the week. Hanni had business there, and her family had a weekend cottage. They were so busy at work, it would be difficult for both of them to go.

"So we take a week off," Hanni had said. "While we wait for fabric orders and the workrooms. That won't kill any of our clients. Relax, Kate. I'm the boss, I say we drive down. You know the movers and shakers in the village better than I. You can help me, it's for a good cause." Hanni had whirled around the studio, kicking a book of fabric samples, twirling her long skirt, her short white hair and gold dangle earrings catching the studio lights, her brown Latin eyes laughing. "We need the time off. We deserve it!"

Kate had known Hanni only slightly in Molena Point when the family was down for weekends. She had always envied Hanni's looks, her prematurely white, bobbed hair, a woman so sleek and slim—those long lean lines—that even in faded jeans and an old sweatshirt, she could have stepped right out of Saks's window.

Strange—if Hanni hadn't been involved with the Cat Museum, very likely they wouldn't be considering the trip home just now.

It was Hanni who had awakened her interest in the Cat Museum, who had shown her photographs of the galleries. Hanni was on the board, deeply involved in the charitable institution's pending sale.

"We have to move somewhere, we're about ready to go into escrow. Twenty million for that Russian Hill property—and the taxes are skyrocketing. And so much pressure from the city—from some friend of the city, you can bet, who wants to build on that land."

Hanni shrugged. "For that kind of money, why fight it? We can build a lovely complex of galleries and gardens, and I think the old Pamillon estate, those old adobe walls and oak trees, might be perfect. That's the way the present museum was built; McCabe started by combining four private homes and their gardens. You need to go up there, Kate. You need to see it."

"Did you say McCabe?"

"Yes. You've read about him? He—"

"I . . . suppose I have. The name's familiar."

Only since she'd moved back to San Francisco had she tried to trace her family, from information the adoption agency was finally willing to release. Her grandfather's name had been McCabe. The agency said he'd been a newspaper columnist and an architect; they said he had not used a first name.

"If we don't find a place soon," Hanni had said, "the art collection will have to go into storage, and we'd rather not do that." Taking her hand, Hanni had given her that infectious grin. "Come with me, Kate. Jim and the kids don't care if I go, and you don't have an excuse. Come help me. You know Molena Point, you know realtors there. I want your opinion of that land."

"But I don't need to go there to tell you what I already know."

"You need a vacation."

Hanni, the mover and shaker. Kate's boss was a top-flight interior designer and a more-than-shrewd businesswoman. Kate loved working with her, she loved

Hanni's enthusiasm. She loved telling people she was assistant to the well-known designer, Hanni Coon. And if Hanni wanted a week in Molena Point, what better excuse than a multimillion-dollar real estate deal?

Striding up Russian Hill, she saw no more "suspicious" men. The morning was bright, the blowing clouds sending running shadows before her across the pale, crowded houses and apartments. Climbing, she was short of breath. Out of shape. Had to stop every few blocks. If she were back in Molena Point for a week she'd walk miles—along the beach, through the village, down the rocky coast.

It would be so embarrassing to go back. She hadn't been home since the afternoon she threw her clothes in the car and took off up 101, escaping Lee Wark. And escaping her own husband. It was Jimmie who had paid Wark to kill her. That came out in the trial.

Everyone in the village knew her husband had gone to prison for counterfeiting, for transporting stolen cars, and as accessory to the murder for which Wark had been convicted—and for conspiracy to kill his own wife.

How had San Quentin let those killers escape? How could a maximum security prison be so lax? The three had overpowered a guard, taken him hostage, using prison-made weapons. A garrote made with sharpened silverware from the kitchen and strips of blanket. That must have embarrassed prison authorities. The guard was not expected to live. They had dumped him in a ditch in Sausalito, where authorities thought the men had split up. Two had apparently stolen cars, and may have taken clothes from the charity Dumpster of a local church.

Had Lee Wark come across the Golden Gate bridge into the city? He could have walked across.

Well, he wouldn't go to Molena Point, wouldn't show his face in the village while Max Harper was chief of police. Harper had come down on Wark with a vengeance, had seen that the prosecuting attorney was aware of every dirty detail, every smallest piece of evidence.

I could go back for a few days. So safe at home. And none of my real friends care that Jimmie's in prison—not Wilma, certainly not Clyde.

The thought of Clyde gave her a silly little thrill that surprised her.

Well, there *had* been something between them, an attraction that she'd never let get out of hand while she and Jimmie were married.

And then when she left Jimmie, Clyde had learned about her double nature, and that had turned him off big time.

As she climbed higher up Russian Hill, the steep sidewalk turned brilliant with sun; the sun on her back felt as healing as a warm, gentle hand. Hurrying upward, stopping sometimes to rest, she fixed her attention on the subtle tone combinations of the many-colored Victorian homes. San Francisco's painted ladies. But, nearing the crest, she stopped suddenly.

He was there. Stepping out from between two houses. The man in the black topcoat.

She swallowed and backed away, ice cold. Wanted to run. Wouldn't give him the satisfaction.

She couldn't see his face. Black hat, pulled low. Black topcoat, collar turned up even in the hot sun so his eyes were nearly hidden. Swallowing, trying to make her heart stop pounding, she casually crossed the street.

Maybe he was some harmless ogler. Nothing more threatening than that.

As she drew opposite where he'd stood, he moved back between the two houses and was gone. Peering across, into the narrow side yard, she saw only a hedge and a patchy scruff of lawn.

And now, up the hill, rose the red rooftops and huge old oaks of the museum. She hurried up toward them, eager to be among people.

But then, as she turned into the museum gardens, it wasn't people who surrounded her, it was the museum cats. Cats sunning under the flowers and bushes and atop the low walls, all of them watching her as she entered along the brick walk and through the wrought-iron gate.

What kind of cats these might be would not be public knowledge—would be the museum's most sheltered secret, if even the museum staff knew.

She wandered the paths for a long time among lush masses of flowering bushes, tall clumps of Peruvian lilies, densely flowering tangles. The scents of nasturtium and geranium eased her nerves. She felt so uncertain about asking to see McCabe's diaries. She was sure they had them, yet had been reluctant even to ask if Hanni knew—because she would have to give Hanni an explanation. And she might, in a weak moment, confess to Hanni that she thought McCabe could be her grandfather. It was all so complicated.

I will simply ask, she told herself. *Ask, and look at what is there, and not* make *it complicated.* Moving toward the door, she pinched a sprig of lavender, sniffed at it to calm herself, stood looking in through the museum's leaded windows at the white-walled galleries.

But as she turned toward the main entrance, she was facing the man in black. He stood just beyond the door, beneath an arbor, his features in shadow, his muddy eyes on her.

Catching her breath, she hurried in through the glass doors and fled to the reception desk, begging the pudgy woman curator to call a cab. She felt hardly able to speak. She stood pressing against the desk, waiting for the taxi to arrive, then ran out to it, sat stiffly in the backseat, unable to stop shaking. She was so cold and shivering that when she got home she could hardly fit her key in the lock. Safe at last in her apartment, she threw the bolts on the doors and turned up the heat.

It had been Lee Wark. She'd seen him clearly. His eyes, the same muddy-glassy eyes.

What if he'd followed her home, in a second cab? Or maybe he took her cab's number, would find out from her driver where she lived? She had to call the police. Report that she'd seen him. Wark was a wanted felon, a convicted killer.

Most of all, she had to get out of San Francisco.

9

Clyde Damen's white Cape Cod cottage shook with the stutter of jackhammers and the thud of falling timbers, enough racket to collapse a poor cat's eardrums. Joe Grey sat on the kitchen counter, waiting for Clyde to make his breakfast, and watching through the window the handsome Victorian home behind them being torn down and fed, timber by splintered timber, to a series of large metal Dumpsters that stood in the wide front yard.

The house's finer fittings, the crown molding, the stained-glass windows, the hand-carved banister and carved cabinets, had long since been sold to an antique dealer, as had the fine Victorian furniture. Seventy-year-old Lucinda Greenlaw had no need any longer for large pieces of furniture since she had married Shamas and moved into his travel trailer and set out to see the world—or at least see more of the West Coast.

All the houses behind Clyde's had been sold. Both sides of that street were being cleared to accommodate a small, exclusive shopping plaza. The constant noise of the tear-down had been too hard on the other cats—

on the three ordinary kitties who could not understand the source of the threatening racket, and on old Rube, the elderly Labrador. Clyde had taken them up to the vet's to board.

Clyde and Dr. Firetti had an arrangement involving hospital and boarding bills swapped for auto repairs, an agreement that worked to everyone's advantage except that of the IRS. Clyde didn't talk about that.

"Another few weeks," Clyde grumbled, staring out at the destruction, "we'll be looking out the window at a solid two-story wall smack in your face. The house will be dark as a tomb. No sunrise. No sun at all. You want to look at the hills? Forget it. Might as well have the Empire State Building in the backyard."

"A handsome stucco wall," Joe said, quoting Dulcie, "to define the back garden—turn it into an enclosed patio."

"That view of the hills was the main reason I bought this house—that and the sunrise. A three-story wall will destroy them both."

"It won't *destroy* the hills and sunrise. The hills and sunrise will still be there. You just . . ."

"Shut up, Joe. Here, eat your breakfast. Kippers and sour cream. And don't growl. You don't have to kill the kippers. You may not have noticed in your enthusiasm that the kippers are already dead."

Clyde set his own plate of eggs on the table beside a bowl of Sugar Pops. The phone rang. Snatching it from the wall, he answered through a mouthful of egg.

He grew very still.

Joe padded across the table to press against Clyde's shoulder, his ear to the phone.

Max Harper sounded grim.

"I have an appointment with the city attorney. Ten A.M. Going to take administrative leave."

"Because of the Marner case? But—"

"Because of Bucky's shoe, Bucky's hoofprints all over the scene. And because of new evidence."

"What new evidence?"

"I just got the report from Salinas. The lab rushed it through. They have the murder weapon."

"Oh. Well, that's—"

"Remember that bone-handled butcher knife that Millie's aunt sent her from Sweden?"

"I remember it. A big, stubby knife with silver inlay."

"One of my detectives found it in my hay shed, under a bale of alfalfa."

"But—"

"The dried blood on it was a match for both Helen and Ruthie."

"That's insane. No one would commit a murder and hide the weapon in his own barn. Where are you? I'll come over. If you step off the case—"

"I've already stepped off. I'm going to ask Gedding to appoint an interim chief until this thing gets sorted out."

"Max, if someone's out to frame you—"

"I've removed myself from the case. There was nothing else I could do. I'm not giving up the search for Dillon. I'll keep on with that, acting as a civilian. And I'm going to have to look for witnesses."

"I can take some time off, help you talk to people. Help you look for Dillon."

"I—we'll talk about it. Every cop on the central

coast is looking for her. Every law enforcement agency in California."

"But—"

"I see Gedding at ten."

"Meet for lunch?"

"Say, one o'clock at Moreno's."

"One o'clock." Clyde hung up, glancing toward Joe.

But Joe Grey wasn't there. Through the kitchen window Clyde saw a gray streak vanish over the fence, heading into the village. Clyde stood looking, swearing softly, but he didn't open the door to shout after Joe.

What good would it do? He couldn't make Joe come back. And, under the present circumstances, he guessed he didn't want to.

If Joe could help Harper, Clyde promised himself he'd never again make one disparaging, discouraging, cutting remark aimed at the tomcat. Would never again tease either Joe or Dulcie. He was, in fact, so upset about Harper that he poured coffee on his cereal and had eaten half the bowl before he realized how strange it tasted.

By the time Max Harper entered Lowell Gedding's office at ten, the two sleuths in question had concealed themselves handily behind a Chinese planter of maidenhair fern, on the wide ledge inside the city attorney's bay window.

Gedding didn't like screens on his windows, nor were screens needed in Molena Point. The sea wind kept flies away. And the decorative burglar grid that covered the window offered ample security. The window could safely remain open, allowing access to no living creature larger than, say, your ordinary house cat.

The morning sun washed pleasantly across the white walls of Gedding's office and across the pale Mexican-tile floor. A white, hand-woven rug was positioned on the amber tiles directly in front of Gedding's dark antique desk. Three walls were bare. On the fourth expanse hung five black-and-white Ansel Adams photographs: stark, hard-edged studies of sand dunes, magnificent in their simplicity.

Gedding sat behind his desk, relaxed and cool. He was a slim, bald, deeply tanned man in his sixties, with the look of the military about him. His gaze was direct, his body well honed, easy in its nicely tailored business suit of a dark, thin fabric. His green eyes were intense.

"Sit down, Max. I gather this is about the Marner murders."

Harper nodded.

"You have nothing further on Dillon Thurwell?"

"Nothing. Search parties are out, her picture on the Web and to the wire services. We—the department has the murder weapon."

Gedding leaned forward.

"Detective Davis found it yesterday. They got the lab report back this morning. The blood of both victims was on it."

"And?"

"It is a butcher knife from my kitchen. It was found in my hay shed."

"Is it a common make, a knife that could be duplicated?"

"It is a one-of-a-kind carving knife made in Sweden. Swedish steel, hand-carved bone handle and silver inlay."

Gedding looked deeply at Harper. "Why would someone set you up, Max, but do it so obviously? Had you missed the knife prior to the murder?"

"I hadn't used anything out of that drawer in weeks except a couple of paring knives. It could have been gone for some time."

"It's not like you not to remember details."

"In your own house? In a place you're so used to, you stop seeing things?"

"I suppose. So what now? You've already removed yourself from the case. You're not here to ask for administrative leave?"

"Exactly why I'm here. Someone took that knife from the house. Someone either borrowed my horse or came up with a set of matching shoes for his own horse, and marked both shoes. Someone with a pair of boots like mine, the soles worn into the same indentations."

"You've checked the house for any signs of break-in."

"The detectives have been over it three times."

"No one has a key?"

"No one."

"Surely a houseguest or dinner guest could have taken the knife, anyone coming in. Have you made a list of who's been there?"

Harper handed a list across the desk. "Everyone who's been in my house the last three months. A few close friends and the plumber. You can see I have a big social life.

"I don't think the killer's name is there. No one comes in my place, Lowell, except friends I trust fully."

"That include Crystal Ryder?"

"She . . ." Max hesitated. "She's been up at my place three times, uninvited. She didn't go in the house any time—that I know of."

"*Could* she have gone in?"

"Yes, I suppose she could have. While I was feeding or working with the horses. I didn't like her coming up there. When she showed up, I went on with my work."

"That's why she isn't on the list." Gedding's tone was cool.

"Exactly why. Because she wasn't inside, to my knowledge."

"That's not the way I heard the story. Talk in the village has you two pretty close."

"Put her on the list," Harper said. "Make a notation that I never saw her go inside, never saw her inside the house."

Gedding leaned back in his chair. "I've received two anonymous phone calls that when you left the restaurant, the day of the murder, you were seen riding your buckskin up the mountain following Helen and Ruthie and Dillon. Riding *up* the mountain, Max, away from your place, not down the hills toward home as you said in your statement."

"There's nothing I can say to that, Lowell. It isn't true. I didn't do that. I went directly home, took care of Bucky and the other animals. Answered the phone—that tip about Baker. I showered and dressed, and headed for Baker's place. You've read my statement."

Gedding sighed. "And you have no changes to make to that statement?"

"None."

"It's turning into a tangle. The best bet—not that I think your people can't handle it, but to get them off the hot seat—would be to call in an outside detective."

Harper nodded. "I think you have to do that. Someone on loan from another district."

"I can talk to San Francisco. I have a friend in the department there. Good detective—Dallas Garza. The family has a weekend cottage down here. I'm sure he'd welcome a change of scene."

Behind the Chinese planter, narrowed yellow eyes met blazing green eyes. Neither Joe nor Dulcie had thought of an outside investigator.

And how had Gedding come up with a candidate so fast?

The cats had thought there was mutual trust here. Joe had heard Harper tell Clyde, more than once, how Gedding had stood by him when the mayor or city council meddled in police business.

What bothered Joe was, one council member had pushed hard to hire Gedding. And that man wanted Harper out of the department. So where did Gedding's loyalties lie?

"Garza's brother-in-law," Gedding said, "is chief U.S. probation officer in San Francisco. I believe Wilma Getz worked with him before she retired. Garza's niece—she's the interior designer that Kate Osborne works for. But you know the family—they have a weekend cottage in the village. Kate and Hanni, when they were small, used to play together."

"I know who they are," Harper said stiffly. "Should I say, *small world,*" he added dryly.

Gedding shrugged and straightened the papers on his desk. "Have you made any other arrangements?"

"When your man arrives, Ray and Davis are prepared to step off the case, if he so chooses. I've put Lieutenant Brennan in charge of the department.

"As for my personal life, I don't plan to stay at home. I've taken my horses up to Campbell Ranch, they'll keep them ridden. As long as I live alone and isolated, there'll be a shadow on my activities. I'm locking up my place and moving in with Clyde. Unless," Harper said with a twisted smile, "unless you plan to put a leg bracelet on me."

Joe Grey felt his belly lurch. Though Harper was joking, the thought of an electronic monitor made him twitch. If Harper had to phone the station for permission to walk out his front door, he might as well be locked in a steel kennel.

It was noon when Harper left Gedding's office, now on official leave. The cats were about to slip out through the window when Gedding made a long-distance call; they subsided again, beneath the potted fern.

Gedding was apparently talking with the chief of police in San Francisco. It was all very low-key. Gedding was as nice as pie; apparently he and Chief Barron went back to college days. Barron seemed to be telling him that Garza was busy on a case and suggesting he send another man. Gedding was gently insistent. He wanted Garza, badly needed Garza. It was a long and oblique discussion that left the cats fidgeting. It ended, apparently, with San Francisco's assurance that Garza was on his way.

"Most informative," Joe muttered as they hurried out along the parking lot.

"Informative, and confusing. Look. Harper's still here."

In the parking lot shared by the courthouse and police headquarters, Harper was putting some cardboard boxes in his king cab pickup; the cats could see a pair of field boots sticking out from the top and a gray sweatshirt.

"He's cleaned out his desk," Dulcie whispered.

"Dulcie, don't be concerned about Harper. No creeping lowlife is going to get the best of Max Harper."

He wished he believed that.

Dropping the box and the boots in the truck bed, Harper closed the canvas cover. He looked more than tired. The minute he drove off, the cats trotted down to Ocean and over to Moreno's Bar and Grill, where Harper was headed.

Padding down the narrow alley past Moreno's front door, they slipped in through the screened kitchen door, pawing it open behind the backs of a cook and two busboys. Past the bar into the restaurant, and through the shadows to the far corner, to Clyde and Harper's usual booth. Sliding beneath the table unseen, they cringed away from Clyde's size tens. The carpet smelled like stale French fries.

"The horseshoes," Clyde was saying. "Your men didn't find any more tracks made with the cut shoe? Didn't find anything on the trail that could have cut the shoes like that?"

"Ray and Davis have been over every inch."

"There have to be two shoes. And you said on the phone that your boot prints were at the scene. But you were up there searching. Of course your prints would be—"

"The prints were under the victim's prints. And partial prints under their bodies. The only time I got off Bucky was when I first arrived, to check the bodies. That set of prints was clear. There were other prints like them, underneath."

"Some son of a bitch has gone to a lot of trouble. How would he get your boots? Could he replicate them?"

"They're Justin's. I buy them up the valley, at the Boot Barn. Those soles were the same shape, same size. No problem there. But they had the same worn places on the left heel and right sole."

"So the guy stole your boots, then put them back. Or he took a cast of your boots somewhere. Fixed up an identical pair. Same with the horseshoes. Somewhere, that night, was there another horse wearing the same shape of shoe with the same scar?"

"I think the guy took Bucky. Came in the house, took my boots and the knife, then returned with them."

"Did he have time to do that?"

"Yes, he would have. I left about three forty-five. Helen and Ruthie were killed around five o'clock. And when I came back to change cars, I didn't go in the house or the stable. He could still have had Bucky.

"And later, when we got the missing report and I went home to get Bucky, he was nervous—irritable and tired. The horse was tired, Clyde. And Bucky is in top shape.

"I'd ridden him for some four hours, then put him up. He'd had plenty of rest—or should have—before I took him out again on the search.

"I was irritated at myself, when I saddled him to go look for the Marners, for not rubbing him down very well, after lunch. He had saddle marks, though I could have sworn I cleaned him up. Had what looked like quirt marks on his side and rump. I thought he'd been rubbing himself again. And his bridle was hung up differently than I hang it. I thought that strange, thought I'd been preoccupied." Harper paused, then, "Pretty unobservant, for a cop."

Clyde said nothing.

"The bridle. The saddle marks, Bucky's condition. The boot prints and hoofprints. And Gedding has received two anonymous phone calls—he thinks from the same man—that I was seen leaving the restaurant at noon riding Bucky up the mountain, in the opposite direction from my place. Following the Marners and Dillon.

"The day after the murder, Davis walked the trail that the Marners and Dillon rode. The first half mile above the restaurant, they rode on deep gravel. No prints of any value. But where you can see hoofprints, there's the same scar-marked print, coming along behind their three horses.

"Not a lot of people ride that trail, it's rough and steep. Davis said that deer trails crossed the hoofprints in two places, heading down to water and back again up toward the forest."

Joe tried to imagine a stranger riding up that mountain following the three riders. A stranger riding Harper's horse? A stranger who had taken Bucky after Harper left for work, and beat it down to the restaurant, to leave hoofprints following the Marners. Then followed them, killed them, and took out after Dillon. And then brought Bucky home, put him back in his stall.

"I've turned the department over to Brennan. Likely Davis and Ray will be off the case when Gedding's man gets here. Dallas Garza. San Francisco PD. I've moved the horses up to Campbell Ranch, and the pups, too. They'll be fine. I need a place to stay—where someone will know what I'm up to."

Clyde was silent for some time. When he spoke, his voice was low and angry. "You're quitting. Just quitting—stepping back like that. If that doesn't make you look guilty—"

"There's nothing else I can do. That's protocol, to do that. Nothing guilty about it. If I stayed in the department, I could manipulate my people, cook the papers, cook the evidence. It's not ethical, Clyde. You know that."

"I'll clean up the spare room. But what about during the day—I can't baby-sit you, Max, while I'm at work."

"I'll make myself visible in the village. And I'm not finished looking for Dillon. I can move around, be seen, keep my eyes open but stay out of the department's way. If I ride out with the searchers, I'll stay with a group. Some of them keep their horses up at Campbell's."

"The department's searched the old Pamillon place?"

"We were all over it that first night and the next day. The detectives have been back three times, have climbed down into every dark, musty cellar that ever existed on that land.

"This morning they had tracking dogs in there. One of them scented something; it started on a trail, then kept doubling back—sniffing around a puff of animal hair caught on the rocks. Dogs got all confused. I don't think they ever did get Dillon's scent, I think it was just a fox or something—maybe that cougar. The cougar's pad marks were back and forth through the old house—that's what has me worried."

From beneath the table, the cats couldn't see their faces. Nor did they need to.

Harper said, "If there *was* some trace of Dillon up there that the dogs couldn't find, it's beyond what any human could detect.

"Every department in California has her description and photo," Harper said. "The local TV channels will keep running her picture, along with a recording of her voice, that her mother gave us. Whatever son of a bitch has her, Clyde, whatever son of a bitch hurts her, I'll kill him."

10

Max Harper's words kept ringing in Joe's head. *If there was some trace of Dillon, that the dogs couldn't find, it's beyond what any human could detect.*

Had Harper been unwittingly asking for other-than-human assistance?

Not likely. Not Max Harper.

But as the two cats emerged from the grass at the edge of the Pamillon estate and trotted beneath the chain barrier, Joe's mind was filled with questions. The scarred horseshoe, Harper's boot prints, the anonymous phone calls to Harper and then to Gedding.

Behind them down the hills, the red village rooftops and dark oaks shone in a bright patchwork against the blue sea—a chill winter day, clear and sharp and filled with potential.

Slipping in among the fallen walls, their whiskers sliding across broken bricks, threading between overgrown rosebushes whose thorns caught at their fur, they knew that something had drawn them here. A scent left undetected? Some small clue overlooked? Something that puzzled them and pulled them back.

Springing up the trunk of a broken oak tree, they studied the massy growth below them, the jungle of tall, wild broom and upturned tree roots. Vines woven across a rusted wheelbarrow. A wrought-iron gate standing alone, slowly being pulled down by vines. A world as impenetrably green and mysterious as Rima's haunted Green Mansions, in the book that Wilma and Dulcie liked to read.

Seeing nothing below them to draw their specific attention, they dropped down again among the foliage where the afternoon light filtered to jade.

Scenting along through the bushes, they could detect no human trail. Only wild green smells and animal smells, filling every pocket of air. They had to rear up, every few steps, to see their way.

Where the ancient adobe bricks had been dished out by fifty years of wear, rainwater was cupped, and the cats drank, lapping among the leaves. Down beneath crushed leaves and broken foliage, the earth was a mass of crisscrossed hoofprints, boot and shoe prints, small animal tracks, and the tracks of the hounds that had come searching.

Hours before the police teams arrived, before anyone knew that the Marners were dead, the civilian search party had ridden here, trampling any amount of evidence, so that later when Harper's people went over the land, they could record only fragments.

Joe and Dulcie came out of the weeds onto a broken terrace so covered with rubble that it was impossible to tell where the rotting timbers of the veranda ended and the decaying floor of the house began.

Carved mantels stood half devoured by creeping vines. Fragments of torn and curling wallpaper hung from broken walls, as delicate as butterflies.

Prowling the parlor through forests of nettles that thrust between the rungs of broken chairs and curtained crippled bookcases, one wondered why the locals hadn't long ago taken every piece of furniture. Vines covered a capsized table to form a den that smelled of raccoon. Scraps of water-soaked, mouse-gnawed sofa cushions had moldered into mush beneath a mass of yellow flowers. All around them, they saw the old house being sucked back into the earth from which it had sprung.

They found no footprints small enough to belong to Dillon Thurwell. They could detect no scent of Dillon. But Joe smelled the cougar, and warily they watched the shadows. And then, near the stink where the lion had sprayed, they caught the scent of the child. Dillon's scent, leading across the parlor and up the broken stair to the nursery.

The morning glories had arrived upstairs long ago, to festoon a cane-backed rocking chair and to crawl up the faded wallpaper across cartoon rocking horses, the vine's heart-shaped leaves and tendrils fingering out through the broken windows. Morning glory crept across the nursery fireplace that stood alone where the walls had fallen into landslides of timbers and bricks.

The fireplace stank of wet ashes spilling out onto the floor. Across the ashes led a trail of small, neat pawprints that continued beneath the fallen wall.

The cats were scenting among the rubble when they heard voices, someone in the garden below.

Padding to the edge of the broken floor, they watched two young women approaching. "Kate," Joe said softly. "Kate Osborne."

"What's she doing here?" Dulcie gawked at the other young woman. "That beautiful white hair. I've seen her before, in the village."

"I think that's the woman Kate works for. Hanni something—this detective's niece. Maybe they came down with him. Detective Dallas Garza." Joe sat down, licking ashes from his paw. "Maybe it was Kate who called Clyde last night. He got all excited. Shouted, 'When did you get in town? Where are you?' I was half asleep. It's all right if he wakes me in the middle of the night. But let me scratch an itch or wash my face, jiggle the bed a little, and it's a federal case."

"So when did Kate come down?"

"Last night, I guess. He made a date for breakfast—was off like a flash this morning, all polished and scrubbed, nearly forget to make *my* breakfast. And he's meeting her tonight for dinner. Didn't give a thought to Charlie. Apparently didn't wonder if Charlie would be jealous."

"It would do Charlie good to be jealous," Dulcie said darkly.

"Clyde called Charlie this morning before he left the house; I think Kate asked him to. Sounded like Kate wants to see Charlie's drawings. I didn't want to shove my ear in the phone; Clyde can be so bad-tempered in the morning."

Below them, the white-haired woman had fished a

camera from her leather tote and was taking pictures of the ruined gardens and house. Kate sat idly on a broken wall in a patch of sunshine, her short blond hair as bright as silk. She was dressed in pale faded jeans and a creamy sweater; Kate always wore cream tones or off white. Hanni's sweatshirt was bright red, her earrings long and dangling.

"The walks could be repaired," Hanni said. "This is a lovely patio, the way the old walls rise around it." She kicked away some rubble to look at the brick paving. "This part looks good. And maybe even some of the old building could be kept and reinforced. And if these plants were pruned and cleaned up—a gardener could do wonders."

"Hanni, I'm having trouble keeping my mind on this, with the murder and the missing child."

"It's terrifying, I know. But there's nothing we can do, Kate. At least at the moment. The department will work overtime—every department in the country has the information, every search team is looking for the child. And Dallas will be down in the morning."

"I keep thinking of Max Harper, suspected of murder. Keep thinking of Dallas investigating Harper as if he were a criminal. It makes me feel sick. Makes me want to rip and claw whoever did this." Kate looked surprised at her turn of speech, looked embarrassed. "I . . . To think that someone has done this terrible thing, has killed and kidnapped people, in order to hurt Harper . . ." She looked hard at Hanni. "There can be no other explanation. Don't people know that!"

"I'm sure they do. But the department has to do it by the book, Kate.

"This kind of tragedy goes with the territory. For every cop who does a good job, there are a hundred guys out there wanting to destroy him, and not caring who else they hurt."

Kate sighed. "And Lee Wark's out there somewhere. He hates Harper."

Hanni shook her head. "The whole state's looking for Wark. He'll have left the country by now."

"I hope. Harper was very kind to me when Jimmie hired Wark to kill me, when I was trying to get away from them. This new city attorney—what's he like? How will he treat Harper?"

"I don't know anything about him. I haven't been down to the village for over a year." Hanni removed a roll of film from the camera and inserted another. "Not to worry, Dallas will get to the truth. He won't let anyone railroad Harper."

Kate rose, looking around her into the tangled bushes. The cats watched her with interest. Usually she was so calm, so in control. Now she moved with a lithe, almost animal wariness, nervous and watchful.

"*Is* there something about this place?" Dulcie said. "About the Pamillon mansion—some strangeness, the way the kit imagines?"

"*I* don't know, Dulcie. I don't feel anything strange. You and the kit—"

A small voice behind them said, "There *is* something. Something shivery."

The cats turned to look at the kit where she sat atop a vine-covered dresser, her forepaws neatly together, her long fluffy tail wrapped around herself, her round yellow eyes intense. "Something *elder*, here in this place."

But Joe and Dulcie's attention was on the dresser top. They leaped up to see better.

Beside the kit's paw, half hidden among the green leaves, lay a piece of shiny metal. Joe pushed away the leaves.

"What is this, Kit? Where did you get this?"

A silver hair clip gleamed among the leaves, its turquoise settings blue as a summer sky. Joe sniffed at it and fixed his gaze on the kit. And Dulcie's green eyes widened. "Dillon's clip," Dulcie said softly. "The barrette that Wilma gave Dillon."

Joe pushed close to the kit. "Where did you find this?"

The kit looked across the jungly nursery to the pale stone fireplace that loomed against the afternoon sky.

"In the fireplace? Show me."

The kit leaped away among the vine-covered furniture and vanished behind the fireplace beneath a heap of fallen timbers beside the chimney. Joe was there in a flash, a gray streak pawing and pushing in where she had disappeared. Shouldering under the timbers, he pushed his head beneath the partly open lid of a long wooden box the size of a coffin—the lid would open only a few inches. The kit crouched within, on the rusted floor. The interior was metal lined; had perhaps, at one time, held firewood.

"Here," the kit said. "It was right in here." Even the inside of the box reeked of wet ashes. They could not smell Dillon. There was nothing inside but the kit. Joe backed out again, where Dulcie pressed close behind him.

"We have to get the barrette to Harper," she said softly. "Or tell him where it is. I suppose whatever prints were on it are smeared with paw marks and cat spit."

Joe Grey flattened his ears. "Harper mustn't have anything to do with finding this."

Her green eyes widened. "But—"

"Prosecution could say he planted it." He looked keenly at Dulcie. "The detectives need to find it here. The department detectives—or Garza."

"Then we'll have to phone the station."

"We're not phoning the station. An anonymous phone tip would make Harper look like dog doo."

"Well what, then?" Dulcie hissed.

"Someone uninvolved could find it," he said with speculation. "Find it and call the station." He looked down into the garden.

"Kate," she whispered.

"Kate," he said and leaped down the broken stairs toward the garden.

Joe didn't know he was being watched, just as Kate and Hanni were being watched.

From higher up the hill above the ruined mansion, the three cats had been observed for some time, with keen and unwavering attention—as had two human creatures.

The movements and noises of the humans puzzled and interested the young lion. The mouth noises of his small feline cousins puzzled him far more.

The cougar was uncertain about whether two-legged beasts should be considered food, but the three little felines were certainly edible. They were nice and fat, and were out in plain view waiting to be taken—except that these small cat creatures made noises like the two-legs, and he did not know what to make of that.

And as Joe Grey descended to the garden, to lure Kate away from Hanni and lead her to the hair clip, above them on the hill the cougar slipped closer, padding among dense cover and silently down the slope. Intensely curious, the lion stalked toward the patio, moving as smoothly and silently as a drifting cloud-shadow, his big pads pressing without sound among the vines and stones, his broad head cocked, listening, his golden eyes seeking to separate possible lunch from possible threat—his teeth parted to taste cat scent and human scent, trying to sort out another strangeness, in a world filled with dangers from the unknown.

11

Charlie Getz was on her hands and knees scrubbing the floor of her one-room apartment when Kate arrived, an hour earlier than they'd planned. Charlie answered the door with the knees of her jeans sopping, her red hair in a mess, and a ketchup stain down her T-shirt. Opened the door to a gorgeously turned-out blond, sleek golden hair, clear green eyes, her creamy merino sweater immaculate and expensive. Charlie felt like *she'd* crawled out of a Dumpster. She'd meant to shower and change, make tea, put the bakery cookies on a plate, try to act civilized. She had never met Kate, only talked with her on the phone last night. If Clyde had told her what a stunner this woman was, she'd have spent the morning fretting over her clothes and trying to do something with her hair.

Kate held in her arms the relaxed and purring tortoiseshell kit. Joe Grey and Dulcie stepped out from behind her, Dulcie's tail waving, Joe's docked tail erect and cheerful, the two cats smiling up at her as they pushed past Kate's ankles into the room. But the expression on Kate's face made Charlie hurry her inside and hastily shut the door.

"What's wrong? There's nothing wrong with the kit?"

"No, she's fine. I'm sorry I'm so early. I'm Kate. Hanni and I were up at the Pamillon place, we hurried straight down to the police, and I . . ."

Charlie led Kate to the dinette table and pulled out a chair. Kate sat, still holding the unprotesting kit, cuddling her as if she needed the kit's warmth. Behind her, Joe and Dulcie leaped onto Charlie's daybed and began diligently to wash, their expressions smug and secretive. Charlie looked at them intently. "Start again," she told Kate, turning on the burner under the teakettle and sitting down opposite her.

"We were—we found something of—that might be Dillon's. I . . ." Kate looked deeply at Charlie. "I found it. I left it there, didn't touch it. I came right down to the police. A silver barrette. With turquoise. They—Officer Wendell has gone up to look. But I . . ." Kate stared absently at the teakettle. When she looked back at Charlie, her eyes were filled with fear and with a strange and powerful wonder.

"What?" Charlie said.

"We saw the lion," Kate whispered.

"The mountain lion? The cougar?"

"Yes. And it saw us. It came toward us. The kit went up my back like a bullet." Kate turned to show the bloody splotches down the back of her sweater. She didn't seem concerned about the wounds or the sweater. Tenderly she stroked the kit. And she began to laugh.

"She clung on my head and she . . ." Kate doubled over, cradling the kit, laughing until tears came.

When she looked up, she said, "You know about them."

Charlie was silent.

"It's all right," Dulcie said softly. "Kate knows—more then you'd guess."

Charlie looked at Kate with speculation. "Then what happened?" she said. "What did the lion do?"

"He came right down into the ruin," Kate said. "Came directly toward us—as if he was curious. He paused not twenty feet from us. We were terrified, we daren't move. He kept coming, watching and watching us. I thought he would attack—but he was so beautiful. I can't explain how I felt.

"The kit was up my back digging her claws in. The lion stopped again and stood looking at us. Just—looking. I wanted to run, and knew you daren't do that. I glanced at Hanni. She was standing stone still. I felt like we were glued to the ground. And then the kit, still digging in—she snuggled down by my ear and whispered, so soft. She told me to look big, to hold my jacket up, make myself look bigger."

From Kate's lap, the kit stared at her, trying to see what was so amusing.

"She told me to look him in the eye and speak clearly. She said, 'Tell him to get lost.'

"I held up my coat and spoke to him just as the kit said. And Hanni—Hanni knew what I was doing. She came up beside me, holding up her coat, and we stood together telling the lion very sternly to go away.

"And he did," Kate said. She sat back in her chair,

hugging the kit. "He turned and melted away into the garden. He was standing on a fallen tree one second and gone the next. I thought he had dropped down behind the log, that he would wait, then attack. But then we saw him far up the hill, standing among the trees. Still watching us."

Charlie had to grin. She felt like she'd known Kate forever—Kate's animal sense, her humor, and the way she loved the kit. All were qualities that drew her to Kate—as did the fact that she and Kate shared the cats' momentous secret. They were bound together, with Clyde and Wilma, in a confidence that, if any of them broke it, would be the most horrible of betrayals.

"And we got out of there," Kate said. "The moment he was gone. Went straight to the police to tell them about the barrette."

"Wilma gave Dillon a barrette," Charlie said. "Silver, set with turquoise strips."

"It was there in the Pamillon nursery. Beside an old firewood box next to the hearth. A box big enough for a young girl to hide."

"But why didn't the searchers find it?"

"The kit found it in the chest, caught up under the lid. Must have pulled off when Dillon hid."

Kate grinned. "The kit found it, and the cats brought it to me while Hanni was distracted."

"And you told Officer Wendell?"

"Yes. What's wrong?"

"I . . . nothing. When you went to the police, wasn't Hanni surprised that you brought the cats down from the ruins with you?"

"No. She wouldn't have left them, with the cougar

there. It seemed perfectly natural to her to bring them down."

Charlie rose to pour boiling water into the teapot. She felt as comfortable with Kate as if she'd known her forever. Setting the teapot on the table, she fetched the lemon cookies, sliding them onto a plate.

Kate's color was coming back. "To see such a thing, Charlie. Can you imagine it? I felt terrified, but I was filled with such wonder. I still can't believe I saw that beautiful beast, so close to us."

How strange, Charlie thought, that Kate's voice seemed filled with envy.

And she saw envy again, a few minutes later, as Kate looked at the pencil and ink studies of animals that Charlie had lined up along the wall, and at the framed drawings hanging above them, sketches of cats and dogs and of Max Harper's horses. "And raccoons," Kate said. "These are all quite wonderful. And foxes. Where . . . ?"

"In the hills," Charlie said, "around Harper's place. We've been working the pups on obedience, those two big pups Clyde found. Working them in Max's pasture."

"And the foxes were watching?" Kate teased.

"In the evenings," Charlie said, laughing. "That big fellow in the drawings, he comes near the porch. He knows when the dogs are shut in their stall. I think he comes to hunt mice. Max never puts out food."

The village of Molena Point imposed a stiff fine for setting out food for wild animals. The area was overrun with raccoons; they turned over trash cans and would break into people's houses, tearing through the screens. Even George Jolly had been criticized for setting out treats in his alley, though the deli was right in the center of the village, not on the outskirts where the smell of food was more likely to attract a wild beast. Raccoons hunting in packs had killed village cats and small dogs—and the raccoons and foxes drew the larger predators: bobcats and an occasional coyote, and now the cougar.

"You've been seeing a lot of Harper," Kate said tentatively, "what with training the pups."

Charlie nodded. "Clyde talked to you about that?"

"He mentioned it."

"And . . . ?"

Kate shrugged. "Clyde's easily made jealous." She grinned. "Not to worry—jealousy's good for him, keeps him on his toes."

"Clyde asked you to pump me. To see how I feel about Harper."

"Would you mind?"

"I—I suppose not. What difference? Our petty feelings, right now . . . What difference? Oh, why did this have to happen! To a good man!"

"That's how you feel about him."

"Maybe. I really don't know how I feel, Kate."

Kate nodded. "Are there any leads to the murder? Any suspects? I know that everyone's looking for Dillon. What a terrible thing this has been."

"There's a parolee in town who might be involved. But I don't hear much. The department keeps pretty tight security." She looked at Kate. "Those officers will do everything that's humanly possible to find the killer and clear their chief."

"There's . . . no chance that Harper, under some kind of stress, in a moment of rage . . . ?"

"Max Harper?" Charlie felt her face go hot. "Kill that woman and her daughter? No way in hell Max could do such a thing." She rose, refilled the teakettle, and put it back on the burner. Turning, she looked at Kate. "You can't believe that."

Kate smiled. "No. I don't believe that."

"Still a fishing trip."

Kate shrugged.

From the couch, the cats watched this exchange with amused interest.

Kate took two more cookies, ate them quickly. "Do you remember when three men escaped from San Quentin?"

"Yes. From death row? You're talking about the one from Molena Point. The one who was sent to prison at the same time—"

"The same time as my ex-husband."

Kate swallowed half a cup of tea. "I think I may have seen him in San Francisco. Someone in the city is murdering cats. He did that, Lee Wark did that." She shivered. "He liked to kill cats."

On the couch, Joe and Dulcie moved closer together, their blood going icy. The tortoiseshell kit turned wide yellow eyes on Kate.

Kate looked back at them sternly. "You would stay far away from a man like that. A tall, thin man, Kit. Thin and hunched and pale, with muddy eyes."

The three cats shivered.

"The man in San Francisco," Kate said, "had a black coat that madc him look squarer and broader. A black goatee. Black hat. But his eyes were the same. Like a dead fish."

The kit crowded closer to Kate. *Frightened,* Dulcie thought. *Frightened down to her little black paws. And so am I.* And she watched the kit, terrified for her.

Lee Wark had tried to kill Dulcie and Joe just as he had tried to kill Kate. And if he got one look into the kit's eyes, Wark would know that she, too, was not an ordinary cat.

But Wark was not there in the village, he would not come there. The very thought made her fur crawl.

"Dallas will be here in the morning," Kate said. "He's very aware of Wark."

"What's he like? What kind of man?"

"I work with his niece, I'm her design assistant. Dallas helped to raise Hanni and her sisters after their mother died. Hanni says he's totally honest. But . . ." Kate laughed. "I guess that's like asking what kind of man your father is. What are you going to say?"

"I . . . have another source, too," Charlie said.

"Your aunt Wilma? She worked with Hanni's father at one time."

"Yes, in the San Francisco probation office, before he was appointed chief. She knows Garza by reputation. Wilma says he's okay."

"Hanni says no little girls ever had better raising. They learned to ride, to hunt, to handle firearms—and to clean house and cook. Hanni says Dallas is a wonderful cook. Kate, he has to be a good man, to take such care in raising his dead sister's children."

But Joe Grey, watching the two young women, thought, *Even crocodiles take care of their helpless young. Even Mafia parents see that their kids learn what they want them to know.*

Charlie said, "Whoever's out to get Harper, I hope Garza sees them burn in hell."

Joe Grey hoped so, too. Though the haste with which the city attorney had suggested Garza, and the pressure that Gedding had put on the chief in San Francisco to get Garza left him wondering—hoping the source of this cold-blooded setup to destroy Harper didn't reach clear to San Francisco via Molena Point City Hall.

The balance of Max Harper's life now lay in the hands of Dallas Garza. And Joe Grey, stretching out across the daybed, considered how best to monitor Detective Garza's moves.

Meantime, he'd like a look at confidence artist Stubby Baker, Harper's unwitting and apparently useless alibi.

12

A cat could travel for blocks above the village of Molena Point never setting paw to the sidewalk, crossing the chasms above the streets on twisted oak limbs or by leaping the narrow alleys between skylights and attic windows, by trotting between shingled peaks so precipitous that even with all claws out, one couldn't help but slide, landing on a swinging sign below or a roof gutter. At only a few streets must the feline traveler come to earth like a common tourist and run across behind the wheels of slow-moving cars.

Stubby Baker's apartment was a handsome penthouse on the second floor above a row of exclusive clothing shops. The kit led Joe Grey and Dulcie there as if she had invented surveillance. "That's where he lives," she hissed, clinging to an oak branch beside Joe, three floors above the street. "Right in there across that balcony behind those big glass doors, the man who kicks cats."

From the tree in which they crouched, the cats looked down on a long tiled balcony and a pair of many-paned French doors. Despite the bright day, a light was on within. Baker sat at a dining table littered with papers, just inside the glass doors. He was a tall well-knit man totally unlike his nickname, his dark hair neatly trimmed, his smooth skin well tanned. A man the women would find appealing.

The apartment had high, dark beams against a white plaster ceiling, white walls, a skylight through which the sky shone blue and clear. Used brick formed the floor and the corner fireplace, beside which hung eight small, well-framed reproductions of Richard Diebenkorn's landscapes, gleaming rich as jewels. An opening behind the fireplace apparently led to a bedroom. Before the fire, three tan leather couches formed a luxurious conversational group, their cushions deep and inviting, perfect for kneading claws.

Baker seemed totally absorbed in the official-looking documents he was reading, making occasional notes or corrections. He wore clean chinos and a tan golf shirt. Expensive sandals graced his thin, tanned feet. He gave every impression, both in his person and in his environment, of a well-to-do businessman of some stature, not an ex-con with a laundry sheet that would stretch a city block.

The cats, slipping along the branch closer to the window, had a fine view down onto the papers that occupied him: documents marked with seals and notary stamps, and a land map marked off into individual parcels. Pens and a ruler were aligned beside it. Joe read the larger print upside down, a talent he had developed during interminable breakfasts when Clyde hogged the front page.

"Deeds of trust," he said softly. "Copies of wills and

property transfers." He studied the land map. "The way the coastline runs, that *could* be the Pamillon estate."

On an end table, among a clutter of dog-eared paperbacks, lay a stack of bills. The paperbacks didn't seem to fit Baker's image; the covers looked like lurid, cheap fare. The utility bills were of greater interest, particularly the phone bill on top, showing half a dozen long-distance calls to one Marin County number.

Joe peered closer, committing the seven digits to memory just as he had committed his own phone number, Dulcie's, and several numbers for Max Harper.

He might not want to explore some of his more bizarre inherited talents, but the memory bank within his gray sleek head was of considerable use to the tomcat.

Marin County, some thirty miles north of San Francisco, was the home of San Quentin State Prison. And Lee Wark hadn't been the only convicted murderer incarcerated there thanks to Harper.

Repeating to himself the number and prefix, he was trying to figure how to get inside the apartment and paw through the rest of the bills when Dulcie hissed, staring down at the street.

Almost directly beneath the balcony, in the line of halted traffic waiting for pedestrians to cross, sat an open black Mercedes convertible, its radio blaring rock music, its driver staring above her up toward Baker's windows. Her honey-colored hair was tied back with a yellow scarf. Her tan shorts revealed long, tanned legs. Her brown eyes scanned the portion of French doors that she must be able to see above the angle of the balcony. Beside her on the front seat sat three loaded grocery bags. The cats could see peanut butter, a jar of jelly, some kind of cereal. The traffic moved on.

Dulcie watched narrowly as the convertible slid away. "What was she looking at?" Dulcie said.

"Maybe at us." Joe leaped to the roof, away from the branch and Baker's windows. "Maybe she's a cat lover."

"Oh, right." She joined Joe and the kit on the roof, her green eyes glowing. "Could she be checking on Baker? Is there a connection between Crystal and Baker?"

"I don't—" Joe began. But Dulcie was gone, streaking across the rooftops, following Crystal's convertible as it crept in the line of slow-moving cars. Joe saw her disappear over the edge and reappear on the roofs of the next block, lashing her tail with annoyance—very likely after dodging too close to slow-moving wheels. He wished she wouldn't do that. The village's daytime streets, though crowded and slow, belonged to the cars of upscale tourists. That, he had pointed out to Dulcie, was why they used the rooftops.

The early-morning village streets, before the tourists were out of their beds, boasted more careful drivers. Those streets smelled better, too. Smelled of the sea and of newly watered gardens, while the midday village smelled, to a cat, of exhaust fumes–deodorants–shaving lotion–perfume–chewing gum–restaurant cooking and too many human bodies.

Joe caught up to Dulcie, the kit crowding close, and they followed the black Mercedes for eight blocks, crossing the streets twice among the feet of the tourists, enduring endless remarks about the cute kitties and constant attempts to pet them, dodging away from reaching hands.

But when Crystal's car turned right, traffic moved swiftly again and the cats couldn't keep up; they ran until they were panting. Standing on the sidewalk, Joe stared after the Mercedes, frustrated. Joe and Dulcie didn't see the black SL again until the following week.

But the kit saw Crystal's car later that evening and followed it, alone. Galloping along the sidewalk, dodging between tourists' feet, she was wildly excited to be on a trail that the two big cats had lost.

The time was just dusk. She had been out for a prowl through Jolly's alley, because no matter how well Wilma fed her, she could never get filled up, and Jolly's had such delicious offerings, all that lovely smoked salmon.

Leaving the alley licking her whiskers, she saw the open Mercedes go by, saw Crystal's tawny hair blowing and smelled Crystal's perfume. She followed, running seven blocks after the car but careful about crossing streets, followed until Crystal pulled into a drive and parked before a closed garage door.

Crystal hurried up the wooden stairs, the kit following so close on her heels that when Crystal pushed in through the front door it slammed in the little cat's face. Backing away, the kit leaped to the windowsill, pressing her nose to the glass. There was a curtain drawn across.

Rearing up, she couldn't see over it.

Taking the direct approach she mewled at the door, her cries ever louder and more desperate, in the age-old classic plea: *I am abandoned, I am starving, I am so terribly hungry and cold.* She worked herself into such a frenzy, convinced herself so well of her plight, that she was all a-tremble when Crystal flung open the door and dumped a pan of water in her face.

The kit fled for Wilma's house.

13

Dallas Garza arrived in Molena Point at 8 A.M., the morning after the three cats spied on Stubby Baker. He was a big, broad-shouldered man dressed in civilian clothes—faded jeans, a tan shirt, charcoal V-necked sweater, and a tan corduroy sport coat, clothes that blended well into the milieu of Molena Point, comfortable layers to be removed as the fog burned off and the day turned warm. Garza's thick black hair was trimmed short, in a well-styled, no-nonsense haircut. His chiseled, square face, brown as oak, seemed carved into lines that were all business—a look that won immediate confidence from law enforcement and nervous reluctance from those who would screw with him.

During his twenty-three-year career he had been put on loan three times to other departments when their internal affairs got into a tangle, carrying out investigations of fellow officers—once in Redding on a drug-related case, and twice in southern California on charges of moral misconduct. This was the first time he had been called in to investigate a murder.

He had never met Max Harper. Garza didn't socialize on his vacation time; he kept to himself. He didn't like the fact that his case was Molena Point's chief of police, an officer well thought of in the village and among other law enforcement agencies in the state.

But he owed Lionel Gedding. And Garza was rigid about paying his debts.

He was uncomfortable, too, that Hanni was here and had opened the cottage, as if they were down for a family vacation.

He didn't stop at the cottage to drop off his bag, but drove directly to Molena Point PD. In the police lot behind the station, he swung a U and backed into a slot against the back wall. Sitting in his car, he took in the blank, two-story brick wall on his right where the jail was housed, and the single-story police station on his left. The station was connected to the courtrooms and city offices behind him by an enclosed passageway.

Garza had worked in San Francisco for ten years. Before that, he had put in five years on a SWAT team in Oakland. He would be forced to retire at age fifty-seven because his work was considered hazardous duty. He had no idea what he would do after that. He was four years younger than Molena Point Police Chief Max Harper. He had read the file on Harper the night before.

Leaving the police parking lot, he walked two blocks toward Ocean to have breakfast at a favorite small café. Sitting in the patio with his back to the restaurant wall, he ordered three eggs over easy, ham, biscuits, and coffee. He ate slowly and neatly, watching the village street. A lot of the locals out this time of morning were dog walkers. And the tourists were walking mutts, too. Several hotels in the village catered to pets. Folks liked to bring their dogs along where the little poodles and spaniels—and a few big dogs—could run on the beach, show off up and down Ocean—four-legged conversation pieces—and sit with their masters at the outdoor cafés.

It amazed him that people with money, people who drove expensive foreign cars, had mongrels instead of well-bred animals. Mutts. Absently he counted nineteen dogs; only two of them were purebred, and neither of real good breeding.

If Garza was a snob in any way, it was in the matter of canines. A well-bred pointer or setter, a handsome big Chesapeake or Weimaraner of really good bloodlines was one of the finest accomplishments of mankind.

A far finer accomplishment, in many respects, than man himself.

But that was a cop's view.

Paying the bill, tucking the tip under the sugar bowl, he walked to Molena Point PD, entering by the unlocked front door into the big open squad room. His first look at the department didn't please him.

In the big open room, all functions seemed to be carried out with little thought to privacy or security. And certainly minimal attention to neatness. This surprised him. Harper had a reputation for running an orderly shop, but these officers' desks were piled with papers; a case of soft drinks had been left by the front door;

several officers had hung their jackets over the backs of their chairs; two had laid their guns atop their desks; a pair of field boots stood next to an overflowing wastebasket. They didn't use shredders? Even the dispatcher's area contained stacks of papers that he would never have allowed. He did not, as he began to make the rounds of the room, find much to admire in Max Harper's department.

Joe Grey and Dulcie spotted Garza leaving the restaurant as they stepped out of Jolly's alley after a leisurely post-hunting snack. The man's solid build and his military walk and air of authority drew their gaze. Dulcie's green eyes widened; her dark, striped tail twitched with interest. "Who's that?" The broad-shouldered, dark-haired Latino was an imposing figure.

"Either a full bird colonel or some kind of law enforcement. My guess would be our detective from San Francisco. Garza's due to arrive this morning."

They followed him, padding along the curb and through sidewalk flower gardens until the broad-shouldered stranger entered Molena Point PD. As Garza stepped in through the glass door, the cats beat it into the courthouse, whose front door was easy enough to claw open, galloped down the hall into the squad room, and took cover under Max Harper's desk.

They couldn't see much but the jungle of desk and chair legs and officers' shoes spreading away across the linoleum, but they could hear Garza working the room, introducing himself to individual officers. They listened with interest to the casual wariness exhibited by Harper's men and women as they took Garza's measure.

"Talk about a roomful of tomcats," Joe said, grinning.

"So what would you expect? Garza was sent here to do *their* job and possibly to help prosecute their chief."

Joe slipped out from under the desk far enough to see Garza sitting at Detective Davis's desk with Davis and Ray. They seemed to be going over field notes, Garza reading his copy and asking questions. Joe felt nearly invisible, with all officers' eycs on the threesome while trying to look busy with their own affairs. When at last Garza headed for Harper's desk, carrying the detectives' thick sheaf of reports and photographs, Joe was deep under the drawer section beside Dulcie.

Sheltered from Garza's feet, they dozed as the detective shuffled papers. Periods of silence indicated that he was reading. He rose occasionally to refill his coffee cup from the large coffeemaker on the credenza behind him. Joe was soon cross-eyed with boredom.

They had meant, coming out of the alley, to head for Dulcie's house and make that call to Marin County—Joe had a feeling about that phone number. The same kind of feeling as when, though he couldn't see or smell a mouse, he knew the little beast was close. He wanted to make that call in an empty house, without any human listening, and Wilma would be at work.

Telephones still amazed him—sending his voice over that unseen cable to manipulate someone invisible at the other end. That joining of humanity's electronic wonders and his own remarkable feline skills gave him a huge sense of power. A real twenty-first-century, state-of-the-art jolt.

And right now, while they marked time on the dusty linoleum under Harper's desk, learning nothing of value, that Marin phone number bugged him.

They listened as Garza arranged to see the stable manager where the Marners had kept their horses, and to see several Marner family members who had arrived soon after the tragedy and were staying in the village. He set a time to see Charlie Getz and to interview the staff at Café Mundo. The problem with all this was that Joe and Dulcie would be privy to nothing, no more inside line to what was happening than if they'd been a thousand miles from Molena Point.

Garza told Lieutenant Brennan that he would talk with the Marners' neighbors in their condo building, and he made an appointment for that evening with Dillon Thurwell's parents. That would be a hard call, for Dillon's mother and father to talk with police again, when there was only that one slim lead to finding Dillon, only the lost barrette.

At least they knew she'd escaped the killer at one point. But nothing after that. Nothing more than that one small piece of jewelry that had been described in the paper just after the murder, the barrette Dillon's mother said the child had been wearing when she left the house Saturday morning. Nothing else to give them hope that Dillon was still alive.

Garza made no appointment with Joe's housemate, though Clyde was Harper's closest friend. Other than this omission, the detective seemed to be starting out in an efficient and businesslike manner. Maybe he was going to descend on Clyde's place unannounced, hoping to catch Harper off guard.

When Garza finished with the phone, he nodded to Detectives Davis and Ray, and the three of them headed back to the conference rooms, Garza carrying the reports Davis had given him, as if he meant to go over the meat of the case in strict privacy. The cats were crouched for a swift race down the hall to listen, when they heard the conference room door slam closed.

Slipping into the shadows of an adjoining room, they pressed their ears uncomfortably to the wall—cats' ears are not made for wall-pressing; it hurts the delicate cartilage. Even with their superior hearing, they could make out only indistinct murmurs, and the conference rooms had no windows that might be open to the bright morning. Their source within Molena Point PD had dried up faster than canned tuna left in the sun. Sometimes even a cat, the most facile and adept of snoops, gets outshuffled.

"Come on," Joe said, and he headed down the hall, through the courthouse, dodging behind the heels of a pair of attorneys—you could always tell attorneys, they had briefcases growing out of their hands—and down the street to Dulcie's house, hot to get at the phone.

14

Joe and Dulcie spied the kit in Jolly's alley as they were headed for Dulcie's house and the phone. The kit sat smugly beneath the jasmine vine beside an empty paper plate.

Dulcie nudged her. "Come on, kit. Is that your second breakfast?"

The kit smiled. Her face smelled of caviar and roast lamb.

The two cats hurried her along out of the alley and down the street—like herding fireflies. She was everywhere, up the bougainvillea vines that climbed the shop walls, up into the oaks and across the roofs and down onto balconies and awnings. When they nosed her through Dulcie's cat door, she charged at a plate of scrambled eggs that Wilma had left on the floor and inhaled yet another meal.

"I saw Wilma walking to work," she said between bites. "She looked elegant. Those beautiful pale jeans and that new black blazer and cashmere sweater."

"Just jeans," Dulcie said. "Not so *very* fancy, kit."

"Elegant," the kit repeated. And Dulcie had a sharp sense of the kit's fascination with beautiful clothes—a hunger perhaps as keen as Dulcie's own covetous craving. She wondered if the kit had ever stolen a silky garment from some house when she traveled with that rebel band of homeless cats. Wondered if the kit, just as she herself, had ever innocently lifted a silk nightie from someone's clothesline or nipped in through an open window to snatch a lacy teddy or a pair of sheer stockings.

Well, Dulcie thought, *I don't do that anymore.*

At least, hardly ever.

She missed having those lovely garments to snuggle on. Oh, Wilma gave her pretty things. But the stolen ones were nicer.

She was ashamed of her failing, and secretly reveled in it. She didn't consider herself a thief. She always gave back the stolen items, in a way—leaving them in the box on the back porch that Wilma had provided, where the amused neighbors knew to retrieve their "misplaced" clothes. *Not* stealing, she thought, following Joe through the dining room and onto Wilma's desk.

Joe pushed the phone from its cradle, squinched his paw small, and punched in the San Rafael number. He was unusually nervous. The kit bounced up beside them to watch, round-eyed. And the three cats bent their heads, listening to the measured ringing.

A man's gravelly voice. "Year. Alby? That you, Alby? You're two minutes early."

Joe said, "Is this Davis Drugs?"

"What the hell? Who's this? Who you calling?"

"Davis Drugs." Joe repeated the number he'd dialed.

"You got the wrong number, buster. Get off the friggin' line."

Joe pressed the disconnect, scowling. "That didn't net much."

"Didn't it?" said Dulcie. "Wait a few minutes, and try again."

He waited, then punched the redial, checking the little screen to be sure he'd dialed the right number the first time. The kit watched every move.

A different voice answered. Smooth but equally abrupt. "Yeah? Who you want?"

"Hello?" Joe said inanely.

"Who you want to talk to?"

"I was calling Davis Drugs. Can you tell me what place I've reached?"

"Davis *Drugs*! That's a good one! We ain't got that brand, buddy. Who you calling?"

"Can you tell me what place this is? Maybe I have the . . ."

A clanging, metallic voice sounded in the background, its vibrating rumble so loud they couldn't make sense of the words. Sounded like "Wall uh—uh—ers heave ta ecc—ecc-ecc-ed wall at once." A man shouted, "Come on, Joobie. Get off the damn phone! I got a call coming." Then a click and the line went dead. In a moment the recording came on telling Joe to hang up and dial again.

He slapped his paw to silence the offensive message. "What was that all about?"

Dulcie sat scowling, trying to make out the words. She lifted her paw. "Let me try."

She punched the redial and the speaker button so they could all hear. She sat washing her paws, listening with all the sophistication of a debutante buffing her nails while monitoring the call of a dull-witted suitor. The gravelly voice answered. "Start talking. It's your nickel."

"Hi, honey. This is May."

"May who?"

"Maybe I could give you a good time, baby."

He guffawed, his laugh so loud that Dulcie backed away. But her voice was sweet and smooth as cream. "Honey, are you the handsome one?"

"You bet I am, baby. That's me." The guy bellowed a rasping laugh. "Handsome as a hound pup. Who is this? Where you calling from, honey?"

"My name's Chantelle. What's yours?"

"Baby, this is Big Buck Brewer. You calling from near here? Why don't you come on up? Have us a little conjugal visit."

Dulcie rolled her eyes at Joe. "I'm just a few blocks away, honey. Maybe if I come up there, we could party?"

"Baby, if you can figure out how to get in here, I guarantee you'll have a party."

The loudspeaker went again. "Waaalll pr—boom—boom—boom—out of the . . . yar—yar—yard . . ." And the phone clicked and went dead. Dulcie looked at Joe, her green eyes huge.

"A prison," Joe said softly.

Dulcie nodded. "Prison loudspeaker. 'All prisoners out . . . out of the exercise yard'?" Her eyes were wide and gleaming, her ears sharp forward. "A prison, Joe? How could we call inside a prison? What prison?"

"There's only one prison in that area code." And Joe Grey thanked the great cat god—or the great phone god—that Pacific Bell was so explicit in its billing, listing each city along with its long-distance number. "San Rafael, Dulcie. San Quentin State Prison." He showed his teeth in a wicked feline grin. "San Quentin, temporary home of every serious felon and convicted murderer in the state of California."

"But . . . *how* could we phone into a prison? Were those inmates—how could inmates answer the phone? What am I missing here? They're locked up, they're supposed to . . . They wouldn't have *telephones*."

"Right. And I don't have claws and whiskers."

She only looked at him, her green eyes wide with shock—and with growing excitement.

The kit gaped at them both. She was beyond her depth.

And Joe Grey looked like he'd swallowed a whole nest of mice. "This is from the horse's mouth, Dulcie. Straight from Harper's men, at the poker table. There are pay phones all over San Quentin. Maximum security prison, but the inmates can make a call to anyone, any time they please."

"You're putting me on."

"Not a bit. They can call out, and can receive incoming calls if they stand around and wait for them. Like, say, their outside contact calls at a prearranged time."

Dulcie shook her whiskers, her green eyes narrowed with disgust. "What's the point of putting them in prison? I thought it was to get them out of circulation. What good, if they have all that contact with the outside?"

"Exactly. But the phones are only part of it. Those prisoners have computers, e-mail, the Web, you name it."

Dulcie sighed.

"The Justice Department wants to crack down on the phones, though. Justice thinks the prisoners are making too many drug deals and orchestrating too many murders from behind bars."

"Now you're kidding."

"Dead serious."

"*Too many* drug deals? And just how many is too many? *Too many* murders?" Her tail lashed with rage. "What's happening to the world?"

"You have to make allowances. You're dealing here with humans."

"Oh, right."

"Bottom line—the state earns a lot of money from those pay phones. Harper said the take in California alone last year was something like twenty-three million bucks from prison pay phones."

"Come on, Joe."

"Knight Ridder Newspapers—the wire service," Joe said authoritatively. "Harper was so angry about it, he clipped the article to show Clyde. It gave statistics for Illinois and Florida, too. Said in Illinois, in one year, inmates placed over three million long-distance calls—and the deal with the phone company is, the state gets half the take."

Dulcie's ears went back; her eyes darkened with anger. "Why do we even bother to try to catch a killer, if that's all it means? He gets free room and board, free computers, free phones so he can do his dirty drug deals—and the state of California rakes in twenty-three million dollars." She was so worked up she growled at Joe and the kit both. "Those cons sit inside like some Mafia family in its Manhattan penthouse arranging drug sales and murdering people by remote control."

"That's about it," Joe said. "Used to be, prisoners were allowed maybe one call every three months—and those were likely monitored. Now they can use the phone all day. That's who you talked to, Dulcie, some inmate waiting for a call."

And Joe Grey smiled. "Lee Wark escaped from San Quentin, but his accomplice in the Beckwhite murder is still there—and Osborne is not on death row. Osborne's serving life. He'd have unlimited phone privileges. And he isn't the only no-good that Harper helped put in Quentin. Kendrick Mahl's there, too."

Max Harper had helped see Mahl convicted for the murder of Janet Jeannot.

Joe and Dulcie had also helped—though only two people in the world knew that.

Joe sat down on the blotter. "This could be not one felon setting up Harper, but a partnership. A whole squirming nest of rats."

"Fine," Dulcie said. "Our source of department information dried up. Harper knows no more than we do. And when we can't pass on the tiniest little tip without implicating Harper."

Joe said nothing. Pacing back and forth across the

desk, his ears and whiskers were back, his scowl deep, pulling the white splotch down his face into washboard lines.

The fascinated kit lay belly-down on a stack of bills, looking from one to the other as if watching them bat a mouse back and forth.

"So how are we going to play it?" Dulcie asked. "How are we going to lay this on the new detective? Clyde's right about the phone tips. We try an anonymous tip with Garza, he thinks Harper's trying to manipulate him.

"Still," she said, "when the tip proves to be true . . ."

Joe rubbed his whiskers against hers. "We don't want to blow this, Dulcie. I want to think about this."

He gave her a broad grin. "I could move in with Garza."

"Oh, right. Play lost kitty, as well fed as you look?"

Joe dropped his ears, sucked in his gut, and crouched as if terrified, creeping across the desk as though someone had beaten him.

"Not bad."

"Add a little roll in the dirt, scruff up my fur, and I'm as pitiful as any homeless. You're not the only one who can play abandoned kitty."

"But you *can't* play stray kitty for Garza. His niece, Hanni, knows us from when she gave us a ride to Charlie's apartment. Hanni knows you're not a stray."

Joe looked sheepish. He didn't often forget such important matters.

He had to get hold of himself. This worry over Harper was fogging his tomcat brain.

"So I stroll in the front door, look Garza in the eye.

Don't offer up an excuse. Make myself at home. Demand food, lodging, and respect. I think Garza could relate to that."

"I think Garza would boot you out on your furry behind."

"Or Kate can grease the wheels. She can say Clyde asked her to keep me for a few days, until the demolition is finished. Say I'm a bundle of nerves from all the noise. That I've gone off my feed. Twitching in my sleep."

Dulcie smiled.

"Oncc I gct insidc, I make friends with Garza, and I have free access. I can figure out how to let him in on the Quentin connection, if he doesn't already know."

"And what if he does know? What if he's part of it?"

He only looked at her.

"Joe, this is beginning to scare me."

"Hey, we're only cats. Who's to know any different?"

"Lee Wark would know different."

"Lee Wark isn't here. Wark wouldn't dare show his face in this village."

"So when are you moving in with this high-powered San Francisco detective?"

"Soon as I can set it up with Kate—and with Clyde," Joe said, thinking how unreasonable Clyde could be.

"Clyde's going to pitch a fit. You know how he—"

"I don't need Clyde's permission. I'm a cat, Dulcie. A free spirit. A four-legged unencumbered citizen. I don't need to answer to Clyde Damen. I'll tell him what I'm going to do, and *do* it. If I want to freeload on Garza, that's my business. It's none of Clyde's affair."

"You're getting very defensive, when you haven't even talked to Clyde yet."

Joe only looked at her. Then he dropped off the desk, beat it through the house and out the cat door.

And Dulcie sat listening to the plastic flap swinging back and forth in its little metal frame. Pretty touchy, she thought, feeling bad for Joe.

It wasn't easy to have his best line of communication dried up—and the source of that information, the man he admired so deeply, the brunt of a plot that would destroy that man. Couldn't the city attorney see this? Couldn't the movers and shakers of the city make a few allowances?

But she guessed that was part of being human—humans ideally had to stay within the law. Once they'd made the rules, the point was to follow them.

15

Midmorning sun washed the village with gold, laying warm fingers into Joe Grey's fur as he galloped through the streets, dodging dogs and tourists' feet. Sliding in through his cat door, he heard the washer going. The time was ten-fifteen. Maybe Harper, who had moved in last night, was getting domestic. Strolling into the laundry, he found Clyde was still home, sorting clothes, tossing the whites onto the top bunk, which belonged to the cats, and his colored shirts onto the lower bunk. The fact that the dirty clothes were picking up animal hair was of no importance in this household.

"What're you doing home?" he said softly, glancing in the direction of the spare bedroom. "Harper's not still asleep? You feeling okay? You take the day off?"

"Took the morning off. Harper's riding with one of the search groups."

Joe leaped into the bottom bunk, onto old Rube's blanket, and began to lick dust from his paws. "Has he heard anything more about the case? Anything from his officers?"

Clyde didn't answer. Continued to sort clothes.

"Well? What? You don't need to act like *I'm* the enemy."

"You know how I feel about your meddling."

"I'm meddling? Harper's career is on the line, his whole life is on the line, and I'm *meddling*? And what about the evidence we've already found?"

"What evidence? What are you talking about?"

"The barrette, Wilma's barrette. Didn't Harper . . ." Joe stared at Clyde. "Didn't anyone tell Harper about the barrette? The one that Wilma gave Dillon? We found it up at the Pamillon place—the kit found it."

Clyde looked blank.

"I can't believe Harper wouldn't tell you—that someone in the department wouldn't tell him. His own men . . ."

Clyde laid down the shirt he was clutching. "How do you know this? How do you know it was the barrette Wilma gave her? And that she was wearing it Saturday? If it was the same barrette, she could have lost it anytimc. Where on the Pamillon place? She could have been up there weeks ago, fooling around, she—"

"She was wearing it that day, that was in the paper, Clyde. With a description of it—silver, with turquoise bars. Her mother said she was wearing it that morning when she dropped her at Harper's place. And Dillon had it on when she and the Marners met Harper for lunch. The waitress in the café remembered it. *That* was in the paper."

Clyde looked hard at him. "And *you* found the barrette. After the detectives went over that place three times."

"So?"

"They need to know that, Joe! What did you do with it? You shouldn't move evidence. Why didn't you call the department? You could at least have told me!"

"*We* didn't *move it. We didn't* touch *it. The department* knows *about it. What do you think we are, idiots?* Why in the world would we move it? Why would we disturb evidence?"

"Cut to the chase, Joe. Did you call the station? Who did you talk to? An anonymous tip right now could really mess Harper up. When was this?"

Joe glared.

Clyde sat down on the bottom bunk, ducking under the top rail. "You didn't call Garza?" He fixed Joe with a cold glare. "You didn't lay one of your anonymous phone tips on Garza. If you start this stuff with Garza . . ."

"Start what stuff?"

"Start these insane, unwanted, disruptive, and probably illegal telephone calls. If you start that with Garza—"

"If you really need to know, we found the barrette on Tuesday. Garza wasn't here yet. And it wasn't me who informed the department. Nor was it Dulcie."

Rising abruptly, narrowly missing a crack on the head, Clyde snatched a wad of shorts and socks from the top bunk, flung them in the washer, and turned back to scowl at Joe. "Not the kit! You didn't teach that innocent kitten to use the telephone." His face had begun to flush. "Tell me you have not laid your despicable and alarming habits on that little innocent kitten."

"It wasn't the kit. The kit is afraid of phones. She thinks telephones transmit voices from another world."

Clyde let that one go by. "Who, then? Who called the station? Not Wilma. You haven't laid your dirty work on Wilma."

"If you must know, it was Kate. We found the barrette upstairs in the nursery. Kate pretended she found it, and she reported it—told them where to find it. Do you really want to put those red T-shirts in with the white stuff? You have a sudden yearning for pink Jockey shorts?"

Clyde snatched out the offending shirts. For a long moment, both were silent. Then, "You laid that stuff on Kate?"

"For all intents and purposes, Kate found the barrette. She went directly to Molena Point PD, as any law-abiding citizen would do. I'm surprised no one at the station told you or Harper."

"They're not *supposed* to tell *me*. They're working a murder case. This is serious business. The department's not supposed to talk to Harper, either."

"Who made that rule? He ought to be able to step back without being completely cut off."

"Lowell Gedding made that rule."

Joe swallowed. "Harper needs to know about the barrette. He needs to know that Dillon got away—at least for a while."

"And I'm elected to tell him."

"Who else?"

"And how do I explain that I came by such information?"

"Kate told you, of course. Fill her in—but get your stories straight." He studied Clyde a moment, then curled up on Rube's blanket and closed his eyes. Let Clyde sort it out.

He hadn't told Clyde about their spying on Stubby Baker, and about Baker's connection to San Quentin. He had to think about that. If Harper knew, he might be so angry, and so hot to follow up, that he'd do something foolish, maybe blow the case himself.

Oh, right. Harper had been a cop all these years, to do something stupid now?

Still, with the pressure on, and Harper so rudely excluded from the information loop, who knew?

This whole scene, Joe thought miserably, made him feel like he was clinging to a broken branch that was about to fall, hard, on the concrete.

Clyde said, "Lowell Gedding has complete confidence in Garza."

Joe opened his eyes. "Confidence in him to do what?"

Clyde glared.

"Confidence that Garza will come up with evidence to clear Harper? Or that Garza will stack the evidence to please those guys on the city council who'd like to see Harper out of there? Who'd like a softer brand of law enforcement?"

"You're letting your imagination run overtime. Harper *asked* Gedding to call in an investigator. That had to be done, to put Max at arm's length. Harper knows Garza's reputation, *he* has confidence that

Garza will clear him. And if Gedding wanted to dump Harper, why would he call in an outside investigator?"

"Why would he *not*? Make it look good. Make a solid case against Harper. An investigator who's in Gedding's pocket."

Clyde's brown eyes blazed with indignation, but then with uncertainty.

"Gedding was mighty quick to suggest Garza," Joe said. "He had Garza right on the tip of his tongue, primed and ready, when Harper suggested an outside man."

"How would you know that?"

"I heard him. Dulcie and I heard him."

Clyde poured soap into the washer and slammed the lid, closing his eyes as if in pain. "I don't want to know how you two were able to hear Lowell Gedding and Max Harper, in a private conversation, behind a closed door, inside Lowell Gedding's private office."

Joe Grey smiled. "What I'm telling you, Clyde, is that Gedding came up too fast with the name of Dallas Garza. As if he had it all planned." He sat up straighter, studying Clyde. "Your face is awfully red. You really ought to think about the damage that stress does to the human body. How long since you've had a checkup? You really shouldn't get yourself so tied in knots."

Clyde turned on his heel and left the laundry.

Alone, Joe pawed a nest into Rube's blanket, and settled down, considering his options.

Despite the dangers and drawbacks, moving in with this new detective was the only thing he knew to do, if he wanted a line into Molena Point PD.

He could make a run every day into the squad room. Spend his time underneath Garza's desk—until he got caught and pitched out on his furry ear.

And from beneath the desk, what would he learn? He could hear phone calls and conversations, but he'd get no look at department correspondence or at Garza's notes and reports. And as to interviews, Garza had arranged all his appointments away from the department.

Rolling on his back, he shoved Rube's blanket aside. Long-term surveillance beneath the detective's desk would be about as productive as hunting mice in a bathtub.

He was going to have to move in with Garza, give it a try, hope that Garza brought work home at night, away from the department and from the officers who were close buddies with Max Harper.

He imagined Garza, late in the evenings, making his notes and listening to his tapes in private. Quiet evenings in a cozy cottage, perfect to think over the facts, see how they added up; and a good time to place sensitive phone calls.

Particularly if he meant to frame Harper.

Clyde returned with an armful of sheets, tossing them practically on top of Joe. "What are you grinning about?"

He stepped atop the pile of wrinkled bedsheets. "Why would I be grinning? This situation is not a matter for levity."

Clyde began to sort through his dark shirts, dousing spot remover liberally on shirt fronts and inside collars, forcing Joe to endure a fit of sneezing.

"Tell me something, Joe. I know I'm opening a can

of worms here. But what, exactly, *is* your take on the Marner murders? What do *you* think happened up there?"

"You're asking me? You want my opinion? The lowly house cat?"

"Cut it, Joe."

"You never ask me anything. All you ever do is—"

"Kate and I had dinner last night. I think it's interesting that she didn't tell me a thing about the barrette."

"Maybe the department told her not to. So what's your point?"

"She told me—this wasn't in the *Gazette,* only in the San Francisco papers—that Lee Wark escaped from prison three weeks ago, with two other death row inmates."

Though he knew this, a chill coursed down Joe's spine. Knee-jerk reaction to the mention of Lee Wark.

"Kate said prison authorities thought Wark might be in San Francisco."

"I hope Harper knows this," Joe said.

"Harper's not in the most talkative of moods." Clyde looked at him deeply, the kind of look that made Joe pay attention. "Kate said there's been a spate of cat killings in the city.

"She's terrified it might be Wark. That's why she came down here, to get away. I don't have to tell you, Joe, that scares the hell out of me."

"It doesn't make me feel like party time." Joe sat very straight. "Do you remember when Wark was sentenced? His outburst in court, that he swore he'd get Harper?"

Clyde nodded. "That he'd get Harper. And Kate.

And anyone else who helped do him." Clyde fixed Joe with a keen stare. "Wark knows you cats helped."

He reached to touch Joe's shoulder, looking at him deeply. "Kate says that for a week before the Marner murders there were no cats killed in the city. Two days after the murders, they started again."

Fear sparked between Joe and Clyde.

The idea of Lee Wark slipping around Molena Point made Joe Grey as shaky as if he'd eaten a poisoned rat.

16

Like a cave in the side of the hill, the Garza family cottage nestled against a steep wooded slope above the north end of the village, its living room windows affording a view of the village rooftops, while its kitchen windows looked up into the back gardens that crowded above it.

The rafters and paneled walls were washed antique white, and the living area divided by a creamy stone fireplace behind which was a small, open study. Beyond the study were Garza's bedroom and bath. At the other end of the large, airy great room, before a deep bay window, stood a dining table big enough to seat a vast tribe of Garza relatives. A stairway tucked next to the kitchen led down to two additional bedrooms and a bath.

On the shelf of the bay window among a scatter of patchwork pillows, Joe Grey sat eating broiled shrimp and pilaf from a flowered plate. At one end of the long table, Dallas Garza and Kate and Hanni enjoyed larger portions of the same fare, and a green salad in which

Joe had shown no interest. The detective glanced up at Joe occasionally, amused possibly by Joe's excellent appetite, or possibly comparing him unfavorably to members of the canine persuasion. From the photographs on the walls, it was obvious that Garza was a dog man. Joe was surrounded by professional-quality color shots of businesslike hunting dogs. Pointers, setters, two Labradors, and a Weimaraner, each picture accompanied by the dog's extensive pedigree and a list of his field honors.

Some of the photos were not posed portraits but had been taken in the field, the dog carrying a pheasant or quail or duck to Garza or to Hanni; in many instances, Hanni was just a little girl—she'd had black hair then, but you couldn't miss those dark, laughing eyes.

Joe knew of dog-oriented families where cats came under the heading of vermin—right down there with a cockroach in the kitchen cupboard. He was surprised Garza had let him in the door.

Shortly before supper, Joe and Kate had made their entrance, Kate carrying Joe over her shoulder, asking nicely if the tomcat could stay for a few days. She said cats in the house upset Harper and made him sneeze, and that Clyde and Harper were painting the interior of Clyde's house, to keep Harper occupied in the evenings while he wasn't working. She said paint fumes were death on cats. It was true about the paint; Kate's manipulation of Clyde had been extensive, Joe thought, smiling.

Garza had studied Joe with the same expression that, Joe imagined, he used on a particularly seedy transient arrested for mugging old ladies. "Can't Clyde take the cat to a kennel?"

"Clyde put the other three cats and his Lab in the kennel. But Joe pines away. He won't eat. The last time Clyde boarded him, Joe worried and paced until he made himself sick.

"And Wilma Getz couldn't take him; her cat has the sniffles—like kennel cough, you know." She had given Garza that lovely bright smile. "I don't want him to be a problem. It's just that . . . I volunteered, I guess. I could take him to a motel."

Garza snorted. "You know you can't get a motel on short notice—particularly with a cat in tow."

Kate had watched Garza diffidently, glancing at Hanni.

It was then Joe made his move.

Leaping down from Kate's shoulder and looking the detective square in the eye, he had meowed twice, boldly, the way a dog would speak, and lifted a paw to shake hands. Such pandering disgusted him—but he was doing it for Harper.

Garza had widened his eyes and burst out laughing, a hard, bawdy cop's laugh.

Joe had kept his paw raised, watching the detective with the same keen intensity he had seen in the expression of an attentive German shepherd.

Garza, possibly impressed, certainly amused, had leaned down to shake Joe's paw. "I guess he can stay. As long as he doesn't spray the furniture. Who taught him to shake hands?"

Kate said, "Clyde's taught him a number of tricks.

Clyde says sometimes he seems almost as smart as a dog."

Joe cut her a look.

"Can he roll over?"

"Roll over, Joe. There's a good boy."

He had flopped down on the rag rug and dutifully rolled over, an appalling display of submission. He was going to kill Kate.

Amazing what indignities a good sleuth had to endure, for a little inside information.

"He can fetch, too," Kate said. Wadding up a piece of paper into a twist, she tossed it across the room.

Joe fetched the paper back to her, quickly expanding the list of embarrassments he was going to visit upon Kate Osborne. She had sensibly ended the list of his talents with the fetching routine.

Now, finishing his shrimp, he sat on the window seat washing his paws and observing the human diners, wondering if he could work them for seconds. With a few more "cute" exhibits of caninelike intelligence, Garza might have offered a glass of wine.

Thus began Joe's surveillance of the man who had been appointed to clear—or to destroy—Max Harper. When, after dinner, Kate and Hanni went for a walk in the village, Garza retired to his desk and turned on his tape recorder. And Joe leaped nimbly onto the protruding end of the mantel, where he had a clear view of the top of Garza's desk.

The first interview tape that Garza played, with Dillon's parents, made Joe feel deeply sad—and then angry.

The Thurwells blamed Max Harper for Dillon's disappearance.

Even with the heartbreaking tragedy of their missing child, they had no right to blame Max Harper. Harper had treasured that child, had been so proud of her increasing riding skills, of the way she handled Redwing.

He supposed the Thurwells had to blame someone. Supposed that to blame Harper was only human. But Harper had taken such pains with Dillon, had taught the little girl a valuable discipline.

The Thurwells were good to Dillon, but, as Dulcie pointed out, they didn't seem to see the need a growing child has for some direction in her life. Harper knew about that kind of need. He had given Dillon the goals she'd hungered for, had fostered the skills and the strength of mind that could keep her from going off suddenly on some tangent when she hit her teens. Dulcie said you didn't have to be a human to recognize that universal need.

When Garza had rewound the Thurwell tape, hc played Harper's statement to Detective Davis, and as the tape ran, he made detailed notes on a large yellow pad.

The detective played back interviews with various personnel at the ranch where the Marners kept their horses, and with the manager and the three waitresses who had been on duty at Café Mundo the day of the murder. There was nothing in their answers to conflict with Harper's statement.

Garza played, three times, his interview with the

witness who claimed to have seen Harper following the three riders up the mountain, directly after lunch. The man was a tourist staying in the village, a William Green. He said he had been out biking, that he had recognized Harper because Green had lost his car keys the week before, and had gone into the station to identify them after a foot patrol found them, that Captain Harper had come in while he was signing for his keys, and he'd heard an officer call him by name.

Fishy, Joe Grey thought.

Green was very sure about his details. Joe felt easier when Garza made a note to check out the man's home address and background.

At twelve-fifteen, Garza called it a night. Kate and Hanni had come in around ten and gone downstairs to bed. Switching off the desk lamp, Garza turned suddenly toward the fireplace, looking directly at Joe.

"For all the attention you've given me tonight, tomcat, I'd say you were some kind of snitch."

Joe's belly did a flip-flop. He purred hard and tried to look stupid. He could feel his paws sweating.

Garza grinned. "Working for Max Harper? And does that mean you're working for the killer?" Garza's eyes were as black as obsidian, totally unrevealing. Joe regarded him as coolly as he could manage, considering he had a bellyful of hop-frogs.

"Instead of spying on me, you might make yourself useful. This cottage has been shut up for months. It has to be crawling with mice."

Garza tousled Joe's head as he would rough up a big dog, and headed for the bedroom.

Well, maybe it was only Garza's way. Joe had heard

him tease Hanni with the same dry wit, and had seen him ruffle her head, too.

Retiring to the window seat, he curled up, listening to the night sounds through the slightly open, locked-in-place window. The small clock on the kitchen pass-through said 12:19. An occasional car passed on the street below, and later a party of raccoons began to squabble, chittering and hissing, and he heard a garbage can go over. He woke and dozed, and when next he looked at the clock, its illuminated face said 4:40. Something had waked him. His head raised, his ears sharp, he lay listening.

The sound of footsteps reached him softly from up beyond the kitchen windows, and the rustle of bushes, sounds so faint that only a cat would hear.

Dropping to the carpet, he sprang to the pass-through and padded silently across the kitchen counter. Keeping to the shadows behind the bread box, he peered out beside the curtain into the night.

A man stood among the bushes on the hill, a dark shadow nearly hidden among the black masses of foliage and trees, a thin, tall man, looking down into the house.

Was he stoop-shouldered like Lee Wark? Through the glass, Joe could catch no scent, but the look of the man made him choke back a stifled mewl, his voice as tremulous as a terrified kitten. In panic, he dropped to the floor, crouching behind the refrigerator, and stared up at the window, half expecting the man to slide it open and climb in. He was ashamed to admit the fear that swept him; he was scared down to his tomcat paws.

But *was* it the Welshman? The shadow blended so

well into the overgrown gardens that he really couldn't see much. And now, his nose filled with the stink of dust from the refrigerator's motor housing, he couldn't have smelled Wark if the man had stood on top of him.

Leaping to the counter, he peered out again, but the figure was gone. He could see only the crowding houses and massed bushes, could detect no human shape within the indecipherable tangles of the night.

Pacing the house, he worried until dawn, prowling in and out of bedrooms, making the round of partly open, locked windows both on the main level and downstairs. Twice he imagined he could smell Wark, but the next instant could smell nothing but pine trees and the lingering stink of raccoons.

If that was Wark, had he come here looking for Kate? Joe began to worry about Dulcie and the kit; he wondered if they were out hunting, in the night alone. At 5:00, pacing and fretting, he leaped to Garza's desk, pushed the phone off its cradle onto Garza's blotter, and made a whispered call, watching Garza's closed bedroom door.

Wilma answered sleepily, a curt and irritable "Yes?"

"I think Lee Wark may be in the neighborhood, prowling around the Garza place, but now he's gone. Watch out for him. Are they there? Tell Dulcie she needs to be careful."

"They're here. I'll see to it." Wilma asked no questions, wasted no time getting up to speed. Thank God for a few sensible humans.

Beyond the closed bedroom door, he heard the detective stir. Pawing the phone into its cradle, he fled for the window seat, had just curled up when the bedroom door creaked open and light spilled out—and Joe was gently snoring.

Maybe he'd been wrong, maybe it wasn't Wark out there. Could it have been Stubby Baker? Could Baker be interested in Garza's notes and tapes? Baker was tall and slim like Wark, and about the same height. He was straighter and broader of shoulder, but in the shadows, might he have appeared hunched?

By 5:20 Garza had showered, made coffee, and was frying eggs and bacon. Joe, strolling through the kitchen, yowled loudly at the back door.

"At least you're housebroken." The detective gave him a noncommittal cop stare and opened the kitchen door.

From the garden, Joe glanced up at the window, expecting to see Garza's dark Latin eyes looking out, watching him, but the lighted glass remained blank. He found, beneath the window, the waffle prints of a man's jogging shoes incised into the damp earth; large shoes, certainly larger than Clyde's size 10s. Carefully prowling, he studied each area of bare soil, tracking the prints clear around the house, pausing where the man had stood looking into the downstairs bedroom windows.

Surely neither Kate nor Hanni had been awakened and seen him. They'd have called the department—or come upstairs to wake Dallas. Presumably, Dallas was the only one with a firearm. Heading around the house again, he pawed at the kitchen door, bellowing a deep yowl.

Kate opened the door. He stepped in, sniffing the aromas of breakfast. Kate and Hanni were showered and dressed, all polished and smelling of Ivory soap.

Hanni sat at the kitchen table across from Garza, drinking coffee as Garza ate his fried eggs and bacon and sourdough toast. The detective glanced down at Joe absently but didn't offer to share.

Evidently no one had pointed out to Garza, and he probably didn't know, that any ordinary cat, moved to a new house, would be kept in for a couple of weeks so he would become oriented and not run away.

When no one offered him a fried egg, Joe fixed his gaze on Kate, licking his whiskers.

Kate fetched a can of cat food.

He looked at her, amazed. *Cat food?*

"Cat food," she said, shaking the can at him. "I'm not cooking eggs for you. Dinner was one thing—you can share our dinner, but I'm not laying out caviar and kippers at six in the morning like Clyde does. Besides, you're getting fat."

He hated when someone threw insults and he couldn't talk back. *Fat?* Kate didn't know muscle when she saw it. Under his gray velvet fur he was as solid as coiled steel. Studying the can Kate had flipped open, and taking a good sniff, he was relieved to know it was the fancy kind, the brand that, the commercials implied, should be served on a linen tablecloth from a crystal sherbet dish.

He guessed Kate hadn't seen the commercials, because she plopped the fish concoction into a cracked earthenware crock and plunked it unceremoniously on the floor.

So much for early-morning amenities.

Grinning with sadistic pleasure, she turned her back on him.

Garza, finishing his breakfast, rose and stepped to his desk. Joe heard him lift the phone and punch in a number—it was local, seven digits.

"Max? Right. You want to come down to the station? I'll want another statement. Then I want to go up to your place, have a look at the house and stable, then on up to the scene. That fit with your plans?"

All very friendly and low-key.

And Joe was stonewalled. He considered hiding in Garza's car, riding up to Harper's with the detective, then following the two men up the mountain—but he knew that wasn't smart.

Garza, pulling on a suede sport coat over his jeans and shirt, headed for his Chevy coupe. When he had gone, Joe looked with meaning at Kate.

She opened the door and followed him out, leaving Hanni deep in the arts section of the morning paper.

Joe's whisper was hasty. "Someone came prowling last night. Stood outside your bedroom. Did you see him?"

Kate turned pale. "No. Not a thing. Who . . . ?"

"Tall and thin. It could have been Wark."

She went completely white.

"There are footprints. Good ones. Garza needs to see them."

"I—what'll I do?" She was clearly shaken.

"Call the station. Tell them you just found the prints—that they seem fresh to you. That they go to the kitchen window, then on around the house. They'll send someone."

"Shall I call Dallas? I have the number of his cell phone."

"I—let the department handle it," Joe said, not certain himself what to do. "And walk around the house yourself first. So they'll believe you. Don't step on his prints." And he hurried away to make sure that Dulcie and the kit were safe, despite Wilma's promise. Racing down the sidewalks dodging early-morning shadows, he kept seeing that brief, muddy gleam of the man's eyes, looking in through the kitchen window.

17

It was still dark when Dulcie set out to find the kit. Prowling the village among the blackest pools of night, it wasn't hard to follow the tattercoat's smell, which had taken on a potpourri of eau de bath powder from Wilma's dressing table.

Awakened by Joe's predawn phone call, she had galloped into the living room to make sure the kit was safe in her basket, and found her gone. With her mind on Lee Wark, she had stormed out her cat door, tracking the kit's boudoir scent over the roofs and across gardens and streets until she found herself doubling back to her own street some five blocks above Wilma's house.

The kit's trail led to a neglected duplex built over a pair of double garages, a property unusual in the village for its shabbiness, the yard overgrown with weeds, the clapboard walls badly in need of paint. The stairs led up to a deck that ran the length of the building, dark at the far end but light beneath the windows of the nearer unit; she could see a lamp burning within, but no movement. The kit's scent led up the stairs to the deck, where an unlatched screen had been pulled out a few inches; Dulcie spotted a hunk of dark fur clinging. She was about to leap up when Joe Grey appeared from the shadows.

She turned a slow green gaze on him. "You following me or the kit?"

"Both of you." He was all claws and nerves. "I have a bad feeling about Wark."

Above them, the sky was the color of Joe's coat, heavy gray without any promise of sun, though the time must be nearly seven.

Joe looked the building over. "Shoddy. Why would the kit come here?"

"Who knows what's in that wild little head?"

Leaping to the sill, he tried to see through the muslin curtains. There was a screen, but the glass was open a few inches. Dulcie followed, the two cats balancing awkwardly on the slanted, narrow ledge. They were looking into the kitchen and could see one big room to their right, apparently a studio apartment. It was sparsely and cheaply furnished. Pushing in under the screen, they stepped onto the old, cracked tiles of the counter, icy beneath their paws. Dropping silently down, they followed the kit's scent across the battered linoleum, beneath the scarred breakfast table and into the studio. They heard the courthouse clock striking seven. The room contained a decrepit metal chair meant for outdoors, a scarred coffee table littered with clothes, and a pullout couch made up into a bed. The bed was occupied, the woman's tawny hair spilling over the pillow. Crystal slept soundly.

And in the rusty metal chair, the kit slept, curled up tight and so deep under that she was not aware of them.

"What the hell?" Joe said softly.

"Beats me."

"Has she been slipping away to visit Crystal? Why would she do that?"

Crystal's sandals and riding boots were tossed in the corner beside a pair of high heels. Her purse lay on the coffee table among the tangle of clothes, beside a blue folder. Joe reared up to have a look, front paws on the coffee table.

"Sarden Realty," he said softly. The folder bore the familiar tree-in-a-circle logo of the local real estate firm. As he reached a paw to flip it opcn, thc kit woke.

She gazed from one to the other with eyes like yellow moons. "How did you find me?"

"Shhh," Dulcie said. "She'll hear you."

Joe pawed open the folder. He was silent for a few moments, then looked at Dulcie. "It's a sales contract and closing statement. Escrow papers. For this address, Dulcie. Crystal has bought this place."

"Crystal? This dump? Why?"

"The previous owner was Helen Marner," Joe said. "The escrow closed two weeks before Helen was murdered. Crystal paid four hundred and eighty thou, with forty thousand down."

Dulcie looked at him wide-eyed, trying to process this. "What does this mean? Can we get this to Garza? Can you slip the papers out?"

"Oh, right. Crystal finds the papers gone, knows someone's been in here."

"But . . ."

Creeping toward the bed, Joe studied Crystal for signs of waking. She seemed deep under.

Something wasn't right here. Something was making his fur crawl. He felt as edgy as a mouse in a glass bowl. "Peninsula Escrow," he whispered, leaping onto the table. "Garza can get a copy from them." Standing among Crystal's wrinkled clothes, he looked intently at the kit. "What are you doing here, Kit? What made you come here?"

"I followed a man. He was in Wilma's garden. And then I followed Crystal."

"You're not making sense."

"Yes, I am. A man came in Wilma's garden and looked in the window."

"What man? When was this?" Joe felt his fur going stiff. "What did he look like?" He stared into the shadowed hall that led, apparently, to a bathroom and closet, but saw no one, could scent no other human in the apartment.

"What did he look like, Kit?"

"Muddy eyes. Bent over, like his shoulders wouldn't hold him real straight."

Every hair on Joe's back went rigid.

"When he looked in the window, I dropped off Wilma's desk and hid. When he went away, I followed him."

"I thought you hated that cat door."

"I hate it, but I wanted out. I followed him to where that oak tree grows through the middle of the street and there are pictures of a blue dog in the window and that place where Wilma likes to eat breakfast."

"The Swiss Café. Then what?"

"She was standing by the oak tree."

"Crystal?"

"They argued. They got so mad—mad as raccoons fighting over garbage. The man said that someone named Mel owed him money. Crystal said, 'You think I'm stupid? How could he owe you money when you didn't *do* anyone. You think he pays for nothing?' "

The kit looked from Joe to Dulcie, her round yellow eyes darkening. "What did that mean? How could he *do* someone? Do what?"

Joe dropped off the coffee table, nudging the kit out of the chair and toward the kitchen. "Did she call the man by name?"

The kit mewed a laugh, then hushed, staring back at Crystal's sleeping form. "She called him 'you stupid bastard.' She said, 'The deal wasn't with you, you dumb Welsh bastard. What makes you think . . . ?' Then he interrupted her."

The three cats leaped to the kitchen counter. "How can you remember all that?" Dulcie said. "How can you repeat all that, word for word?"

"The big cats taught me—the cats I lived with. Well, then the man said, 'Don't be such a bitch. Who do you think did them? They're dead, ain't they?'

"Was he talking about those women? Is that what it means—to make them dead?"

"Yes, Kit," Joe said gently. "What else did they say?"

"She said, 'We'll see about that, you no-good deadbeat,' and she left. Walked away real fast and mad, and I followed her."

"Did Wark see you?" Dulcie said. "Did he know you were there?"

"I stayed way deep in the shadows. I followed her up and up the hill past the shops and saw her come in here. The light came on inside. I found where the screen was loose. I watched her until she went to bed, then I slipped under just like you would. And here I am," she said proudly.

Joe and Dulcie exchanged a look. Dulcie sighed. She wanted to cuff the kit's inquisitive little nose—and wanted to hug her. Across the room, Crystal stirred but didn't wake. Beside the cats, the kitchen window was brightening with dawn.

"Before she turned the light off," the kit said, "the phone rang."

"And?" Joe said impatiently.

"She listened but didn't say anyone's name. She said, 'Of course I met him. What do you think?' Then a pause. Then, 'No. I haven't the faintest. I'm still looking for her, you know that.' She was real angry. She shouted into the phone, 'Oh, right. And let them hang me, too? You think I want to spend the rest of my life in T.I.?'

"What's T.I.?" said the kit.

"It's a prison," Dulcie said shortly. "Go on, Kit."

"She hung up. And she opened up the phone and took out something. Like a little box. She put it in that drawer and put another like it in the phone. Then she poured a drink of that sharp-smelling stuff, there by the refrigerator. She drank it down and went to bed. And I came inside to see what I could see.

"What was that box?" the kit said. "What was she doing? After she went to bed I curled up in the chair to watch her, but I guess I went to sleep. Then you were here." The kit looked deeply at Dulcie, the tip of her tail twitching. "It's scary."

"What's scary?" Joe said. "Being in here with Crystal? Then why did you go to sleep here?"

She looked bright-eyed at Joe. "It's scary spying on humans. Coming into their den to spy on them."

"Then why did you *do* it?" Joe growled.

"Because you would have. Because humans do bad things, and you know how to make them stop. Because if you know enough about them, you can make them pay for being bad—like you did before, when that man was killed on Hellhag Hill. I followed her because she's a mean person."

Joe Grey sighed, and hid a grin, and pawed open the drawer beneath the counter.

Two reels of miniature tape lay inside, the kind used in answering machines. They were tucked down among some packages of plastic spoons and forks. Joe picked them up in his teeth and dropped them on the counter.

"Those paper towels behind you, Dulcie. To keep the drool off."

Nipping at the towels, Dulcie managed to pull one free. She was wrapping the tapes, folding the towel with her paw, when Crystal rolled over and pushed back the covers.

Joe glanced back at the escrow papers, then snatched up the package of tapes. Dulcie pushed out the window behind him, nosing the kit along, and they fled down the stairs and underneath.

Crouched in the damp shadows, they heard Crystal moving around in the kitchen above them, heard water running, then the sucking of a coffeemaker. A lone car passed, its tires hissing along the fog-damp street. Above in the apartment, a door slammed; the pipes rumbled as if Crystal was taking a shower.

Joe dropped the paper packet between his paws. "Now we're getting somewhere."

"Now," Dulcie said softly, reaching to pat at the packet of tapes, "one of us will have to phone Garza."

"Maybe," Joe said. "Maybe not. I can leave the tapes tucked into the morning *Gazette*."

"But what about the escrow papers? If she bought the house from Helen and didn't *tell* anyone . . . And if that *was* Wark she met last night . . ." She looked deeply at Joe, her green eyes burning. "What does this all add up to? *Did* Crystal pay someone to kill the Marners? How does this apartment sale fit in?"

Carefully, Joe Grey washed his front paw. "I guess, if Garza got a phone call from an escrow officer, that wouldn't be the same as an anonymous call."

"Except," Dulcie said, "he'd check it out with the escrow company. When there's no one there by that name—"

"So I get the name of the escrow officers. I think most of them are women—and you've been dying to call Garza. You can ask him to keep it confidential."

Dulcie purred. "You did very well, Kit. I can't believe you remembered that long conversation."

"I told you. The clowder cats. They tried to do magic, but they never could. I learned to say the spells the way they did. But they never worked, never made anything different. I was still cold and hungry."

Joe Grey licked the kit's ear. "You're fine now, Kit. You're just fine." And he picked up the packet of tapes and led the ladies away from Crystal's, through the bright, chill dawn.

18

The Garza cottage smelled of spaghetti sauce laced with marsala. Beyond the windows, the February sky was dark but clear. A thin sliver of moon shone above the treetops. The ringing of the phone mingled with the chiming of the courthouse clock from down in the village. When Garza answered, Joe Grey was already stretched out along the back of the mantel, his eyes closed, his studied breathing deep and slow, feigning sleep. The time was 7 P.M. He could just hear the crackle of Dulcie's voice from the other end of the line.

Garza listened. "Peninsula Title Company?" Then a long pause. Then, "Yes, of course I'm interested. Can you tell me your name?"

He listened again attentively, making notes on a pad. Dulcie's voice would have, Joe knew, that soft, insinuating tone that so annoyed Max Harper. The name Garza jotted down was *Caroline Jacobs*. Joe wondered why Dulcie had chosen that name, from the list of four woman officers he'd given her. Maybe because it had a nice rhythm.

Duplex, Dolores above First. Helen Marner to Crystal Ryder. $480,000. Closed February 9.

"Oh, yes, this is very helpful information. Any information we receive about Helen Marner is of course of departmental interest. Can you get me a copy of the escrow papers?

"I see. Yes, of course I understand. I will simply make an inquiry. If Miss Powers wants to furnish us with a copy, I'll send a man over." Garza paused. Joe cocked his head, straining toward that faintest murmur from the other end of the line. Dulcie, at this moment, was most likely stretched out on Wilma's desk blotter, taking her ease beside the handset, and feeling smug. These little tips to the law really brought out the ham in his lady. Maybe she should have her own talk show.

"Tell me," Garza said, "were you responsible for making a delivery to my home this morning?"

Whatever Dulcie's response, Garza grunted as if unconvinced. "Do you know anything about such a delivery? Whatever you say will be strictly confidential.

"I see. But you do know where I live," Garza said. "You did have my phone number."

The premise didn't necessarily follow, but it was a good try. Joe heard a faint click from the other end.

Garza stared at the phone until the canned recording came on, then hung up. Joe settled back into his relaxed sprawl and shut his eyes, waiting for Garza to play the tapes that the detective had found inside his morning *Gazette*. Garza had unwrapped and examined them and dropped them in his pocket.

And he did not play them now. He rinsed out his coffee cup, slipped on his jacket, and left the house for an appointment.

Joe spent a restless night pacing the cottage. Kate and Hanni were at a play, and Garza had not returned when he grew too impatient to stay inside, and went to hunt, slipping out a loose downstairs window, through the burglar bars. He did not look for Dulcie and the kit; they had promised to stay inside. Keeping to the local gardens, he contented himself with house mice. He ended up at home in time for breakfast.

Slipping in through his cat door, past a tuft of tortoiseshell fur, he stopped in the living room, laughing. Thc kit had learned very quickly to taunt Clyde.

"Why *can't* I sit on the table? Joe Grey sits on the table! And I don't *want* scrambled eggs. We had breakfast. We dined in Jolly's alley," the kit said grandly.

"Hush," said Dulcie. "Let me finish."

"It's a really shabby duplex," Dulcie was saying. "But a lovely location and view. Charlie would love it."

Clyde said. "Would *you* like a scrambled egg, Dulcie?"

"I would," Dulcie said softly. "The kit ate all the blintzes."

Joe shouldered into the kitchen, to see the kit, looking hurt, jump onto the table. He watched Clyde pick up Dulcie and set her beside the kit, apparently in the interest of fairness. Leaping up beside Dulcie, Joe stretched out across the open newspaper. Clyde, scowling at him, added two more eggs to the skillet.

"It was Wark that the kit saw," Dulcie said. "It had to be. And it was Wark Joe saw snooping around the Garza cottage."

Clyde looked at Joe. "Did Garza catch him?"

Joe flicked a whisker. "None of them saw him; they slept right through, even our big-time detective."

"You sure it was Wark?"

"I'm not sure. Could have been Baker. But the kit saw Wark talking with Crystal."

Clyde sighed. "Did the man at the cottage see you, Joe?"

"Of course he didn't see me."

Clyde dished up the eggs, setting the cats' three plates on the table. Having nowhere to put his own plate, he stood at the stove to eat. "If you were looking out the window, those white markings would shine like neon."

"You think I don't have sense enough to keep away from the glass? That is so insulting."

"You think he was looking for Kate?"

"I have no idea. Maybe looking for Kate. Maybe checking on Garza. If he was involved in the murders—"

"He could have been looking for you and Dulcie. You'd better come home where you're safe."

"Why would I be safe at home? Wark knows where I live. He was all around this house, if you remember, after Beckwhite was murdered. Looking in the windows—right in my face. Scared the spit out of me."

"Then you can move in with Wilma. No, you can't do that. He knows where Dulcie lives."

Joe said, "Dulcie and the kit can stay with Charlie. Not likely Wark knows about her."

"And you can stay there, too. You don't need to be hanging around Garza's."

"Where do you think Garza makes his sensitive phone calls and tapes his notes? Kate set that up for me, and you helped her—I'm not tossing that away."

Clyde just looked at him. That ever-patient, put-upon expression of a defeated human.

"I'll keep of sight," Joe said.

Clyde said, "I'll talk to Charlie about Dulcie and the kit."

Joe dropped to the floor. "Even Charlie's apartment isn't the safest. There's only one way out, just the front door, down the stairs and through that little foyer to the street. Wark breaks in, you're cornered. No back door, no side windows. And that window over the street—you can't reach anything from there, not a rooftop, not so much as a vine. It's only one floor down, but all concrete. Splatter a cat like—"

"Hush," Dulcie said. "It's a perfect setup. Charlie can fix a way for us to slip out to the roofs—through a vent or something. You know how clever she is. Wark would have to bring a ladder to get up on the roofs. And he can't jump from roof to roof, or run across a branch, or leap six feet between buildings."

Joe was unconvinced.

"Anyway, he's after Kate," Dulcie said. "This time, Joe, he's not after us. He followed Kate in San Francisco. It's Kate you should worry about."

"Kate knows he's here," Joe snapped. "Besides, with a warrant out for him, the department will pick him up—haul him back to Quentin."

Clyde poured a fresh cup of coffee. What he appeared to need, Joe thought, was a double Prozac. With his coffee cup so full it sloshed, he sat down at the table, looking deeply at the cats.

"However this turns out, you two have opened a whole can of worms with Garza. The guy comes here to do a legitimate piece of police work and—"

"That's a matter of opinion," Joe said darkly.

"To do a straightforward investigation, and he starts getting anonymous phone tips."

"One phone call," Dulcie said, "from a legitimate employee of Peninsula Escrow."

"And unexplained tapes are left at his door that might be evidence and might not. That might be a plant. Don't you think Garza—"

"So what were we supposed to do?" Dulcie said. "Hold back information?"

Clyde sucked at his coffee. "Crystal Ryder has been in town for maybe six months, living in that duplex. Why, all of a sudden, did she decide to buy it?"

"She had a lease/option," Joe said. "Apparently she decided to move on it. My question is, why just two weeks before the murder? And it would be interesting to know, as well, why Helen owned a place in Molena Point, when she's lived for years in Santa Barbara."

"I can answer that," Clyde said. "She had half a dozen rentals in the village. Max told me that. She had them with a rental agency."

"A pretty shoddy agency," Dulcie said, "or they'd have insisted she paint the place."

Clyde rose to rinse the dishes. "You three have an opinion on everything. You have an inside line to Garza's investigation. You have spied on Stubby Baker. You have tossed Crystal Ryder's apartment and tampered with critical evidence. And you—"

"If you mean the tapes," Joe said, "if we'd left them there, and Crystal hid them, Garza might never know they existed."

"And what about the barrette?" Clyde said.

"We had no contact with the police over that," Joe told him. "Kate reported the barrette to the police, they told her they'd go right up there, photograph where they found it, and book it in as evidence. It's probably, right now, sitting in the lab being dusted for prints and particles caught in the setting. They—"

"Probably they are going to find cat hairs."

"Why must you always drag in cat hairs? Why must you always tell us we're messing up an investigation? Do I really have to remind you, Clyde, of the murders in the past, where with our help Harper has made a case?" He looked at Clyde sadly, hurt written in every line of his gray-and-white face.

"The three of you are going to Charlie's. You're going now. And you're going to stay hidden."

"Dulcie and the kit are going. I'm settled in with Detective Garza and I intend to stay there."

Clyde slammed down the plate he was drying, nearly breaking it. "At least you won't be here in the house taunting Max Harper, making *his* life miserable."

"We are trying to save his life. And when have I ever taunted Harper?"

But then Joe said, more gently, "How *is* he doing?"

"Not good. Won't talk about the case or about anything else much. He's quit going out with the search parties. Afraid he might taint some piece of evidence."

"How would he . . . ?"

"If they find her—when they find her—someone might claim he tampered with evidence or slowed the search, maybe made counterproductive suggestions, that kind of thing. He's getting . . ."

"Paranoid," Joe said. "That's not like Harper."

"He talked last night about quitting the force. Retiring. After he's cleared, of course. Talked about going to Alaska."

"Alaska!" Joe yowled.

"Max Harper," Dulcie mewed, "leave Molena Point? I don't believe that."

"There's more than that to believe." Clyde looked at the cats deeply. "I think there's something between Max and Charlie."

The cats widened their eyes, trying to look amazed.

"I wouldn't be surprised to see them, when this thing is over, take off together for Alaska."

Dulcie stared at Clyde, then turned away, washing furiously.

Clyde said, "Max *had* been talking, the last few months, about reorganizing the department. He has five new officers and a new clerk. They're getting crowded in that one-room setup. But now . . ."

"He has basement space," Joe said. "Where they store the old files, where they have the shooting range and emergency operations room."

Clyde nodded. "He's done some really nice plans to redesign the building, give officers more space and privacy. Add an up-to-date report-writing room, more room for communications, a bigger evidence lockup, more security.

"But since the Marner murder, it's as if he never heard of a redesign. Has no interest. Seems like he doesn't give a damn about the department."

"When this is over," Joe said, "he'll launch into it. Bounce back. Reorganize the space. That would be just the ticket, get his mind off what those buzzards are trying to do to him."

"If we only knew which buzzards," Clyde said. "I don't know, I've never seen him like this. Years ago, in Salinas, after a bad bull ride when Max got gored in the shoulder, when he was all broken up and in the hospital—and didn't have a dime—he was still joking. Still on top of it.

"His shoulder got infected, he had a high fever, three ribs broken. I was scared he was going to cash it in. But he hung in there—joking all the way, with that dry humor.

"Even when Millie died, even though he's never gotten over it or stopped missing her, he was never like this.

"You had the feeling, when Millie died, that no matter how destroyed he was, he knew things had to get better. That he knew that's the way life works—that we all take our bumps and keep ridin'. But now . . ." Clyde shook his head. "Now, he doesn't seem to believe that anymore."

Joe just looked at him. Sometimes all these human problems were too much; sometimes he thought the household animals were the lucky ones. All they had to do was nap on their soft beds, gobble their three squares, enjoy lots of petting, and no worries over humankind's disasters.

Except he remembered too clearly that other life, before he realized his ability to speak. He wouldn't want to return to that. He'd been bored out of his tomcat mind.

As a young cat, it had been a big deal to invent some simple new entertainment—find some new diversion in one of the several shabby apartments he'd lived in, a new way to tease some human in one of the interchangeable families who'd taken him in. Stupid kitten stuff. He'd never had a real human friend until he met Clyde. Or he'd find some smaller, skinnier kitten abandoned in an alley, someone weaker than he, that he could tease and torment.

When he moved in with Clyde, he'd graduated to intimidating Clyde's lady friends. How amusing, to terrorize those lovely young women, faking lethal claws, treating them to loud snarls and flashing teeth—all because life could get so yawningly, nerve-deadeningly, mind-numbingly dull.

But now, with his newly discovered skills, there was no time to be bored. He hardly had time for a nap or a good rabbit hunt—the sleuthing life took every claw-clinging ounce of creativity he could muster.

And now, as a pattern of clues was forming in the Marner murders, a morass as intriguing as a crisscross of fresh rabbit tracks, he had no time for discontented thoughts—except in terms of the final retribution for this killer.

This case was more than a fascinating puzzle. This time, he wanted not only justice, he wanted revenge. Sweet, sharp-clawed revenge. This time, he was out for blood.

19

Dressed in the oversized T-shirt she'd slept in, Charlie Getz stood on a ladder in her small bathroom, removing the vent fan from the ceiling. She had gone up on the roof last night, removed the fresh-air grid and wiped out a quarter-inch of accumulated dirt from inside the vent pipe. The four-inch tunnel didn't allow much room—peering along its length at a small circle of sky, she went queasy at the tight quarters through which the cats must push. Six feet of claustrophobia leading from her apartment out to the village rooftops. She guessed Dulcie and the kit could slither through, but Joe Grey had better not try.

Coming down the ladder, glancing in her bathroom mirror at the reflection of her milk-white legs, she had a sharp vision of Molena Point's pretty, tanned blondes in their tennis shorts. The only tan she had was what her grandmother had called a farmer's tan, brown only on her neck and hands and lower arms. Not a body to bring the men flocking.

Not the face, either, she thought. *But I have a warm*

heart. And I have nice hazel eyes, if anyone bothers to look.

She wished Max Harper would bother.

Lifting the disconnected ceiling fan from atop the ladder, she nodded to Dulcie and the kit where they crouched in the doorway peering up.

"That should do it. Your own private tunnel. I'll leave the ladder for you to climb.

"But I warn you, Dulcie. If a rat or a bat comes in through that vent—if so much as a wool moth comes in—you're dog meat."

Dulcie smiled. Lashing her tail in reply, she leaped up the ladder into the hole and was gone through the ceiling. Charlie imagined her slipping along above the bathtub, popping out of the wall above the roof like a swallow from its hole. The kit followed her, her fluffy tail twitching as it disappeared, probably to race madly across the rooftops.

She'd done a drawing once of Dulcie and Joe running across the roofs. But it wasn't a cheerful piece, it was dark and frightening. Though it hung in a prominent place in the Aronson Gallery, still it disturbed her.

Clyde had brought Dulcie and the kit over last night, like a father bringing his children to stay with a favorite aunt. Clyde had treated her like an aunt, too, making it obvious that he knew how she felt about Harper. When he left, she'd been really down. Had she hurt him terribly? She'd queried Dulcie, but Dulcie had little to tell her.

"He's . . . would the word be stoic?" Dulcie had said. "Understanding?"

"*Stoic,* Dulcie?"

"Max Harper is his best friend. You are, in a different way, his best friend. He's so caught up in Harper's problems just now . . ." Dulcie, sitting on the end of the daybed, had looked up quizzically at her. "You are asking me, your friendly neighborhood cat, about your love life?"

"Come on, Dulcie. You sound like Joe."

"What can I tell you? He loves you both. He knows Harper needs someone just now."

"You're saying he's glad to dump me on Harper."

"No, he—"

"He's seeing someone else."

"No! But—but when Kate called him that night, when she got into town . . ."

Charlie had sat back against the pillow, hugging herself. Kate. Kate Osborne. That beautiful blonde. It seemed a hundred times harder to lose a man to a beautiful woman than to some pig. If her rival were ugly, she could tell herself Clyde didn't have any taste. But Kate Osborne . . .

But why did she *care*? She'd been mooning over Max, feeling guilty that she was longing for him, that she was hurting Clyde.

And now here she was green with jealousy because Clyde wanted someone who was more beautiful than she could ever hope to be.

"Perfidy," she had told Dulcie. "Perfidy and capriciousness."

Dulcie had smiled and turned away to wash.

"It is all very well, Dulcie, to have a nonchalant wash-up when you want to end a discussion. But such behavior isn't very informative."

Dulcie hadn't answered.

The bottom line, Charlie told herself, was that she wanted what she couldn't have.

And that didn't say much for her depth of character.

And through this conversation, the kit had prowled the one-room apartment poking into every box and cranny—making herself immediately and totally at home. Taking over just as she had taken over Wilma's house and, before that, Lucinda and Pedric's luxurious RV. Claiming every surface—Charlie's few pieces of furniture, the kitchen counters, the packing boxes Charlie used for cupboards, as her own feline territory. Leaving little face rubs and tufts of black-and-brown fur as fine as silk, to mark her conquests. Clyde said the kit was the greatest feline opportunist ever born, and Charlie believed it.

But who could blame her? The kit had never had a home. Always on the move, tagging along behind a clowder of cats that didn't want her, never sleeping in a warm, safe house or knowing the friendship of a human, until she went to live with Lucinda and Pedric Greenlaw.

Charlie smiled. The kit had learned pretty fast.

Stashing the ceiling fan in the cabinet beneath the bathroom sink, she put her tools by the front door with her purse, nuked her cold cup of coffee, and sat down to finish her sweet roll, using her paper napkin to wipe Dulcie's and the kit's pawprints from the table. This business of having cat houseguests was like living in a dream straight from Lewis Carroll. It was one thing to take your meals with cats who could carry on a dinner conversation, one thing to go to bed at night with two kitties who said, "Good night, Charlie," like some feline version of *The Waltons*. But cats who peered over your shoulder at the pages of the latest Dean Koontz, one trying to learn to read while the other offered off-the-wall opinions of Koontz's writing style and baroque setting, was a bit too much.

At least Dulcie was well read—and her opinions of Koontz, though wild, were always upscale and positive.

Finishing her breakfast, Charlie pulled off her T-shirt, showered, dressed quickly in jeans and a clean shirt and tennis shoes, and headed out the door. She had two houses to clean today, a garden fence to repair, and a roof to mend.

But as she climbed into her old Chevy van, she took a moment to look up toward the roofs and say a silent prayer for Dulcie and the kit, and for Joe Grey. Her wish, as she turned out of the alley, consigned Lee Wark to a far more uncomfortable fate than incarceration in the Molena Point jail.

And while Charlie's prayer coiled itself into the wind to be sucked up like celestial e-mail by the forces that rule the universe, one subject of her concern was quickly and stealthily pawing through Dallas Garza's papers, scanning a stack of police reports on ex-cons who, apparently, Garza considered possible suspects in the Marner murders. This turn of events was heartening: the tomcat was in a very up mood. The prospect of half a dozen additional contenders cheered him considerably. Maybe Garza *was* going to give Harper a fair shake.

Unless these documents were for show, simply to make his investigation look good.

The time was 8:15. The cottage was empty, Garza gone to work, Kate and Hanni headed for the Pamillon estate to make measurements and take additional pictures. This time they had a cell phone, two canisters of pepper spray, and, tucked in Hanni's belt, a .38 automatic that she intended primarily as a noisy deterrent to scare away the cougar.

But was the cougar all they might encounter? Joe wondered if the old adage was true, that a murderer would return to the scene.

Of the six ex-cons in the police reports, four were on parole and two were under house confinement. One of those on parole was Stubby Baker, who had served twelve years on seven counts of embezzlement and fraud. Garza had files on both Baker and Lee Wark. Joe was drawn to the information on Wark in the same way a rabbit is drawn to the mesmerizing form of a weasel that stands deadly still, waiting for his prey to approach.

Wark was thirty-two years old, had brown hair and light brown eyes (muddy). He was five-ten, 160 pounds, pale (make that pasty) complexion, hunched posture. (They got that right.) He had no facial scars. He had been born and raised in Wales, had become a U.S. citizen at the age of twenty-three.

In the photograph Wark wore his hair trimmed short and neat. Joe had seen it only shoulder length, always greasy. Wark's current legal address was San Quentin State Prison.

Wark's interests while in prison had included reading lurid space operas, girlie magazines, and Celtic history. He took no more exercise than the prison demanded. He had socialized with only two other inmates: James Clayton Osborne, Kate's ex-husband and Wark's partner in the murder of Samuel Beckwhite, and Kendrick Mahl, whom apparently neither man had known before they were incarcerated. Both Osborne and Mahl were serving life without parole.

Joe knew from the newspapers that the guard whose throat had been lacerated with the prison-made garrote was still hospitalized but that doctors now thought he would survive.

At the bottom of the stack of files and reports was a document Joe had not expected. It was not a police report but a three-page memo from LAPD, on a witness in a seven-year-old fraud trial.

He forgot to listen for anyone approaching the cottage. He forgot he was *in* the cottage. He did not realized he was digging his claws into the page. He read avidly, his stub tail twitching. The witness was Helen Marner.

While art dealer Kendrick Mahl, now serving time in San Quentin, was married to Janet Jeannot, whom he later murdered, he had an affair with Helen Marner, a society reporter and aspiring art critic for the *Los Angeles Times.*

Joe and Dulcie had helped Max Harper amass the evidence that would convict Mahl—including the decisive clue, which the police would never have discovered without the curiosity of someone small enough to crawl twenty feet through a mud-filled drainpipe.

The memo said that Mahl saw Helen Marner whenever he flew down to L.A. to conduct business with clients. During this time, Helen realized that Mahl was accepting part of the sales price for each painting under the table, thus circumventing the artist. She had blown the whistle on Mahl. In the case that ensued, she had testified against him.

Mahl had not been convicted; he had received only a reprimand and probation and had had to pay restitution. At about that time, as Joe remembered, Mahl's marriage to Janet had started to go awry.

Later, when Mahl went to prison for killing Janet, he had not kept in touch with Helen Marner. But he had kept in contact with the woman he was then dating. Joe was so fascinated that he startled himself with his loud, intense purring. If ever he'd hit the jackpot, he'd hit it this morning.

Or, rather, Garza had hit the jackpot.

The question was, what was Garza going to do with this information? Mahl and Crystal Ryder had been hot and heavy when Mahl was sent to Quentin. Joe couldn't wait to hear the phone tapes—if he got to hear them.

Joe was still on the desk chewing over the facts when a car pulled into the drive. Glancing through to the kitchen windows, he saw Garza heading for the back door. He was crouched to drop to the floor behind the desk, when he changed his mind—if Garza had come home to work, he wouldn't see much from the floor. Leaping to the mantel, he settled above Garza's desk in his classic improvisation of deep, deep sleep.

The back door opened. He listened to the detective

moving around the kitchen. Sounded like he was making a sandwich. Refrigerator door, sound of knife on cutting board, sound of a jar being opened, the smell of pickles. Lying limp as a rag, Joe considered the suspects, to date.

Kendrick Mahl had to hate Helen Marner for blowing the whistle that he was ripping off his artist clients. Mahl was mean-tempered anyway, a vindictive sort who had made Janet's life miserable.

Lee Wark and Jimmie Osborne had both been in residence at San Quentin when Mahl was convicted. Very likely the three men had been drawn together by their mutual connections in Molena Point and their mutual hatred of Max Harper.

And Mahl's contact on the outside, Crystal Ryder, was a friend of Stubby Baker, who also had no love for Harper.

Garza came into the study carrying a plate and a cup of coffee. The smell of ham and cheese and pickles filled Joe's nose. Setting his lunch on the desk, Garza opened the morning paper, then turned to look at Joe. Joe kept his eyes closed, didn't flick a whisker, but he felt his heart pounding. He imagined Garza's intense black gaze on him, a penetrating cop look. Couldn't a little cat catch a morning nap?

Only when Garza sat down at his desk did Joe open the old peepers enough to peer over the detective's shoulder.

He didn't see the two miniature tapes he'd been hoping for. Were they still in Garza's pocket? Or had he left them at the station, properly checked into the evidence vault? He was wondering if he'd ever get to hear them—how he could manage to hear them—when the phone rang.

Pressing the speaker button, Garza continued to enjoy his sandwich.

"Detective Garza, I got your number from the newspaper. I don't understand. Why does the paper keep saying there were no witnesses to where Captain Harper was the afternoon of the murder? Except that man who said he saw Harper on his horse, following the riders?"

"He is the only witness we have," Garza said, laying down his sandwich.

"I made a report the day after the murders. You must have a record of that."

Garza clicked the phone's record button. Joe could see the tape rolling. "Could you give me your name, please?"

"This is Betty Eastmore. I manage Banton's Jewelry, across the street from where the captain was parked, the afternoon of the murder."

"And you made a police report to that effect?"

"Yes, I gave it to Officer Wendell while he was on patrol. He had some blank report forms, I filled it out right there in my shop and signed it. He said he'd take care of it for me. Is it just that the paper didn't want to say there was a witness? In case—"

"Would you like to meet me at the station? I can be there in five minutes."

"I'm not at home, I'm in Sacramento. I fly back tonight."

"How did you know about the article?"

"My daughter called me. She thought it was strange."

"When can you come in?"

Betty Eastmore made an appointment with Garza for the following morning. He offered to meet her at the airport, at the time her plane was scheduled to land, and give her a ride back to the village.

Was that really very professional, Joe wondered, meeting her away from the station to take her report?

For the rest of the afternoon, lying on the mantel behind Garza's head, Joe listened to the detective play back interview tapes and record his observations. He did not play Crystal's tapes. Just before dinner, Garza played his interview with Max Harper. The detective's questions, and his dictated notes, were upsetting. By the time the tape was finished, Joe didn't want any supper. Garza had really bored into Harper. Oh, he'd started out very friendly, all buddy-buddy cop stuff, but when he couldn't make Harper change his story, he had come down hard, taunting Harper.

Harper had handled the interview calmly, with no change of voice, and of course no discrepancies in the facts. But later when Garza played back his own recorded memos, he had constructed a scenario where Harper could have galloped up the mountain the short way, meeting the Marners at the crest. Garza had calculated that Harper would have had time to kill them, get home again, change clothes, and get to the station by five. The tape was made before Betty Eastmore called him. The detective made it clear that there was no witness to Harper's whereabouts between four and five, when Harper claimed to be watching Stubby Baker's apartment.

During Harper's interview, Garza had questioned the captain's relationship with Crystal Ryder and with Ruthie Marner—he had asked a good many questions about Ruthie, and about how her mother viewed their friendship.

"She viewed it just fine. We were friends, riding companions, Crystal and the Marners and Dillon—I rode with them because of Dillon, because I didn't want to be riding alone with a minor."

"I can understand that."

But later, in his notes, Garza discussed in some detail Harper's leave schedule for the past two years. Harper had taken three short vacations down the coast to Cambria, where he could have met either Crystal or Ruthie or Helen, could have spent several days with any one of them.

Nonsense, Joe thought. *That is totally reaching for it.* But only once did the tape make Joe's fur stand rigid.

During the time that Garza and Harper walked the Pamillon estate, while Garza taped their conversation, they had seen the cougar's pawprints, and had discussed the possibility that the lion might have found Dillon as she hid from the Marners' killer. The discussion sickened him. He wondered if he should go back there and search again.

But what good? He and Dulcie had been all over that property, and so had the search teams.

And what did Garza intend to do with the Eastmore woman's statement? The detective's interview of Harper left him feeling decidedly irritable.

Dropping down from the mantel, he retired to the window seat, all claws and bad temper. He was lying on his belly, sulking, when Kate and Hanni returned. Hanni, setting her camera and purse on the dining table, stopped to stroke him. Angry and out of sorts, he hissed and slashed at her.

She jerked her hand away, her brown eyes widening.

He hung his head, ashamed. And Kate descended like a whirlwind, grabbing him by the nape of the neck.

Hanni stopped her. "Don't, Kate. Maybe he hurts somewhere. Maybe I touched a wound from fighting."

"I doubt it. Let me feel, Joe. Are you wounded?" Kate glared at him and poked him, pushing and prodding with a familiarity that even Clyde would hesitate to inflict. "You growl at anyone again, Joe Grey, you're dog meat."

He wanted to claw Kate as well.

"Can't find anything," she said lightly. "I'll watch him for swelling. Probably he has a hair ball." She gave him another scowl, her amber eyes blazing with such a catlike temper herself that he wanted to yowl with laughter.

But later at dinner, Kate and Hanni together fixed him a nice plate of lamb chops, cutting the pieces up small. Serving him on the window seat, Hanni reached again to stroke him.

He gave her a purr.

"Friends?" she said.

He rubbed his face against her hand; though, in truth, his mood hadn't brightened much.

Why hadn't Garza tossed Stubby Baker's apartment? Why hadn't he searched Crystal's duplex? Did he not have sufficient cause? Didn't he think the judge would issue warrants?

Or did he have no need to do those things?

Did Garza already know where Dillon was?

Watching the detective, he told himself he was letting his imagination run crazy, that he was too emotionally involved. But he felt as restless as bees on a skillet.

Well, maybe Garza *didn't* have probable cause to do those searches. But not every player in this game needed a warrant.

Giving Kate a look of urgency, as if he really needed to go out, he headed for the back door.

20

The time was 9:30, the night sky clear, the slim moon and stars as bright as polished diamonds. On the village sidewalks, traffic was beginning to thin, late diners emerging from the restaurants, heading home or to their motels. While the tourists dawdled, looking in the shop windows, Joe Grey hurried along, brushing past their ankles, dodging across the narrow streets between slow-moving cars until soon he had left the shops behind and was among the crowding cottages. Passing Wilma's house and moving up the north slope of the village, he paused before Crystal Ryder's duplex.

Above the two double garages, with their closed, unwelcoming doors, Crystal's windows were ablaze. In the far unit, only a faint light burned. Two different kinds of music came out—modern jazz from Crystal's side, country from her neighbor, the two mixing in nerve-jangling discord.

Padding up the tall flight of wooden stairs, he leaped to Crystal's window.

The screen was still loose, but the window itself was

locked. He was peering between the curtains when the garage door rumbled open below him. Dropping to the deck, he looked over, watching Crystal's black Mercedes back out, the top down, Crystal's amber hair catching the light from the overhead. Behind her, as she headed down the hill, the door rumbled closed again. He watched until she was out of sight, then tried the front door, leaping up to swing on the knob.

Locked.

Galloping down the stairs, he fled around the building and up the grassy hill, to where the back windows might be accessible.

From the steep slope, he peered across a six-foot space to a lone window, very small, perhaps the bathroom window. The top half was open a few inches.

No light burned in the bathroom, but light seeped through from the studio. Springing across to the sill, he leaped for the top of the double-hung. Under his sudden weight, it crashed down so hard it nearly sent him flying. Scrambling over, he dropped down inside, narrowly missing a cold bath in the commode. He was just congratulating himself on his graceful entrance when the garage door rumbled up again and he heard the Mercedes pull in.

Had she forgotten something? If he only waited a few moments, would she drive away again?

Since he and Dulcie had followed the kit and found the tapes and escrow papers, he hadn't been able to shake his uneasy feeling about this apartment. Call it overactive curiosity, call it senseless fear. Joe thought of it as the kind of feeling a cop got—he'd heard plenty of stories over the poker table as he lolled across the cards, getting in the way. Sometimes an officer just *knew* something was amiss. Knew that the perp had a gun stashed in the seat behind him. That the innocent-looking high school girl batting her eyes at him from the driver's seat had a trunkful of drugs. No rhyme or reason. Just a feeling. He had it now, about this apartment.

Crouched in the bathroom where he'd landed, he heard a door open in the garage, then close again, and a lock snap or slide home. Heard Crystal come upstairs within the house, heard the door at the top open, heard her cross to the kitchen.

He peered out. The door to the stair stood ajar. The smell of garlic and tomato sauce filled the stairwell. He beat it down to the garage before she came back.

He heard her cross the room, heard the door close above him, heard her crossing back and forth, heard the water running, then in the kitchen heard her pull out a chair, then silence.

The garage was empty and neat, not like many village garages, filled with cast-off furniture, moldering storage boxes, and greasy yard equipment.

This two-car space had been swept clean. It contained only Crystal's black Mercedes, a broom standing in the corner, a square metal furnace, a washer and dryer, and some empty metal shelves fastened to the wall. Beneath the stair was a small wooden door. He could hear, from within, a soft shuffling noise, then a tiny thump as if rats were at work on whatever was stored there.

The aroma of spaghetti clung around the door.

Sniffing beneath the door, he caught a scent that

made him rear up, pawing at the bolt, then leaping and fighting, trying to slide it back.

The sounds from within ceased.

Above him, footsteps crossed the room. The door opened, spilling light. Crystal came down, opened the little door, slipped inside, and closed it behind her.

In the small space, the two female voices echoed sharply, one young and angry, the other haughty.

"I want to call my mother. I want to tell her I'm all right. If you really mean to help me, I don't see why—"

"How many times do I have to go over this? He's bound to have a tap on their phone. One call, and he'll find you. And if he finds you, Dillon, he'll kill you. You're the only witness."

"I'm tired of being shut in this stinking place. I'm cold. I'm tired of the dark! I'm tired of using a bucket for a bathroom."

"It's better than being dead."

"Not much. Why can't I come upstairs with you! I hear you moving around, I hear the TV and radio. I hear the water running—the shower! I want a shower! And last night I smelled steak cooking."

"I brought you spaghetti. And here's some Hershey bars. Eat them and shut up. You should be thankful that I got you out before he found you. Thankful I'm taking the trouble to protect you. If I hadn't found you, you'd be rotting dead up there on that mountain."

"You could've taken me to the cops. Why didn't you take me to the cops?"

"What would they do? Question you and take you home. And the minute you're home, he'd have you.

Your parents couldn't protect you. You told me they don't keep a gun. He breaks in, kills you all. Kills you first, Dillon. In front of them. Then kills your mother and father."

"I don't want to stay here! I want out!"

The sounds of a scuffle. Dillon yelped as if Crystal had hit her. "Leave me alone! And what *do* you get out of this? What *do* you get for saving *me*?"

No answer.

"I want to call my mother. I'll make her promise not to tell anyone."

"The worst thing you could do. No mother would keep a promise like that; she'd hightail it right to the cops. And he'd find you. Now shut up. It won't be much longer."

"Much longer until *what*?"

"Until I can set you free. Until the coast is clear and I can let you go."

But in the shadows, Joe Grey had a different interpretation, one that made his skin crawl.

There was only one window in the garage, a small dirty glass high in the back wall, just below the ceiling. He had noticed it from the hill, but it did not lead into the house. He thought Dillon might squeeze through, if he could get her out. But she would need a ladder. He could see no ladder, nothing to stand on but the Mercedes, and it was too far from the window. Maybe Dillon could push the dryer across. All she'd have to do was unplug it, and the dryer would be lighter than the washer.

Right. And it would be noisy as hell—and first he had to open the locked door.

Crystal came out, ducking through the low door and sliding the bolt home with a hard clunk. Hurrying up the stairs, she slammed that door and slid the bolt across. The dissonant jazz music had ended long ago. From next door, the cowboy lament was filled with misery.

Leaping at the bolt, he found it immovable, hard and ungiving. He tried for some time; then, crossing the garage, he tried the lock on the pedestrian door, thinking he could go for help.

It, too, was beyond his strength. And he realized he was as much a captive as Dillon.

Looking up at the ceiling, he studied the automatic opener, then prowled the garage until he found the button to operate it, to the left of the washing machine. That would be easy enough to spring.

Right. And bring Crystal on the double.

He fought the bolt on Dillon's door until his paws throbbed. His thudding battle must have terrified her. "Who is it? Who's there?" Dillon's voice was both frightened and hopeful. "Please," she whispered, "who's there?"

He was sorely tempted to speak to her.

Oh, right. And blow his cover forever, him and Dulcie both. Enough people knew about them. And a kid—even a kid as great as Dillon—was too likely to spill. In one trusting moment, tell someone.

He had started to search for a vent, to see if he could tear off its grid or screen and slip through, when the upstairs door opened yet again, the light spilling down around Crystal as she descended. Swinging into the

Mercedes, she raised the garage door, and backed out, the big door rolling down again like a giant guillotine.

He could have streaked out beneath it, except his passage would have made it halt. He guessed he could have leaped over the electric beam, left it unbroken. But he didn't want to leave Dillon, he was afraid for her, he had a gut feeling he shouldn't leave her.

He was pacing the garage trying to think what to do when he heard a police radio. Light flared under the garage door as the unit pulled up the drive.

All right! Help was on the way.

But what had alerted the patrol? Was this only a routine neighborhood check?

He had to get their attention.

The car door opened, he heard hard shoes on the concrete, heard the officer walking along the front of the duplex, then hushing through the bushes.

Joe followed the sound as the officer walked around the building, all sound lost at the far end, then came back behind the building through the tall grass of the hill. Heard him try the pedestrian door, then cross the drive again, and double-time up the front steps.

The bell rang three times, then a key turned in the lock—or maybe some kind of pick; Joe could hear the metal against metal. He followed the hard-soled footsteps above him as the officer prowled the house.

That was the way it sounded. Like prowling, not just walking around. Joe heard him open the closet door, then the shower door. What—or who—was he looking for? Did he have a warrant? Not usual, even with a warrant, to come into an empty house. When he stopped beside the door leading down to the garage, Joe slid behind the washer, his heart pounding. Who was this, which officer, prowling Crystal's apartment?

The bolt turned. The door at the top of the stair was opening when, out in the drive, a siren began to whoop and the light beneath the garage door turned pulsing red. *Whoop, whoop, whoop. Flash, flash, flash.*

The officer pounded across the room and down the front stairs, jerked open the car door. The siren stopped. Joe heard him walking the front yard as if looking for whoever had entered his vehicle. He left at last, slamming the door, burning rubber as he backed down the drive.

Collapsing against the washer, Joe felt as limp as a slaughtered rabbit. He was staring at Dillon's door, trying to figure out how to get it open, when up the stairs the door swung wide and light spilled down—silhouetting a small tabby-striped figure, her tail lashing.

He reared up, watching her. "How did you know I was here? How did you get in?"

"Through the bathroom window," she said, galloping down. "Same as you." She smiled and nuzzled him. "You're not the only one who can break and enter—or follow a trail of scent." She sniffed at the door beneath the stair. "Dillon! Oh, Joe! Is she really there?" she whispered.

"Alive and well. Who was that, tramping the house?"

"Officer Wendell. He didn't open a drawer or cupboard, but he checked everywhere a person might be hidden, the closet, even under the sinks and in the shower. Stood on a chair and pushed up the little door into the attic, swung his torch all around. He checked the food in the kitchen and the clothes in the closet." She narrowed her green eyes. "Looking for little-girl clothes? And why did he come so secretly? This isn't his beat—he's on day watch, south side of the village."

"Did *you* set off the siren?"

Dulcie smiled. "I saw Crystal at Binnie's Italian, saw her come out with two cartons of take-out. On a hunch, I nipped on over here. Caught your scent. Went on in. Then Wendell came snooping."

"Nice," Joe said, nipping her ear.

Together they tried the bolt, leaping and grabbing and twisting, but they couldn't budge it. They daren't speak beyond the faintest whisper. They could hear Dillon just inside, softly breathing, as if she was pressed against the door.

"When we get her out," Dulcie whispered, "where can we take her? We can't take her *anywhere*. We can't *talk to her*."

Joe didn't have an answer. "The first order of business is to get her out."

She touched his paw. "The minute we set her free, she'll run straight home. And that's the first place Crystal will look. You can bet she's armed, Joe. If she gets there before they call the station . . . Dillon's parents are such—gentle types."

"Only her father. Her mother has spunk."

"But—"

"We'll think of something. I don't want to leave her here. If we knew how long Crystal will be gone . . ."

"She went to meet someone. She called him but didn't use his name. Just, 'I need to talk with you,' then, 'I can't. Meet me the same place.' "

"Wark?"

"I'm guessing it was Wark."

Leaping across the garage, Joe toppled the broom with one swat, where it leaned against the wall. Pushing and pulling together, they got it across the floor and upended, angling it against the bolt. They were forcing the broom with teeth and claws, pushing it against the bolt, when a furry warmth thrust between them, trying to help.

"How did you get here, Kit?" Joe snapped.

"Followed Dulcie," she whispered, pushing with all her might.

From beyond the door, Dillon's muffled, frightened voice cried, "Who's there? What are you doing? Crystal, is that you?" The cats imagined her cowering in the small, dark space while a stranger—quite possibly the killer—pried at the door to get at her.

They tried again, with the kit pushing too—she was stronger than she looked—but the bolt seemed frozen in place.

"We need help," Dulcie said, licking her bruised paws, crouching to race up the stairs—flying to the kitchen, to knock the phone from its cradle.

21

Charlie was so scared she was almost sick. Parking around the corner from the duplex, she left the van's street-side door open as she'd been instructed. She didn't fear Crystal, she feared whoever had killed the Marners and would be looking for Dillon. Dulcie said that already Officer Wendell had come prowling, in a way that was more than suspicious.

Hurrying along the dark street, she looked warily into the black interiors of the scattered cars parked against the curb, ready to run if someone stepped out to grab her. But despite her fear, she had to smile. She felt like Alice Through the Looking Glass for sure, stumbling around in the night, following orders from a cat.

Quickly up Crystal's drive into the shadows, she moved along the side of the garage until she found the pedestrian entrance, a black rectangle where the door stood open. She could see nothing within. Clutching the hammer that she had pulled from her toolbox, she wondered if she'd be quick enough to use it if someone grabbed her.

A voice from inside made her jump. "She's across the garage," Dulcie said. "Under the stairs. We couldn't slide the bolt—we finally did loosen this one. Hurry. Crystal's gone, you can use your flashlight. Oh, hurry."

Flipping on her flashlight, softly pulling closed the door behind her, she fled across behind Dulcie, her light sweeping across washer and dryer and furnace, pausing on the door beneath the stairs.

She slid the bolt. The door flew open in her face, knocking her backward. Dillon hit her in a tackle that sent her sprawling, the girl's shoulder in her stomach. She couldn't get her breath.

"Get off, Dillon. It's me—it's Charlie." For a thirteen-year-old, the kid was strong. Fighting for her life, she crouched over Charlie, punching, blind with fear. When Charlie grabbed her hands, Dillon kneed her in the stomach, broke her grip, and ran, taking the stairs two at a time. She was halfway across the apartment when Charlie caught her, grabbing Dillon's red hair, upsetting the coffee table, nearly strangling the child before she got her stopped.

"Hold still! Be still! It's all *right.* I'm getting you out of here. Away from here. I'll hide you."

"That's what *she* said."

"Stop it! I'm Clyde's friend—Harper's friend—you know that!"

Dillon stared at her, didn't know her well enough to trust her. Charlie wished she'd brought Wilma. "I'll explain when we're out of here. Explain as much as I know. We—I think there's more than one person wanting to kill you." She scanned the apartment, half expecting Crystal to appear.

"Just let me go. Let me go home."

"I can't." Dragging the child, Charlie stepped to the windows.

The drive below was empty. There were no new cars on the street. "Come on."

"Where? I don't want—"

"My place. You can hide at my place."

"Take me to the cops or I won't go! Captain Harper will—"

Charlie held her shoulders, looking down at her. "Harper is under suspicion for your kidnapping. And for the murder of Ruthie and Helen Marner. We know he didn't do it. It gets complicated. You'll have to trust me. If you want to save yourself and help Harper, we need to get out of here."

"Just take me to the station. Is that so hard? Take me to Max Harper." The kid was incredibly stubborn, not nearly as mild-mannered as her parents. Had Harper taught her that, to stand up for what she wanted like that?

"Harper isn't at the station. He's taken administrative leave. *He* can't hide you. How would it look if you turned up at his place, when some people think he kidnapped you?"

"*He didn't! Harper didn't kidnap me!* He *didn't kill them!*"

"I know that. That's why you're in danger. That's why Crystal kidnapped you. Because you're the only witness."

"But Crystal rescued me from that man."

"What man? The killer? Who is he?"

"I didn't know him. It was nearly dark. I thought at first it was Captain Harper. It wasn't. It happened so fast."

A car came up the street. Crystal's black convertible, turning up the steep drive, its lights sweeping across the windows. Charlie pulled her away from the glass.

"Dillon, Crystal's been in touch with the man we think killed them. We think she's using you to blackmail him. That when she's done with you, when you're no use to her, she means to kill you."

"I don't—"

As the garage door rumbled open, Charlie pulled her out the front door, dragged her running down the steps as the overhead door closed again. Charlie couldn't remember whether she'd shut the door under the stairs. They ran, Charlie holding Dillon's arm, racing down the street and around the corner, falling into the van.

She didn't switch on her lights; she hit the overhead for only a second, staring into the back among the ladders and cleaning equipment.

Three pairs of eyes shone back at her. She doused the light and took off, spinning a fast U-turn as Dillon crouched on the seat, her hand on the door handle. Charlie jerked her hand away.

"If you don't trust me, you trust Wilma. I'll take you there."

Something furry brushed by Charlie's cheek and landed in Dillon's lap, purring.

"Dulcie!" She hugged Dulcie, stroking her, nicely distracted. "Why are the cats with you?"

"I'm cat-sitting."

"You brought them *with* you? Into . . . ?"

"They—followed me when I left, and I couldn't take the time to get them back inside."

Dillon looked at Charlie hard-eyed and skeptical. "How come you're here? What made you come here? How did you know where I was?"

"I—you won't believe this."

"Try."

She glanced over at Dillon. "I had a dream. I dreamed of you and Crystal and a locked door." Charlie looked again at the child, trying for a gaze of wide-eyed innocence.

"No. I don't believe that."

Charlie sighed. Did the kid have to be so tough-minded? She thought as she pulled up in front of Wilma's darkened house.

"I'll just get out," Dillon said. "I'll wake her."

"In the dark? Alone?" She reached behind the child, and punched the lock. "With Crystal and the killer looking for you? I don't think so." She gave Dillon a steady look. "We think he's been watching Wilma's house for you. She's seen a strange car cruising."

Dillon hesitated, her eyes qucstioning, holding Dulcie tight in her arms the way a smaller child would hold a teddy bear.

Charlie looked at the black yard, at the looming bushes and trees. "How about we bring Wilma with us?" Charlie handed her the cell phone. "Call her, wake her up. Tell her we're out here. See if she'll come."

Dillon just looked at her.

Charlie took the phone, dialed Wilma's number.

Dillon's brown eyes searched Charlie's. Her red hair was lank, needed washing.

The phone kept ringing.

Dillon said, "I want to see Harper. That man was dressed like him. And he was riding Bucky. I thought—when he first came up the trail, came over the ridge, I thought—we all thought it was the captain. I waved to him and shouted, and he . . ."

Dillon stared at Charlie, her eyes wide and expressionless.

"Did he hurt you?"

"I got away. He was . . . So much blood. And their screams . . . I—Redwing got me away." Dillon bent over Dulcie, hugging her so hard Dulcie couldn't breathe.

Charlie sat idling the engine, letting the phone ring and ring, watching Wilma's dark windows, and watching ahead and in her rearview mirror for car lights. Or for a car without lights creeping up the street. Why didn't Wilma answer? She never stayed out this late. Charlie wanted to get out and bang on the door, look in the garage to see if her car was gone. But she wasn't leaving Dillon.

She hung up at last. She was redialing when a black Mercedes came around the corner, no lights, heading straight for them.

Crystal was not alone. Beside her in the open car sat a tall man that Charlie didn't know. As the car slid against the van, Crystal's passenger leveled a large-caliber revolver at them, first picking out Dillon, then moving a quarter inch so his sights were on Charlie.

22

The gun aimed at Charlie's face looked as big as a cannon. Had to be a .45 caliber. The man's hands wrapped around it were thin and long. He had a thin face, dark eyes, short dark hair. Aiming at her, he kept both eyes open in the manner of an experienced shooter. Was this Lee Wark? Stubby Baker? Or someone she'd never heard of? She couldn't stop looking at the gun. He waved the barrel, motioning for Dillon to get out. Dillon didn't move. Dulcie had vanished, sliding to the back of the van. Charlie couldn't help looking at the man's long fingers overlapped around the revolver, at his one finger curved tight to the trigger.

"I want the girl! Now! Both of you—out of the van!"

Charlie stomped on the gas and jerked the wheel hard, crashing the van into the Mercedes in a metal-screeching sideswipe that threw the shooter off-balance and dropped Dillon to the floor. She took off, burning rubber. "Dial the cops! Dial them now! Nine-one-one. Do it!"

But Dillon was already dialing.

A yowl of protest rose from the backseat.

"Shut up," Charlie snapped. "One more sound, Joe Grey, and I'll pitch you out the window."

She took the corner on two wheels, her rearview mirrors blazing with lights careening behind her.

"There's static!" Dillon shouted. "I can't make them understand. They can't—Was that a tire? Did we blow a tire?"

"Duck!" Charlie shoved Dillon under the dash as another shot boomed. Four more explosions. Dillon hit the redial. Charlie took a corner so fast she thought she'd topple the van. They were in the middle of the village; she prayed no one was on the streets. She was heading for the police station when a siren screamed behind them. She gave it the gas, watching in the mirror as a black-and-white wedged the Mercedes against a parked truck.

"Give me the phone. Watch behind us. Tell me what's happening!"

Shoving the phone at her, Dillon fled between the seats to the back of the van, where she could see. "It's Officer Wendell. Alone in the patrol car. He hasn't made them get out. My God, he's just standing there talking to them. Just *talking*! No, he's getting back in his unit. *Letting them go.* Charlie, he's letting them go. What kind of cop . . . ?"

Charlie turned up Ocean fast, without lights. "Is Crystal coming after us?"

"No, she . . . Yes. Step on it, she's coming."

She made a fast right. "Where's Wendell?"

"Turned left back there."

Was Wendell trying to cut them off? Charlie swung another right, into the narrow, unlit alley behind Beckwhite Automotive. Parking in the blackest shadows, she punched a one-digit code into the phone, listened to it ring and ring. When finally Clyde answered, she was shouting, couldn't make herself speak softly. She didn't think her plan would work, but she didn't know what else to do. She glanced up at Dillon.

"Stay here. Stay down."

Keeping low, she moved out of the van to a wide, sliding door in the back of the building. Using her flashlight long enough to punch three numbers into its digital lock, she slid the door back. Why didn't Clyde have an automatic door?

But why would he? This wasn't the main garage, only the paint shop. She could smell the automotive enamel, sharp and unpleasant. Running out again, she fell into the van, and they roared into the dark building.

Three cars left the big garage. The first, an old green Plymouth running with only parking lights, turned toward Ocean. Clyde drove slowly, slipping around the darkest corners until he saw Crystal's Mercedes pull away from the curb where it had been parked with the lights out—as if watching for a car, any car, to come out of the dead-end alley. As Crystal settled in to follow, he concentrated on some fancy driving, as if seriously trying to lose her.

The other two vehicles left by a different route, running dark, heading east toward the hills. The dull, primer-coated BMW, reflecting no light, might have been only the ghost of a car. It turned northeast. Behind it, the black station wagon headed south.

Crossing above the Highway 1 tunnel, the BMW sped up into the hills, its driver and four passengers enjoying the luxury of the soft leather seats. Dillon and the kit were snuggled together next to the driver, in a warm blanket, Dillon half asleep, so tired that even fear couldn't keep her awake. Joe and Dulcie prowled from front seat to back, peering out, watching for approaching vehicles.

Neither cat saw the black station wagon double back to follow them where it would not be seen.

Moving higher along the narrow winding road, soon they had gained the long, overgrown drive into the Pamillon estate. Charlie wiggled the car in between the detritus of tumbled walls and dead oak trees, parking behind a ragged mass of broom bushes. Only when she cut the engine did she hear another car directly behind them, the sound of its motor bringing her up, ready to take off again.

Then she saw it was Harper. She had already cocked the .38 Clyde had given her, when they switched cars at the shop. Easing the hammer down, she holstered it and nudged the sleeping child. "Come on, it's Harper. Guess he decided to come with us—guess he lost Crystal. You okay? You remember how to get down there?"

Yawning, Dillon bundled out of the van and took Harper's hand. "We have to go through the house." The cats streaked out of the van behind her, pressing close to Charlie's heels. When Harper saw them, he did such a classic double take that Joe almost laughed.

Charlie looked at Harper blankly. "They were in the van, I didn't have time to get them out."

"They changed cars with you fast enough."

"I couldn't leave them in the shop, Max. Those paint fumes would have killed them; cats can't take that stuff."

Harper scowled at her and didn't point out that she could have let the cats out of the shop, that they'd been only a few blocks from home.

He looked down at Dillon. "What makes you so sure Crystal won't think you'd come here?"

"She found me here. Down where we're going. I was so scared, nearly in hysterics. So scared I couldn't talk."

"Then why . . . ?"

Dillon looked up at him. "Later when I sassed her, she threatened to bring me back here—to leave me alone down there. I got hysterical. She thinks—I hope she thinks—I'd do anything to keep from coming here."

Harper grinned. "Good girl. And you're not scared to hide down there again?"

"Not with you here."

Harper made a sound halfway between a grumble and a laugh. Charlie glanced at him, wishing she could see his face.

Moving deeper in through the fallen limbs and dense growth and heaps of adobe bricks, Harper used his torch sparingly, turning it to a thin, low beam that the night seemed to swallow. Listening for any sound behind them, Charlie and Harper kept Dillon close between them. The three cats padded very close, pushing against Charlie's ankles, Joe and Dulcie peering into the grainy shadows, expecting to see yellow eyes flame suddenly in the torchlight. They might envy the king of cats, but they had no desire to be hors d'oeuvres. The kit, though staying close, seemed more fascinated than scared.

"Talk," Harper said as they moved in between the fallen walls. "Talk loud and bold. If the big cat's around, he won't bother three big, loud humans. Walk tall, Dillon."

Dillon stood straighter, holding tightly to Harper's arm, reaching several times to direct his light.

"Is it the old bomb shelter?" Harper said. "Is that where we're heading?"

"I guess that's what it is. It has bunks, scraps of blanket the mice have chewed up, old cans of food all swollen like they'll explode. It's down beside the root and canning cellars. Part of the roof has caved in, but you can hide back underneath."

"I know the place." He didn't sound thrilled.

"You've been down there," Charlie said.

"Didn't hang around. Those crumbling walls and stairs . . ." He shone his light among the standing walls of the house as if looking for an alternative place to hide Dillon.

This was not, Joe thought, an orthodox way for a chief of police to be rescuing a kidnapped child.

Which only pointed up that he, Joe Grey, was not the only one who mistrusted Wendell.

He hated that, hated the thought of corruption

among Harper's cops—corruption aimed straight at the captain.

And, like Max Harper, Joe wondered if it was smart to take refuge in a confining cellar where they might have only one route of escape.

Beside him, Dulcie was tense and watchful. But the kit padded along eagerly, listening to every tiniest sound, big-eyed with the thrill of adventure.

Charlie said, "I don't like it that Wilma didn't answer her phone."

Harper didn't seem concerned. "Maybe she unplugged it. She does that sometimes."

Charlie glanced down at Dulcie. Dulcie blinked in agreement.

"Here," Dillon said. "In the old kitchen, the stairs are here. They're crumbly."

As they started down, the cats caught the old, fading scent of puma. The stairway led down to a long, low-ceilinged cellar with thick adobe walls and heavy roof timbers, a chilly cavern that had been used for canning and root storage, in the days when families had to be self-sufficient. The human's footsteps echoed. Joe didn't like this descending into the earth; it made his paws sweat.

He'd never liked tight places, not since his San Francisco days of narrow, dead-end alleys where his only escape from mean-minded street kids was often down into some stinking cellar, with no idea whether the boys would follow him or not.

Dillon walked leaning against Charlie, nearly asleep on her feet, her head nodding, the blanket from the

BMW that Charlie had wrapped around her half fallen off and slipping to the ground.

A door at the back of the long cellar led through a thick wall and down four more steps to the old World War II air raid shelter, its roof and one wall fallen in, open to the kitchen, above.

"When I hid here before," Dillon said, "I thought maybe a cougar wouldn't prowl so deep. That maybe he wouldn't come down here?"

"No sensible beast would come down here," Harper told her. "A cougar doesn't use caves. They want to see around them."

Right on, Joe thought, exchanging a look with Dulcie. *No sensible beast, only humans. And cats stupid enough to follow humans.*

But the kit padded ahead of them, all pricked ears and switching tail, looking about her bright-eyed at the mysterious and enchanting depths, her hunger for adventure and for deep, earthen places supplanting all caution.

The very tales that made Joe shiver, the old Celtic myths that spoke of wonders he didn't care to know about, drew the kit. The old Irish tales of a land beneath the earth, and of cats who could change to humans. The kit thrived on those stories; she hungered for the kind of tales that made Joe Grey cross.

She's young, Joe thought. *Too young. Too trusting. Way too curious.* Padding behind Harper's beam into the black maw of the air raid shelter, he felt he was stepping into a gaping and hungry mouth.

The shelter had had two rooms. Where the first had

caved in, they could see the ruins, above, and the clear night sky.

The door frame of the second, roofed portion still stood. The heavy plank door had been ripped off and lay on its side across the opening, barring the lower half. Behind it, someone had pulled a rusty set of shelves across, to further block the entrance. The shelves still held ancient cans of food, rusted tight to the metal surfaces.

Harper moved the shelf unit aside, glancing questioningly at Dillon.

"I pushed it there. Like a fence—it was all I had."

He swept his light across the small concrete room. "I can't believe these three cats have come down here with us. Sometimes they act more like dogs than cats."

Joe and Dulcie exchanged a look. He wished he could give Harper an answer to that one.

Within the closed, damp room, they could smell the fresh scent of cougar, his trail coming down the earth slide, a track newly laid within the last few days. The kit backed away from the scent, her eyes huge, and patted at a lone pawprint in the loose earth.

Perhaps the young male had come here out of curiosity, had come down into the excavation to look and to mark, the way a cougar would investigate a new house under construction, stopping to spray the open, studded walls, to sniff at a hammer or at bent nails or at an empty beer can left behind by the building crew—leaving his pawprints for the carpenters to wondcr and laugh over, and perhaps feel the cold sting of fear.

Joe, imagining the cougar padding down that insubstantial earth slide, didn't know he was growling.

"What?" Charlie said, kneeling before him. "Has someone been here?"

Joe laid back his ears, giving her a toothy snarl.

"Cougar?" Charlie said, her eyes widening. "Has the cougar been here?"

Joe's eyes on Charlie told her all he needed to say.

Charlie rose to face the door and the open pit beyond, her hand resting on the .38.

23

Chunks of concrete had fallen where one wall was crumbling, and rising from the debris stood a rusted, two-bunk bed with mouse-chewed mattresses. On the floor beside its iron legs were stacked more bulging cans of food, their labels presenting stained and faded pictures of tomatoes, beans, and corn—ruined cans ready to poison anyone foolish enough to sample their contents. Or, as Dillon had said, ready to explode in your face. Atop one can was a limp box of disintegrating matches and a grime-covered first-aid kit. The dozen gallon bottles of spring water against the wall ought, by this time, to be growing frogs. In the far corner lay a heap of animal bones and a strip of hide with short brown hair. "Deer," Harper said, picking up a leg bone with hoof attached, and a jawbone that had long ago been licked clean.

"No puma would drag his kill down here. The deer might have been sick, stumbled and fallen, then foxes and racoons were at him."

Joe wanted to tell Harper that a cougar *had* been

there, that his scent was fresh, that he had come prowling long after those bones were abandoned, and that this male might have a lay-up somewhere else among the ruins, maybe even in the standing portion of the house itself. That he might, scenting their fresh trail, return to have a look.

A curious cougar, if alarmed and cornered, could turn deadly.

Dillon yawned, looking longingly at the upper bunk. Tossing her blanket on top, she was about to climb up when Harper put his arm around her.

"Give us a minute. You're so tired—if you lie down you'll be gone. We need to talk. Come sit down, let me ask a few questions, get it on tape. Then you can sleep."

Dillon sat down on the floor between Harper and Charlie, her back to the concrete wall, the three of them watching the cavernous opening that yawned beyond the frail barrier—though Joe would far rather see the cougar approaching than Crystal and her friend. Light from the flashlight bounced against the wall, brightening Charlie's carrot-colored hair and Dillon's darker, auburn bob. The tape recorder that Harper took from his pocket was no bigger than a can of cat food.

"Do you mind the tape?"

"No. We do tapes at school."

"You hid here after the murder?"

"Yes, he was chasing me," she said, yawning.

"Who was?"

"The man who killed Ruthie and Mrs. Marner. The

same man who shot at us tonight. Crystal said his name was Stubby Baker."

Harper raised an eyebrow. "Did you know a Stubby Baker?"

"No. I didn't know that man."

"The evening of the murder, did you see the killer's face? Could you identify him if you saw him again?"

"His hat was pulled down and his coat collar turned up, but I got one good look. When his face was close to me. Thin face. Bony. Those eyes—black eyes. The same man as tonight, with the gun. And he was riding Bucky."

"You're sure it was my gelding?"

"Of course I'm sure. I know Bucky. Your horse, your saddle. Bucky's bridle—that nice silver bit. The man's hat and clothes looked like yours, too. When he rode up to us, with the hat pulled down, I thought it was you. I thought how strange you had your hat pulled down because the sun wasn't in your eyes, it was behind you, real low in the sky. Then I saw—saw it wasn't you."

"You saw his face clearly."

"At first, just his eyes. The sun was all dazzle behind him. But he looked right at me. Whispered, 'Help. Help me,' and he went limp over the saddle, limp down over the horn like he'd fainted or something. He grabbed at the horn and slid down, fell on the ground. Mrs. . . . Mrs. Marner got off to help him. He . . . Do I have to tell more about it now?"

"We can talk about it later. How much did you see of his face? Tell me again, the general shape of his face. Was he clean-shaven?"

"He . . ." She looked at Harper, frowning. "His face was thin like yours. No beard or mustache. Smooth, no black stubble." She held her hands to her own face, indicating where his hat was pulled down and his collar turned up. "Thin, long face, like yours," Dillon said apologetically. "But no wrinkles. And—real high cheekbones. And black eyes. *Not* you, Captain Harper. Not your eyes. Cold black eyes. And his mouth—a thin, hard mouth."

Harper glanced at Charlie. "You don't have paper or a pencil?"

"I don't have my purse, only my keys."

"Later, would you try a sketch?"

She nodded, as if etching Dillon's description into memory.

"We'll do a lineup," he told Dillon. "When he grabbed Helen, how did you get away?"

"He hit her and cut—I saw him cut her throat." Her voice shook, but she looked at him steadily. "Ruthie and I were kicking and hitting him, from our horses, trying to get him off Mrs. Marner. He grabbed Ruthie's leg and pulled her off. It was all plunging horses and blood and screaming. I couldn't . . . I hit and kicked, but when he grabbed for me I kicked Redwing, slapped my reins into his face, and whipped her." Dillon looked at him desolately. "I ran away—I hung on to the saddle. He was pulling at me, I was nearly off. I kicked Redwing and hung on hard, kicked him and hit her, and Ruthie screaming and screaming behind me. I—I left them, Captain Harper. Left them there. I ran away." She hid her face, crying. He put his arms around her, held her tight, letting her cry, looking over her head at

Charlie, his face so filled with pain that the cats wanted to hold Harper safe, the way he was holding Dillon. And Charlie reached to touch his cheek.

But when Dillon could stop crying, Harper held her away. "Then what happened?"

"I kept going, as fast as Redwing could run. He came pounding behind me. When I looked back at him, I saw the other man back there. He had Ruthie, I could see her white blouse. He was hitting and hitting her. Then I ran into a branch, it nearly knocked me off. I had to lean low, kind of dizzy. Redwing was running full out. It hurt and I felt so dizzy I was scared I'd fall—or that she'd fall, stumble and fall. It was getting dark. He was getting closer. Bucky's so big and fast, he was coming so fast, and the Marners' horses were running after his horse, all wild, their reins and stirrups flapping."

She blew her nose.

"And then?" Harper didn't let up: he was going to have it all before he let her sleep.

"Then I was around the bend—that bend in the trail, by the ruins?" she said tiredly.

"Yes?"

"I knew he couldn't see me there, it's all trees. You know the place. I slid off and whacked Redwing hard; sent her flying, and I hid in the bushes.

"When he'd gone past, ducking low under the branches and beating Bucky, I doubled back and ran.

"I thought if Redwing kept running it would be awhile, under those trees, before he saw I wasn't on her. I ran through the bushes and into the old house and upstairs so I could see if he came back.

"He did," she said, swallowing. "I saw him coming. That was the worst time, when I saw him coming back. I was so scared I didn't think I could move.

"I hid in the nursery, in that box beside the fireplace, under all those pieces of wall piled around it. I didn't know where else to go. I knew I could get the box open without moving all the stuff, I'd looked in it once. You don't really notice it—just looks like part of the junk."

Dillon shivered. "I heard him coming up the stairs, heard him moving around the room. I was so scared. The box was like a coffin, and I'd trapped myself in there.

"I had the pocketknife Dad gave me, I had it open. Thinking, what good would that little knife do? He was bigger than me, he'd take it away from me.

"But I thought if he grabbed me and didn't see it, if he pulled me up to his face the way he did Mrs. Marner, jerked her right up to his face, I'd jab it in his throat before he ever saw. I was trying to remember where the carotid artery is, exactly. I felt sick. I knew I had to try."

Joe looked at Dulcie. Her eyes were wide with pain and with love for the child. Dillon clung to Harper, clutching his arm. She might be thirteen and nearly grown, but at that moment she seemed only a little child, wanting to be protected. And Dillon reached to Charlie, pulling her closer, hanging on to them both.

People talked about therapy, Joe thought. Talked about crisis counseling. What a child really needed was to be held tight and loved, and helped to talk it out.

Harper said, "You heard him leave the nursery?"

"I thought he left. I wasn't sure—maybe he was waiting. I stayed still for a long time."

Harper nodded. "How long do you think you stayed in the box?"

"I don't know. Maybe an hour. It seemed like forever. When I came out it was really dark. I peeked out first. It was quiet, I couldn't hear him. But I waited some more, until I had to pee, bad. I didn't hear anything but the crickets. When I came out, I crawled over to the edge where the floor ends and looked down.

"It was dark but the moon was coming up. I could see the pale garden walls, so if Bucky was there, I thought I'd see him—except if the man had hidden him, and was waiting for me. He killed Helen and Ruthie—or hurt Ruthie. I knew what he looked like. He'd have to kill me.

"Captain, Ruthie was only twenty-something, like my cousin. She was still in college."

Harper nodded.

"I knew, when he chased me, I should have ridden fast down the hill for help. That I might have saved Ruthie. Except, that other man already had her. And going down the bare hills where I couldn't hide, he would have caught me. I was sure they were dead. I knew Mrs. Marner was dead."

She looked up at Harper. "But I feel so . . . I'm alive, Captain Harper. And they're dead."

He said nothing, he simply held her.

"I wanted to go home, but I was afraid he'd find me. And afraid of the mountain lion, afraid it would smell blood and come prowling. I was bleeding, my hand was cut." She showed him the scar, with the dirty mark where a piece of tape had come off. "Crystal bandaged it.

"I didn't see Bucky, but I could see a gleam of metal off through the trees like maybe a car, and that scared me. I thought it might be the man in black, so I came down here—down the broken back stairs and down the cellar stairs. I'd lost my barrette. I kept thinking if it was up there somewhere in the nursery, and one of them found it, they'd know I was there.

"I came down here and pushed that shelf thing across, and lay down on the top bunk, way at the back where he might not see me. I was so scared, I was like frozen."

"I don't think you were frozen," Harper said. "I think you did very well. How long were you down here, do you think?"

"I don't know. Until Crystal found me. It was still dark when she came. She called out to me, from that other cellar."

Dillon looked at Harper. "She'd ridden with us so much, and she's so beautiful, I trusted her.

"She had a gun, I was glad she had it, to protect me. We got in her car, with the top up, and went to her place. She made me some soup and a sandwich and bandaged my hand, and then—then, she said, to hide me, keep me safe, I had to stay in the basement, that she'd lock the door so no one could get in, to hurt me."

Harper nodded and hugged her. The cats had never seen him so tender—as if his own predicament had stripped the cop veneer away for the moment, left him vulnerable.

"The second figure, Dillon. Could you identify the second man? The man in black? Did you recognize him?"

"No, just someone in black, hitting Ruthie. I never saw his face.

"But Crystal knew there were two men. Said she was hiding me from both." She yawned, her eyes blinking closed. "When she locked me up, I knew I'd been stupid to come with her. But then it was too late."

Harper turned off the tape recorder. "It won't be long, we'll get you home. You're safe now. Climb in the bunk and get some rest." He grinned at her. "You did good, Dillon. I'm proud of you. And whoever comes down those stairs, Charlie and I are armed." He grinned. "And mean-tempered."

Charlie helped Dillon up the rusty ladder and fixed her blanket over her. And the kit crept close, snuggling her head under Dillon's chin. Dillon was gone at once, in deep, exhausted sleep.

Dulcie crouched near, on the foot of the bunk, idly swinging her tail, watching the sleeping child and the sleeping kit. Below her on the cold floor, Harper and Charlie sat close together, their backs to the wall, watching the black, empty root cellar and the open rim of the earthslide. They looked, Dulcie thought, as if they belonged together.

When Joe leaped up to stretch out beside Dulcie,

across the mouse-chewed mattress, he lay with every sense alert, every muscle tense, watching and listening; and Dulcie, too, felt safe.

She was just drifting off when Harper said, "How did you find her, Charlie? I didn't want to question her anymore. Did she manage to get to a phone? That brief version you gave me while we were switching cars didn't make a lot of sense."

"She was locked in that tiny room under the stairs, Max. Pitch dark, no windows. No light, no running water. A mattress on the floor. I'm surprised she's in as good a shape as this. She's a tough child."

He looked hard at Charlie. "So now we've had a little diversion. How did you know she was there?"

"Max, you won't believe this."

The captain was quiet. Above them, Joe and Dulcie watched Charlie, ready to yowl and start a fight if she said too much. Would Charlie, in a heady moment of closeness with Max Harper, be tempted to betray them? Share secrets with Harper that later, with a clearer head, she would wish she could swallow back?

She won't, Dulcie thought. Not Charlie, not ever.

But when she glanced at Joe, he didn't look so sure.

"Max, I had a dream. It was so real I woke up sweating, terrified."

Harper's profile went rigid. That hard, ungiving cop look, that I-know-you're-lying look that Joe Grey knew too well.

"It was like Dillon was right there, her face in my face, shouting in my face. We were in a dark, tiny room—all concrete. She was so frightened, was beating at the door—right in my face, beating and pounding on the door, shouting, 'Let me out! Please, Crystal, let me out of here!'

"I've never had a dream like that, not so real."

Harper's profile didn't change. He wasn't buying this.

"I sat up. Knew I couldn't go back to sleep. I thought of phoning Crystal, and knew I daren't do that. I got up, threw on some clothes, and headed for Crystal's. I knew it was crazy, but I couldn't help going.

"Crystal left as I was coming around the corner, I saw her car pull out. I was scared she had Dillon with her.

"I had a hammer in my hand, from my toolbox. I went to the side door, under the house. I was going to smash the glass but it was unlocked, like she forgot to lock it."

On the top bunk, Joe grinned at Dulcie. Charlie was doing it up right, she even had *him* believing. He was mighty glad he had, on the second try, managed to slide that bolt.

"I found the door under the stairs, I *knew* she was there. It was the place I'd dreamed of. All I could think was, get her out of there, get her away."

She looked at Max, lifted her hand to touch his face. "I drove the bolt back, got her out, and we ran."

Harper looked hard at Charlie. He said nothing.

"What, Max? She's a very tough little girl." She rose and stepped to the bunks, stood looking at the sleeping child, raised her eyes to the cats, and winked. Then turned back to sit beside Harper.

"This Dallas Garza, Max. What is he doing? Is he

helping you? Is he honest? Does he talk to you? What does he tell you?"

"He's doing his job, Charlie. He's not supposed to keep me informed—though as a matter of fact, we had a talk yesterday.

"I asked him if Mr. Berndt had filed a report or tendered informal information regarding the case. Garza said not to his knowledge."

Harper eased his back against the concrete wall. "When I was in the grocery yesterday, Mr. Berndt apologized for acting like an old woman about the groceries. I asked him what he meant."

He reached for a cigarette, forgetting he'd quit, then dropped his hand. "Seems Berndt told Wendell, couple of days ago, that he'd noticed Crystal Ryder was suddenly buying a lot more groceries—peanut butter, kid cereal, a lot of kid food. That it made him curious. From what he'd observed, Crystal lives on salads, yogurt, and an occasional steak.

"Berndt had asked one of Crystal's neighbors, a real talkative woman, if Crystal had a child visiting. Molly—Molly Gersten. Molly hadn't seen a child. She can see the front of Crystal's apartment, the front door and windows, from her kitchen.

"Berndt thought it was interesting enough to call the station. Wendell was on the desk, and Berndt gave him the information. Wendell told him he'd pass it on at once, to Detective Garza.

"Garza said he never got it."

Charlie nodded. "Tonight, Wendell stopped Crystal when they were chasing and firing at us. But then he let them go. He had to have heard the shots. But he let them go." She turned to look at him. "What are you going to do?"

"About Wendell?" Harper looked deeply at her. "Time, Charlie. Time, patience, and a cool head."

"I'm not long on patience or a cool head." She studied his face. "Who do you think killed them?"

"Maybe Baker. Maybe Lee Wark. Maybe Crystal."

"Not Wendell."

"Wendell is a follower, not a very bold type. Easily influenced. I inherited him on the force—should have sent him packing."

"But who do you think attacked them—and almost killed Dillon?" she said softly.

"Charlie, you know I can't make that kind of premature call. It muddies the waters. Makes a case harder to work."

"But that's the problem. You're not working this case. Your own future is at stake and your hands are tied. You're not allowed to dig out the facts."

"And that is as it should be."

"I wouldn't be worth a damn as a cop. I'd be champing at the bit all the time, wanting to hurry up an investigation, get to the bottom line."

Harper looked at her a long time, a look so intimate that Dulcie looked away, embarrassed. "You might," Harper said, "make a good cop's wife."

Charlie's face went totally red.

"Well," he said gently, "you can cook and clean. Repair the roof and the plumbing, feed and care for the horses, even train a dog or two. In fact, come to that, you're not a bad shot, either." He reached to his belt. "I'll try the radio, see if we can get a line on Clyde—though I doubt we'll get much, this far underground."

Charlie leaned forward to tie her shoe, as if getting control of herself.

Harper's hand was on his radio when, atop the bunk, Joe Grey froze, watching the short stair and the black cellar beyond. A faint brushing sound, too faint for human ears. Hissing, unable to avoid a low growl, he took off up the steps and up the stairs beyond.

Behind him, Harper extinguished the light and palmed his automatic. Charlie moved to follow Joe, but Harper pulled her back, shoved her to a crouching position at the side of the fallen door. Only Dulcie followed him, racing into the night.

The two humans waited, frozen and silent, the shooters crouched and aiming. And Dillon and the kit slept innocent and unaware.

24

Driving the old green Plymouth, Clyde tried every evasive tactic he'd ever learned from Harper or from watching cop flicks, ducking into driveways, doubling back to slip down an alley, making sure the black convertible was there behind him. With both of them running dark, he prayed no late-hour pedestrian or innocent animal hurried into the street. Crossing Ocean, Crystal stepped on the gas, but at the next intersection she held back as if wary of the brighter streetlight. Glancing back, he lifted a bag of cleaning rags from the seat beside him, let it be seen through the windows as if a passenger had stuck her head up. When Crystal speeded up, narrowing the distance for a better look, he dropped the bag on the seat.

In his rearview mirror, he couldn't see her passenger. Was he lying low or had he bailed out?

Maybe he'd picked up another car, would come slipping out of a side street to cut him off, thinking he had the child.

Or had Crystal's passenger spotted Charlie and Dillon, and was on their tail? They'd be high in the hills now, driving alone on empty, lonely roads, winding toward the Pamillon place. Harper might be following them, or he might not. Clyde was glad he'd given Charlie a gun, glad for their evenings, after hamburgers or Mexican, when he'd taken her to the police range and taught her the proper use of the weapon—glad, he supposed, for Harper's later training, on the nights Charlie went up there to work with the pups. He didn't know how he felt about that.

His relationship with Charlie, though they'd had their moments, seemed to have settled from hot romance into an easy and comfortable friendship.

Was that his fault or hers? He took two more corners, Crystal still on his tail. She'd bolt when she saw where he was headed. Lifting the ragbag again, he dropped it as an oncoming car swerved toward him, its lights blazing on high, moving fast. He tramped the gas, did a hard peel across the intersection on two wheels and down the side street, his rearview mirrors catching the lights as the car screamed on his tail.

It sideswiped him hard, knocking him into the oncoming lane. He managed to spin a U. It hit him again, sent him over the curb and across the sidewalk. The police station loomed half a block ahead. He hit the gas hard. He thought the car was turning away when it spun and hit him broadside—sent the Plymouth sideways into the department's plate-glass window, exploding glass. He threw open the door as a shot rang, and dove in a flying lunge toward the swinging glass doors and through them, nearly trampled as cops came boiling out. Two guys jumped over him where he sprawled. A young corporal stepped on his hand. Three more shots rang out, *bing, bing, bing*. A small-caliber rifle. He saw its flame blaze from an officer's hands, aimed to stop the driver. When it didn't stop him, two patrol cars took off, on his tail.

And two officers grabbed Clyde, jerking his arms behind him, slapping on cuffs. Those two new rookies. He shouted, but no one paid attention. The dispatcher was busy calling the sheriff for assistance. The whole force was in action. Detective Davis spun him around, took one look, looked disgusted, and unlocked the cuffs.

At least he was inside the station, out of the line of fire—maybe.

The offending car was gone, four squad cars scorching after it. He hadn't seen what happened to Crystal; the black convertible had vanished. He sat down on the nearest desk, watching through the shattered window as Davis joined Hendricks, assessing the damage to the building. In a few minutes, two officers came up the street, marching a tall, good-looking guy before them, strong-arming him into the station. Baker. Stubby Baker. Clyde looked him over and went out to look at the Plymouth, his shoes crunching shattered glass.

Shoving through a crowd of onlookers, some in pajamas and robes, and several homeless with their backpacks, who seemed to greatly enjoy the entertainment, he scanned the street for Crystal's convertible. But she'd be long gone. The left side of the Plymouth was totaled.

Moving back inside, he watched as Baker was booked and printed. The well-made, dark-haired man was wide-eyed with surprised innocence. Clyde prayed that Charlie and Harper and Dillon were safe, and he worried about the cats. He'd learned long ago not to argue with cats. Hard-headed and stubborn, they had bulled their way into Charlie's BMW. He guessed, after rescuing Dillon, they had a right to be in on the action—but they were so small and easily hurt. If he let himself worry about them, it tied his belly in knots.

Detective Davis sat down on the desk beside him, her dark eyes appraising. "What's going on, Damen? Why did he ram you? Why was he chasing you?"

He laid out as much of the scenario as he could reveal, told her that Charlie had found Dillon Thurwell in Crystal Baker's apartment, that Dillon had been locked in a cellar, that when Charlie got her out, Baker and Crystal followed and pulled a gun on them. He described his and Charlie's ploy to get Dillon away, their vehicular shell game. He didn't mention Harper.

Davis pushed back her short, dark hair. "So where are they now?" Her brown eyes were unreadable. He saw Officer Wendell beyond her, quietly listening.

"I don't know where Charlie took her. Maybe up the coast. Crystal was after them. Black Mercedes convertible. She was on my tail until Baker started ramming me."

"And where's Harper? He's staying with you."

"I—we started out together. He's in another car."

"Is Charlie carrying?"

He nodded. The department knew he'd had Charlie on the range.

Davis sighed. "If you know anything that you're not telling us . . ."

He looked evenly at the solid, sensible woman. "I want Dillon safe, we need to find Dillon."

"Can you tell me anything more?"

He glanced toward Wendell. Davis widened her eyes.

"I don't know anything more, Juana. I want Dillon and Charlie and Harper safe." *I want the cats safe*, he thought. *I want Joe Grey back in one piece.*

Joe was so enraged by this scam against Harper, that Clyde had no idea what the tomcat would do. He looked solemnly at Davis. "You going to arrest me?"

"What for, Damen?"

Clyde shrugged, and felt easier.

He'd heard the dispatcher call Garza; the detective was on his way in. Clyde didn't quite trust Garza, after what Joe had told him; he was wary of how Garza would handle tonight's events.

If Garza was in on framing Harper, likely Stubby Baker would be out before midnight, free to go on searching for Dillon.

He turned when he heard Garza's voice, watched the tall, broad-shouldered Latino out on the street, talking with portly Lieutenant Brennan, assessing the damage to the building. In a few minutes they came into the station, and Garza nodded to Davis. She glanced at Clyde, jerking her thumb toward the video in the far corner of the squad room. "We're going to question Baker. You want to watch?"

He sat before the screen watching Garza and Davis, in the interrogation room, grilling Stubby Baker, their exchange fed to him through a camera mounted high on the interrogation room wall. Garza let Davis do most of the talking.

"You were with Crystal Ryder tonight in her apartment?"

"No. I was not."

"When were you last in her apartment?"

"I don't remember."

"When were you last within a block of her apartment?"

"Tonight. I followed Harper there. I saw Captain Harper go into her apartment."

"Did she let him in?"

"I don't think so. Looked to me like he used some kind of lock pick. You know? Fiddling around with the lock."

"Did he see you?"

"Don't think so. I'd got out of my car, left it around the corner. I was—ah, in the bushes."

"What time was this?"

"Maybe ten."

"Why did you follow him?"

"I thought he'd be looking for the kid. To do her, you know?"

"Why would he want to do her?"

"Because she saw him kill those women."

"What made you think the child was at Crystal's?"

"I'd been watching."

"Watching what?"

"Watching Crystal come and go. I thought she had someone staying there."

"Why did you think that?"

"She was bringing home a lot of groceries."

"What did you do when Harper went in her apartment?"

"I sat down in the bushes and watched."

"Was Crystal there?"

"The garage door was shut. I didn't see her at the windows."

"Was Crystal there?"

"I guess. She came out later, drove off fast after Harper, after he took the kid."

"How long were you there?"

"Until Harper went off with the kid. When Harper took off, I followed. Afraid he would kill her."

"What time was this?"

"I guess about an hour ago."

"Why did Crystal have her there?"

He looked surprised. Looked right into the camera. "To save her—keep Harper from doing her."

"And what was your interest in the matter?"

"She's just a little kid. I read the papers, I watch the news. A cop gone bad is a terrible thing."

Detective Davis snorted. Garza's expression didn't change. Clyde was glad he wasn't in the room; it would be hard to hold his temper.

"And so you followed Harper?" Davis said.

"I followed him, then that other car came. That old Plymouth. Harper pulled up beside it and got out, and they talked."

"And?"

"There was a lot of moving around, doors opening and closing. I thought he put the kid in the Plymouth."

"Go on."

"I followed it. Driver kept dodging me. I tried to head it over here, toward the station. You know? To get help."

Baker gave Davis that boyish smile. "Well, guess I did get some help. But then I didn't see the kid. Plymouth rammed the station. Well, you saw. And I didn't see the kid. Did you get the kid? Is she safe?"

Talk about chutzpah. Clyde's fists were balled, itch-ing to punch Baker. He waited for Baker to finish, then went back to a conference room with Garza and Davis, and gave his own statement, sipping coffee that tasted like burnt shoes.

"Harper's staying with me, he was there all night, playing poker. We went to bed around ten. Harper snores so loud he rocks the guest room—no way he could have slipped out, even if he'd do such a thing.

"Phone rang, woke me up. It was Charlie. Said she had Dillon. That she was just south of Wilma's house, and Crystal and Baker were shooting at them. Said to meet her at the shop, if she could give them the slip. The back door, up the alley. That maybe we could switch cars and get Dillon away. I woke Harper and we took off."

Davis was recording it all. Somewhere down the line she'd type it up and expect him to sign it.

"I kept wondering, when you questioned Baker, if he and Crystal were the only ones involved. Or if there could be a second man. A man still out there, riding with Crystal, following Harper and Charlie and Dillon."

Davis turned a dark brown, Latin stare on him. "It's possible. Six cars are out looking. Where are they?"

"Try the Pamillon place."

Davis dialed the dispatcher, gave the instructions, then fixed again on Clyde. "I asked you earlier where they were. You didn't know."

"Didn't want to talk in front of Wendell. I don't trust Wendell."

Her response was noncommittal. Garza didn't blink, sat unmoving, watching Clyde. The interview was soon terminated, Clyde none the wiser about what the officers thought. He was heading for the door when a call that stopped him came in. Harper's voice, crackling with static. He moved toward the dispatcher's desk to hear better.

"Code two. I have Dillon Thurwell. The old . . ." Harper went silent, and they heard three shots pop. Clyde didn't wait; he ran for his car, then remembered it was wrecked. Garza was behind him, and Davis. He swung into the backseat of a black-and-white, Garza behind the wheel. The detective spun a U and headed up Ocean, the siren blasting. Clyde was cold with fear for Harper and Charlie and Dillon—but weak, thinking of the cats up there in the middle of the confusion and gunfire, three small cats soon to be surrounded by wheeling squad cars and running officers—three little cats who had saved Dillon Thurwell and now were in danger for their own lives.

And no one knew to care. No one but Charlie would think of protecting them; no one knew how special they were.

25

In the tides and eddies of night, among the broken walls and fallen trees, a figure dressed in dark clothes moved silently and quick, pausing to investigate the two cars parked among the rubble, then slipping toward the ruined house, seeming to know well the layout of the gardens and the abandoned mansion. The time was 5 A.M., some four and a half hours after the three cars left the back door of the automotive shop; the winter night was still black.

Beneath the estate's sprawling trees, no faint gleam shone across the figure's chin or hair, no glint of light fingered the gun that nestled in a furtive hand, nor could one hear the smallest hush of a footstep. The prowler was as silent as the hunter who followed behind on stealthy paws watching with curiosity every move, sniffing at the rank human smell.

As the figure moved into the derelict house through the open parlor and toward the kitchen and stairs, the feline hunter padded closer. Only the cougar was aware of a second two-leg, standing behind them out by the road at the edge of the overgrown gardens. The big cat did not feel threatened. Cocking an ear, he listened behind him, then honed his attention again on the thin figure approaching the stairwell, the black cave down into the earth.

When another hunter entered the scene, slipping up from the earthen caverns below, the cougar caught the scent without interest. The small domestic cat didn't distract him. All his attention was on the two-leg, where it wandered with its back to him, a position that excited him and drew him ever closer—that retreating back enticed him beyond curiosity, to a desire to grab and kill.

Beside the cave-hole, the two-leg paused and seemed to be listening. The cougar paused. And from deep in the shadows, Joe Grey watched the little drama. The four players were positioned as in a game of chess, but this game was played by scent and sound, as rook and knights and king pursued their opposing objectives.

And only one among the players understood the worlds of both his four-footed and two-footed opponents. Only one had the keener senses of the big, four-footed cat, yet the sophisticated mental skills of the two-legs.

Crouched beneath a massy bush of Mexican sage, some fifty feet from the stairs that led down to the cellar, Joe Grey watched the puma slide through the ruined house, stalking the dark-dressed figure, the big cat relaxed and easy, strolling along as if he owned the Pamillon estate. And certainly in his cougar mind, he did own it.

Joe didn't know whether the dark-clad figure the big cat followed was male or female until that player paused at the head of the stairs, and Joe caught the glint of honey-colored hair. Crystal? He couldn't smell her over the garden scents and the stink of the puma. She stood looking around her, listening.

And out on the road, the watcher shifted position, his black clothes darker than the night. Stubby Baker? Had Baker slipped away from Clyde and followed Crystal? Joe wanted to go have a look—but daren't leave Crystal to slip down the steps and take Harper and Charlie by surprise; none of these players had made a sound; Harper would have no reason for sudden alarm. He and Charlie would still be sitting on the floor of the cellar, alert but caught in idle conversation.

Joe didn't know if Crystal was armed. He didn't *think* she would hurt Dillon, but who knew? He thought she had held Dillon as security, to blackmail the killer. He figured Crystal as the go-between, liaison between the killer and whoever at San Quentin had done the hiring.

If Crystal was the banker, the mastermind at Quentin fully trusted her.

How ironic that the money to buy Helen Marner's duplex was money Crystal earned by having Helen murdered.

Moving closer behind the cougar through the rubble of the kitchen, Joe leaped atop a tinder heap of rotting kitchen cabinets. The cougar twitched an ear, but remained intent on Crystal. And in a moment, Joe slipped wide around the big cat, positioning himself to scorch down past Crystal and warn Harper.

But the other figure had slipped nearer, entering the parlor, looming black against the graying sky. It was a man, Joe saw clearly now.

The cougar turned, watching the intruder, the tip of his tail twitching. The black-robed figure didn't see him; he cut through the parlor running. Grabbing Crystal, he shoved a gun in her face. The cougar wheeled, leaping away twenty feet to the top of a broken wall, crouching to watch, his tail lashing.

Unaware, the man shook Crystal and hit her. "Where is she? Where is the girl?" His voice was raspy, whining, icing Joe Grey's blood.

"I don't have her." Fear sharpened Crystal's voice. "Why would I have her?"

Wark hit Crystal again. "Where?"

She pounded him and kneed him. He stumbled, beating her. Above them the cougar crouched. Fighting, the two fell writhing to the ground. The cougar was on them in a hot surge of power, snatching Crystal by the neck, knocking Wark against the wall.

Three shots rang out.

The cougar turned, snarling. Harper fired again into the sky. The big cat dropped Crystal and crouched facing Harper, poised between springing at him and running. His paw still held Crystal. He glanced at her once, licking blood from his whiskers. In that instant, Lee Wark spun away, running. Harper shouted and fired after him—Harper knew better than to run. Nor would he leave Crystal. The gunfire and shout decided the cougar. He fled up the hill into the black forest.

And Lee Wark, too, was gone. Harper looked after him for a moment, then knelt over Crystal, his gun on her as he spoke into his radio. The air stank of gunpowder and blood. Joe could see where the puma had torn her shoulder and arm. He backed away, fading into the shadows—and found Dulcie beside him, pressing close.

And when the two cats looked up the hill above the ruins, the cougar stood watching, sleek and powerful against the silver dawn. The big cat screamed once, wheeled, and vanished toward the wild mountains. They looked after him, shivering.

"Oh," whispered a small voice behind them. "Oh, so beautiful." And the kit pushed between them, her dark little face and round yellow eyes filled with yearning, her furry ears sharp forward as if waiting for another wild scream.

Joe couldn't speak for the kit, but that golden image left him feeling as small and insignificant as a fly speck.

But then Dulcie brushed her whiskers against his, purring, and pressed close to him, and he felt fine and strong again, the boldest and most elegant of tomcats.

And Max Harper turned from his cuffed prisoner, where she lay curled into a fetal position, her head on Harper's folded jacket. Harper had managed to stop some of the bleeding, using pressure. They could hear the ambulance screaming up the hills, and soon they could see its whirling red light and the lights of two squad cars.

As the cats came out from the shadows, Max Harper knelt and, in a rare gesture, reached to stroke Joe Grey. "Thanks, tomcat. With all that hissing and taking off up the stairs, you kept Crystal from slipping down on us. Maybe you stopped the cougar, too." Harper grinned. "Maybe Clyde's right, maybe cats *are* good for something."

26

Driving up the coast with Hanni, Kate couldn't keep her mind off Lee Wark. She leaned back in the soft leather of Hanni's SUV, meaning to enjoy the morning, and spent the entire drive staring into every car they passed, with the paranoid notion that she would see Wark.

The sun was bright, the air just cool enough to be fresh, their windows cracked to an ocean breeze, the sea on their left thundering with sufficient wildness to both beckon and repel. And all she could think of was Lee Wark.

Stubby Baker was in jail, this morning. And that was good news. And Crystal Ryder was under arrest, in the emergency wing of Molena Point Hospital. But Lee Wark was still free, and Dallas had reason to believe that Wark had killed Ruthie Marner.

What an amazing thing, that Crystal had been attacked by the cougar. What a strange end to Crystal's part in a bizarre crime.

Certainly nothing had changed in the threat that she,

Kate, felt from Wark. She was obsessed with the idea that he was near. When Hanni turned off the freeway into the city, just before noon, she was tense with nerves.

And alone again in her apartment, before she must return to work the next morning, she felt the afternoon stretching ahead, peculiarly unsettling.

She needed to lay to rest her fears—at least those surrounding the Cat Museum. That fear, she had come to realize, was in part fear of the museum itself. Fear of what she might learn there, as well as her unease that Wark would find her there and hurt her.

She wasn't home half an hour, glancing through her mail that had been shoved through the door onto the rug, before she grabbed her jacket, locked the door behind her, and headed for the Iron Horse. She'd have a quick lunch, then call a cab. Wark wouldn't be in the city.

He would be too busy, with the Marner murders hanging over him, too busy running from the police to think about her. To think about her possible connection to what she believed was a whole, traceable line of individuals possessed of the spirits of both cat and human. Certainly Wark would not be interested in her search for a man who might have been her grandfather.

Hurrying into the restaurant, heading for her usual table—praying that Ramon wouldn't start about the cat killer—she greeted him with an unusual reserve.

"Buenos días, señora."

"Good afternoon, Ramon."

She felt guilty at his puzzled look, that she hadn't

spoken in their usual joking Spanish. Why had she come in here, only to be rude to him?

"It's good to see you, Ramon."

"You have been away. Did you enjoy your village? Molena Point, *verdad*?"

Kate laughed, telling herself she should be pleased that he would remember. "It was nice to be home in the village, yes." He was such a shy, kind person. There was no need to be rude to him. He was only very curious—and so easy to hurt, easy to rebuff, backing away if he felt unwanted.

There was a reluctant, almost stray quality about Ramon. He was a loner. A shy, needy person and a loner. She gave him a smile. "It's nice to be back in the city. Very nice to see you."

Her friendliness eased him. When he had taken her order and brought her sandwich, he fetched his own cup of coffee and sat down opposite her, glancing at her diffidently.

"You were all right when you were in your village, señora? You had a happy time?"

"Oh, yes, Ramon. Quite happy." What was he getting at? He couldn't know that she had left the city frightened, had been frightened, in a painful undercurrent, the entire time she was at home, and was still scared.

She said, "There have been—no more terrible incidents?"

Why had she said that? She hadn't meant to mention the cat killer, she didn't want to hear about him. It came out before she thought.

"No, señora. No incidents. Maybe that man went away. Except . . ." He glanced out at the street, his white skin going paler, the rust-colored scar on his cheek seeming to darken.

"Except, maybe an hour ago when I took out the trash, I saw three cats running, very frightened, into the alley as if something was chasing them."

"City cats, Ramon. They run from cars, from dogs, from small children."

"I suppose." Ramon finished his coffee and rose. She wanted to ask if he'd gone into the alley where the cats had run. Had he seen anyone chasing them?

But she didn't ask. She was so foolishly obsessed. At least she could keep her fears to herself.

She ate quickly, irritated with herself, paid her bill, and left; she looked back once, to see him standing in the window watching her. He had turned the *open* sign around to read *closed,* and had pulled the sheer white curtain across the lower half of the glass. She supposed he had an errand; he did that sometimes, left after the noon rush, returned in time to prepare for the dinner hour.

Heading up Stockton, she decided not to look for a cab. The sun felt good on her shoulders. She liked watching the clouds racing overhead trailing their shadows swift as birds across the pale hillside houses. She swung along until soon, above her at the crest of Russian Hill, the white walls and red tile roofs of the museum glowed beneath their dark, twisted oaks. Hurrying up the hill, only once did she glance behind her.

Seeing the street empty, she slowed her pace. She entered through the iron gate slowly, taking her time, enjoying the welcoming ambiance of the bright gardens.

The museum's cats were everywhere, sunning on the walks, rolling over, smiling lazily as they watched her, cats as sleek as the marble felines that gleamed on the sculpture stands. Cats peered out at her from the geraniums, looked down from atop the stone walls and out through the gallery windows. She had such a sense of oneness with them, almost as if she could read their thoughts—of sun on their backs, of the warm sidewalk, the taste of water in a bowl.

But then suddenly the cats turned wary, slipping away into the bushes.

Afraid of her? Was her two-sided nature so apparent? And did that frighten them?

Were none of them like Joe Grey and Dulcie, so they could understand her?

Soon only one cat remained, watching her unafraid. A sleek tom as white as alabaster. He looked at her for a long time, then he, too, vanished, just where sunlight struck through the leaves. He'd had dirt on his face, or some sort of rust-colored marking.

Approaching the main door, she paused to read the quotations inscribed on clay tablets along the garden wall.

Some claim that the cat came to us from the vanished continent of Atlantis.

Our companion the cat is the warm, furry, whiskered, and purring reminder of a lost paradise.

That one made her smile. She recognized that quotation, she thought from some French artist.

But the next inscription stopped her.

Dark the cat walks, his pacing shadow small.

Dark the cat walks, his shadow explodes tall,

Fearsome wide and tall.

Ramon's words. That was what Ramon had said, the day he brought the newspaper that had so upset her.

Backing away from the plaque, she sat down on a bench, her hands trembling. *His shadow explodes tall, fearsome wide and tall.*

Ramon couldn't know what those words meant. To Ramon, they would be no more than a poetic image. She read the lines again, trying to put down her unease.

A movement at the corner of her vision made her look up. Ice filled her veins.

The man in the black overcoat stood out by the street. Dense black against the clear colors of the garden.

He stood looking at her, his face in shadow, then turned slowly away, moved casually down the hill to disappear between the houses.

She thought to run after him and get a good look—grab his shoulders and swing him around, get a look at his eyes.

But she didn't have the nerve. She hurried inside through the mullioned glass door to the safety of the galleries.

Losing herself among the rich oils and watercolors, she found some ink drawings by Alice Kitchen, then discovered a Miró and two delightful Van Goghs. And a Picasso she didn't care for. Too stark and impersonal. She stopped to admire the primitive portrait of a black

Manx playing with a mouse, the mouse so real she could almost feel the silkiness of its fur and the prick of its little claws.

Moving slowly through the gallery to the visitors' desk, she slipped her billfold from her pocket to pay the admission fee. The attendant was a stocky, dull-haired woman rather like a box with thick legs. She watched Kate sullenly, looking her up and down.

Why must short, meaty women bristle at her simply because she was slim and tall? She couldn't help how she looked. It embarrassed her when people saw her only from the outside, and didn't care to discover what she was like within.

And *that* thought almost sent her into nervous and uncontrolled laughter.

Even the attendant's eyes were dull, her expression discontented. Maybe she had an unhappy home life. Maybe she longed for a fortune's worth of plastic surgery and cosmetic rejuvenation.

I *can* be catty, Kate thought, amused.

She gave the woman a hesitant smile and laid her hand gently on the marble counter in a gesture of friendship. "It's a lovely museum, the work is magnificent. And the cats look so happy, so many beautiful cats."

"Certainly we have cats." As if she'd heard that same remark more times than she cared to count.

"They're lucky to live in such beautiful gardens." Did she have to add another inanity?

The woman sighed. "They were all strays. Cats who found their way here hungry and lost. Or cats that were dumped by some uncaring person." As she spoke of the cats, a warmth crept into her voice, and she returned Kate's smile. "The cats are our welcoming committee. People seem to slow their pace, watching and petting them, and so take more time to enjoy the galleries."

Kate nodded. "I understand you have a library in the museum? I'm doing research for a magazine article," she lied. "On the history of the smaller museums in northern California. But this museum—this one is special. I just moved to San Francisco. I'd like to learn more about the museum, I'd like very much to join." She opened her checkbook.

The woman handed her a membership form. "I will hold your dues until your application is approved. Are you looking for something in particular?"

"Some diaries. A man who lived in San Francisco in the fifties, a building contractor. I understand Mr. McCabe was a close friend of Alice Kitchen. I'm interested in her drawings, I'm planning a rather long article about Kitchen's work. I understand that Mr. McCabe knew her as a little girl, that he encouraged her talent—and that he designed and built the museum? I've never heard his first name."

"We do not know his first name. He called himself simply McCabe. That was the way he signed his articles for the *Chronicle*."

"And his diaries?"

"They are locked in the vault, very valuable, very special to us. Once your application has been accepted, we can share them with you." The woman bent, reaching beneath the counter as if to retrieve an application form. As she did, Kate saw beyond her, out the window, the black-coated man slipping through the shadows into a pergola of wisteria.

The sight of him there in the gardens made her blood run cold. She looked and looked. She was nearly sure it was Wark. As he moved away behind the wisteria vines, the white cat stepped out of the bushes, warily following him.

"We will process the application quickly," the woman was saying. "Meanwhile, the museum publishes two books, one on the collection, and the other a short biography of McCabe. Both are for sale."

Frightened and edgy, she bought the biography and dropped it in her shoulder bag. She would not run. This time she would not run from him. She would sensibly use the phone, call the police.

But *was* it Wark? How embarrassing, to summon the police if that man was not Lee Wark.

She needed to see for herself.

There was no one around, no one to stop him if he attacked her, only this little woman.

She thought how brave Charlie had been, getting Dillon out of Crystal's garage, getting her away while Stubby Baker was shooting at them. Charlie, too, had been afraid.

Well, she could just go out there into the gardens, get a look at him. If it was Wark, she could dodge him, run back inside, and grab the phone. She had to do this, or she would never be free of him—and he would be free to hurt others.

Slipping out the side door, warily she approached the pergola.

Nothing moved around her. She could see no cats; not a cat was visible.

Had they all gone? Or were they hiding?

Heart pounding, she moved into the pergola, staring into the shadows. The wisteria vines brushed her cheek, startling her.

Wark stood under the vines, his cold eyes full on her. She backed away. He lunged, grabbed her, twisting her arm. What had made her think she could escape him?

"Jimmie still wants you dead, missy. That divorce made Jimmie real mad. Jimmie still means to pay for you dead. And I plan to collect."

He began to whisper; she didn't want to hear him. As he spoke, she had a sense of being watched. When she felt his hands on her throat she fought him, biting and hitting him. He twisted her arm; hot pain shot through her.

But suddenly the cats were there, springing at him, leaping down from the trellis, appearing out of the vines, launching themselves at him, so many cats, dozens of cats. The white cat exploded out, flying at his face, biting and raking him; cats swarmed over him, snarling and clawing. Kate felt nothing for Wark. She stood frozen, watching him cower and cover his face, and she could think only of the poor animals he had hurt.

But then suddenly she'd had enough, she didn't want to see this, didn't want this to be happening.

"Stop," she whispered. "Stop. Let him go."

The cats stopped and looked at her. In that instant, Wark ran, cats dropping off, leaping away.

* * *

She watched him disappear down Russian Hill. She had started inside to call the police, when she knew she couldn't do that.

Covered with bleeding scratches, Wark must not be reported from the phone in the museum. Let Wark get as far away as his running feet could take him.

She fled the garden in a cab, got out at Stockton Street to use a pay phone. Then she hurried home, running past the Iron Horse with the *closed* sign in its window and up her own steps, into her apartment to bolt the door.

She spent the rest of the afternoon huddled on her couch, wrapped in a blanket, sipping hot tea, mindlessly watching her locked windows and bolted front door. Wondering if the police had found Wark. She had not given the dispatcher her name. She was heating a can of soup, watching the little TV in the kitchen, when the local news came on.

Wark's picture filled the screen.

"The first of the three escapees from San Quentin was apprehended this afternoon at Fisherman's Wharf." The anchorwoman was dark-haired, her black-lashed blue eyes looking as if every item she ever broadcast touched her deeply. "Lee Wark, serving a life sentence for murder, was found in the men's room of a Fisherman's Wharf restaurant by a restaurant patron who called the police. Wark had fainted, apparently from loss of blood, from what police describe as hundreds of scratch wounds. Neither police nor hospital authorities have offered an opinion as to what caused his injuries."

The picture on the screen did not show the

scratches; the station had used the same mug shot they had been broadcasting since the three men escaped.

"Lee Wark was serving a multiple sentence in San Quentin for murder and attempted murder and for car theft and counterfeiting. He escaped from prison over four weeks ago, along with James Hartner and Ronnie Cush, who are still at large, wanted by state police. During their escape, the three men seriously wounded a guard. Anyone having information about the two escapees, or about Wark's present injuries, is asked to contact San Francisco police or prison authorities at San Quentin. They will have full assurance of anonymity."

The relief that flooded Kate was more than she would have dreamed. Wark's capture swept away an unimaginable weight. She felt, for the first time since she'd learned of her dual nature, no unease, no fear. If she harbored the nature of a cat within herself, she was what she was. Now, with Wark locked up again, there would be no one to hate her and want to harm her—her private nature would be her own secret.

But she had to smile. She bet the museum's feline population had vanished. She bet no cat would be seen in those gardens until this news was old and stale. Certainly the white cat would have vanished.

She was eating her soup when the phone rang.

"Kate, are you okay? Have you seen the news? Are you all right?"

"I'm fine, Clyde. Yes, I saw the news." She put her hand over the phone, feeling giddy. "I'm fine. Where are you?"

"At home. Drinking a beer and watching the San

Francisco channel. Joe and Dulcie are doing flips, they're so happy. Were you . . . How did Wark . . . ?"

"Leave it alone, Clyde."

"All right, Kate. If you say so. I've ordered in fillets to celebrate. Wish you were here. When are you coming back? We miss you."

"I just left."

"*I* miss you."

She didn't answer.

"Kate?"

"I thought you were dating Charlie."

"Charlie and Max are up at his place, celebrating his return to the department. I think the chief needs her, Kate. And I think Max is what she needs, not a bumbling auto mechanic."

"And you, Clyde?"

"You make me laugh, Kate. You always have. When are you coming home?"

27

Pacing his cell, Stubby Baker looked mad enough to chomp the metal bars, with the sort of rage that made men trash hotel rooms and beat their wives. Baker might be a handsome, boyish-looking fellow, Dulcie thought, with a smile to charm the ladies, but none of that was apparent at the moment. The two cats, looking down at Baker from the high open window, watched Baker's attorney leave the cell and the guard slam and lock the door.

Bars and wire mesh covered the window. The wire-reinforced glass had been cranked open to the warm afternoon. On the sill, Joe and Dulcie crouched beneath the higher branches of the oak tree that sheltered the dead-end alley, the back door of the police station, and the jail. The tree was their highway, their path to all manner of case-related information. It was huge, with rough bark, sprawling twisted limbs bigger around than a cat, and dark prickly leaves. One had only to leap from its sturdy branches to the broad sill to observe the daily lives of the duly incarcerated. A cat could eavesdrop on any conversation that might occur among the residents or between an offender and his jailer or lawyer. The discussion that had just terminated between Baker and his portly attorney had been strictly confidential. The cats grinned at each other, amply rewarded for their three-hour wait atop the hard concrete sill.

Baker was enraged that he'd been picked out of the lineup. Was furious that Crystal had double-crossed him, that she had been hiding Dillon all along. He was mad that Kendrick Mahl and Jimmie Osborne had instructed Crystal to pay him only half the agreed amount, claiming that Wark, not he, had done Ruthie Marner. He said Wark had not been part of the deal, that Wark's escape from Quentin didn't mean he had a right to horn in on a private business arrangement. The attorney, scratching his pale, stubbled cheek, couldn't have agreed more; but he reminded Baker that he *had* been picked out of the lineup, that morning. When the potbellied, bearded lawyer said he was considering how to deal with that little setback, Joe glanced at Dulcie and nearly yowled out a bawdy cat laugh.

The lineup, in which Dillon fingered Baker as Helen's killer, had, in the cats' opinion, been a highly entertaining occasion.

Garza had gathered seven tall, thin people into one of the station's conference rooms, all dressed alike in worn Levi's, western shirts, and boots, their identical western hats pulled low over their faces, and the collars of their jeans jackets pulled up. The subjects had included Stubby Baker, Max Harper, Crystal Ryder sans makeup and with her hair pulled up under her hat, and four strangers whom Dillon wasn't likely to know. Dillon's parents had wanted to be with the child, but Dillon had opted to view the group alone, with only Detective Garza and two attending officers present.

She had not deliberated for more than a moment.

The cats, sneaking into the station during the change of watch, slipping under officers' desks and back through the squad room, had managed to stay out of sight until they were safely concealed beneath the last row of chairs in the appointed conference room. They had peered out at the lineup fascinated. The tall figures, all dressed like the killer, were alarmingly alike, their arms hidden by the long sleeves of their jackets, only small portions of their lean faces visible beneath the broad-brimmed hats. It was hard to tell which was Max Harper—until they looked at the eyes.

The killer's eyes spoke to Dillon, too, the dark, mesmerizing eyes of Stubby Baker. Dillon rose from her chair and drew close, looking up at Baker, then stepped back quickly, swallowing.

"That man. It was that man who killed Helen Marner."

"Are you sure?" Garza asked her.

"Yes. That man, riding the captain's horse." She had gone pale, looking at Baker. Baker's eyes on Dillon burned with such rage that Joe Grey feared for the child. And as he was led away, he cut a look at Harper, standing in the lineup, a fierce and promising stare that chilled Joe.

But Baker would be locked up now, where he couldn't reach Harper or Dillon. And before anyone left the room, the cats had slipped out and raced down the hall, and out to the courthouse lawn, to roll over, purring.

They had contributed in a major way to Max Harper's exoneration. They had discovered Crystal's purchase of Helen's duplex and had found Crystal's phone tapes and gotten them to Garza. The kit had found the barrette, by which Officer Wendell helped to incriminate himself when he didn't report it. They had, most important of all, found Dillon and called in the troops, who had gotten her to safety.

"And," Dulcie whispered, "you very likely prevented Crystal from sneaking down into the Pamillon cellar—from surprising Harper and Charlie.

"You were wonderful," she said. "I was so worried when you left the cellar. But if Crystal had come down there, who knows what might have happened?" She rubbed her whiskers against his. "If Harper hadn't seen you streaking up the steps, he wouldn't have been there to fire those shots and scare away the cougar."

Joe Grey smiled. He felt pretty good about life. And he would far rather see Crystal stand trial than see the puma kill her, if only for the sake of her testimony.

But also, because a cougar who kills a human is in deep trouble. And while he feared the big cat, Joe respected him.

The cats had visited Crystal, over in the women's wing, before settling down to spy on Baker. She'd been in a worse mood than Baker. And she looked like hell, Dulcie had observed with satisfaction.

The bandages on her shoulder and arm were clearly visible now under her loose prison smock, her honey-colored hair was limp and oily, her dimpled smile replaced by a scowl. Her orange prison jumpsuit made her skin sallow. While they watched her, she spoke to none of her neighbors in the adjoining cells, and no one came to see her. They had grown bored at last and headed for Baker's cell, but they were not the only eavesdroppers.

Attached to the cell window, in a position where it could not be spotted by the inmate, was a tiny tape recorder, the smallest model Joe had ever seen. Property of Molena Point PD, it had been in position when they arrived on the windowsill. It appeared to be the kind of machine activated by sound, that would stop recording during periods of silence. The grid for its microphone was directed downward toward the cell. The recorder smelled of hand lotion, the brand worn by Detective Kathleen Ray. Joe was shocked at Kathleen, and highly amused.

There was nothing illegal about a police department installing such a recorder on its own premises. Once a citizen was arrested, the privilege of privacy ceased to exist. The cops had every right—except for the present meeting.

Conversations between a client and his attorney were privileged information—could not legally be recorded.

Kathleen had to know that, Joe had thought, studying the small machine.

But he needn't have worried about Detective Ray's intentions. The conversation between Baker and his attorney was not recorded; the machine didn't activate. Joe thought Kathleen Ray must have been watching for the attorney, and must have a remote control in the station. When the lawyer left, Joe hissed into the machine, and the tape started rolling. It stopped when he stopped. He wondered what Kathleen *had* taped, what would be added to Dallas Garza's report.

Baker had been formally charged with murder, and Crystal Ryder with three counts of conspiracy to commit murder, and with kidnapping.

Lee Wark was languishing once again in San Quentin, nursing his wounds—about which Joe and Dulcie had done considerable speculation. Wark was facing, as well as the state's charge of escape, a charge of murder in the first degree. Wark's blood had been found on Ruthie Marner, and fibers from his sweater on her clothes.

And Joe Grey felt warm and smug. Three no-goods were about to receive the benefits of the American legal system, the system they had tried to manipulate.

The cats had come to the jail directly from the courthouse, from a gathering in Lowell Gedding's office in which they had again assumed the roles of unseen observers, behind the curtain of the bay window.

The city attorney had called the small group together to ease tension among those involved, to clear the air and set matters to rights before the trial began. Those present had included Molena Point Chief of Police Max Harper, duly reinstated; his officers and detectives; San Francisco detective Dallas Garza; Dillon Thurwell and her parents and a few of their close friends; four members of the Marner family; the mayor and five members of the city council; and Clyde

Damen, Charlie Getz, and Wilma Getz, who had sat with their backs to the bay window, effectively blocking any chance glimpse of its occupants.

Gedding had made no accusations as to possible collusion among the city council and the offenders. No innuendos slipped into his statement, yet the cats observed a coolness on Gedding's part, as if perhaps in the next election he might do some heavy campaigning against certain council members. Joe Grey had watched the proceedings with a more-than-relieved air.

The night before, he'd had a nightmare that left him mewling like a terrified kitten. He'd dreamed he was in Judge Wesley's courtroom, that Max Harper stood before the bench facing the judge not as a police officer called to testify, but to be sentenced himself for first-degree murder. The nightmare had been so real that Joe had waked fighting the blanket, growling and hissing with rage.

"Stop it, Joe! What's wrong?" Clyde had poked him hard. "What's the matter with you!"

He'd awakened fully, to find himself lashing out at Clyde. Shocked, he'd stared confused at Clyde's lacerated hand.

"Wake up, you idiot cat! *Are* you awake? Are you having a fit? You clawed me! What's wrong with you!"

From the angle of the moonlight seeping in under the window shade, he'd guessed the time at about 2:30. Rising up among the rumpled blankets, he was still seeing the Molena Point courtroom, watching Max Harper sentenced to life in prison.

A dream.

It had been only a dream.

He'd tried to explain to Clyde how real the vision had been. His distress must have gotten to Clyde, because Clyde got up, went down the hall to the kitchen, and fixed him a bowl of warm milk. Carrying it back to the bedroom, Clyde let him drink it on the Persian throw rug, one of the few really nice furnishings in their rough-hewn bachelor pad.

"That was very nice," Joe had said, licking his whiskers and yawning.

"You didn't spill on the rug?"

"I didn't spill on the rug," he snapped. "Why can't you ever do anything nice without hassling me?"

"Because you spill, Joe. You slop your food, and I have to clean it up. Shut up and come back to bed. Go to sleep. And don't dream anymore—you don't need bad dreams. Harper's been cleared. He's back home, back at work, and all is well with the world. Go to sleep."

"The trial hasn't started yet. How do you know—"

"Go to sleep. With the amount of evidence the department has, what's to worry? Much of that evidence," Clyde said, reaching to lightly cuff him, "thanks to you and Dulcie and the kit."

That compliment had so pleased and surprised him that he'd curled up, purring, and drifted right off to sleep.

But then, all through the meeting in Gedding's office, which amounted mostly to friendly handshakes and smiles, and then later hearing practically a confession from Stubby Baker, he still found it hard to shake off the fear—hard to shake the feeling that this was not a good world with some bad people in it, but a world where any decency was temporal. Where any goodness was as ephemeral and short-lived as cat spit on the wind.

In the cell below them, the lawyer had left, and Joe was prodding Dulcie to do the same when Officer Wendell came along the hall, pausing at Baker's bars.

Wendell looked like he'd slept in his uniform. He spoke so softly that the cats had to strain to hear. Joe glanced at the tape. It was running.

"Mahl called," Wendell said.

"So?" Baker snarled.

"So if you involve him in this, you're dead meat. Said he has people out and around. If you make a slip, you're history."

"Oh, right. And what about you?"

"There's nothing to pin on me."

Baker smiled.

"What?"

Baker lay back on his bunk looking patently pleased with himself. Wendell turned a shade paler—making Joe and Dulcie smile.

Dallas Garza had plenty of evidence to tie Wendell to the murders and to the attempt to frame Harper: Wendell did not file Betty Eastmore's report that she had seen Captain Harper the afternoon of the murder. Wendell did not file Mr. Berndt's report about Crystal's grocery-buying habits, and he did not put Dillon's barrette into evidence until Garza asked him about it. And no one even knew, yet, that Wendell had been in Crystal's apartment looking for Dillon the night that she escaped.

If there was anything Joe Grey hated, it was a cop gone bad.

But now, he thought, glancing at Kathleen's little tape recorder, now the department had additional evidence against Officer Wendell.

"Very nice," he whispered, winking at Dulcie. And they leaped into the tree and down, and went to hunt rabbits.

28

It was late that afternoon that the cougar returned to the Pamillon mansion, prowling among the broken furniture and rampant vines, flehmening at the smell of dried human blood. Investigating where he had downed and bitten the two-legs and where the loud noises had chased him away, he watched down the hill, too, where a small cat crouched, looking up at him, thinking she was hidden among the bushes. It was not magnanimity that kept him from dropping down the hill in one long leap and snatching the kit and crunching her. He was sated with deer meat; he had killed and gorged, and buried the carcass under the moldering sofa. At the moment, his thoughts were on a light nap on the sun-warmed tiles of the patio.

Earlier, before he hunted, prowling farther down the hills, he had sat for some time watching the gathering of two-legs around the fences and buildings of the ranch yard, fascinated by their strange behavior. The sounds they made were different than he had heard before from the two-legs, noises that hurt his ears. He had watched the gathering until he grew hungry. He had studied the horses in the pasture, but they would give him a hard battle, and the two-legs were too close. Trotting away higher into the hills where the deer were easy takings, he had killed and fed.

Now, leaving the carcass buried in the parlor, and glancing a last time where the small cat thought itself invisible, he strolled onto the Pamillon patio and stretched out in the sun.

The kit watched the cougar as he arrogantly put his head down and closed his eyes. She watched until he seemed to sleep deeply. When she was certain his breathing had slowed, she crept up the hill, closer.

Peering out from the tall grass, she wondered.

Could she touch the golden beast? Could she reach out a paw and touch him, and reach out her nose to sniff his sleek fur?

But no, she wouldn't be so foolish. No sensible cat would approach a sleeping cougar.

And yet she was drawn closer, and closer still, was drawn right up the hill to the boulders that edged the patio.

From behind a boulder she looked at him for a long time.

And she stepped out on the tiles.

She lifted her paw. The cougar seemed deeply asleep. Dare she approach closer? Hunching down as if stalking a bird, making herself small and invisible, she crept forward step by silent step.

Claws grabbed her from behind and jerked her

around, deep and painful in her tender skin. A pair of blazing amber eyes met her eyes—and a terrible fear filled the kit.

"Go down, Kit! Go down now, away from here! Away from the lion! Down the hills at once!" Joe hissed. He belted her hard, boxed her little ears. "Go away through the bushes. Stay in the bushes. *Don't run*—sneak away slowly."

The kit slipped away without a word, Joe Grey behind her, the cats keeping to the heavy growth, listening for the lion—and knowing he would make no sound. Sensible fear drove Joe Grey. Terror and guilt drove the kit.

When they were far away, they ran. Down and down the hills they flew, and under the pasture fence, which the cougar could leap like a twig. And across the pasture into the hay shed, two streaks flying up the piled bales.

High up, beneath the tin roof, they looked back across the pasture.

Just beyond the fence, the cougar stood on a boulder looking across the green expanse straight up into the hay shed, staring straight at them.

The kit began to shiver.

The cougar started down along the fence, watching and watching them.

But the cats and cougar were not alone. Jazz music started up again, from the party in the ranch yard. The lion stopped, watching the crowd. The cats saw him flehmen, tasting the strange smells. He laid back his ears at the smells and the loud talk and laughing and the jazz music; he stood only a moment, puzzled and uneasy. Then he wheeled and was gone again, up the hills into the forest.

He left behind a strange emptiness. One moment he had glowed against the hill huge and golden. The next moment, nothing was there.

The kit looked and looked, unblinking.

Joe Grey nudged her. "Did you want to be eaten?"

"I didn't. He is the king, he wouldn't eat me."

"He would eat you in one bite. Crunch and swallow you whole. First course in a nice supper."

"The first course," Dulcie said, leaping up the hay bales. "And all your roaming ways and yearning for another world would end. You and your dreams would be gone, Kit. Swallowed up the way you swallow a butterfly."

The kit sat down on the hay, looking at the two older cats. She was indeed very quiet. She looked at Joe's sleek, pewter-colored face, at the white strip down his face, wrinkled now into an angry frown. She looked into Dulcie's blazing green eyes, and she lifted a paw to pat Dulcie's striped face and peach-tinted nose.

The bigger cats were silent.

She turned away to look down at the stableyard, at the tables and chairs all set about, at the long table covered with food and wonderful smells rising up, at all the people gathered talking and laughing and at the banners whipping in the breeze.

WELCOME HOME, MAX

HAIL TO THE CHIEF, MAY HE REIGN FOREVER

THE FORCE IS WITH YOU

Everyone looked so happy and sounded happy. Someone shouted, "Open another keg," and the kit watched it all, forgetting her fear and shame, and filling up with delight. What a fine thing was this human world, what a fine thing to be part of human life. She wanted to be a part of everything. She wanted to be down there. She wanted to try all the exciting food. She wanted to be petted and admired. She licked Dulcie's ear, forgetting that she was in trouble, and leaped away down the hay and into the middle of the celebration.

Joe and Dulcie looked at each other and shook their heads, and followed her, launching themselves into the party, begging handouts as shamelessly as the kit and the two big hounds. The kit moved among the crowd like a little dancer, galloping, leaping, accepting a morsel here, cadging a bite there until she spotted Dillon.

She went to the child at once, leaped to the bench beside her, patted at Dillon's red hair, then settled down in her lap, purring. Dillon stroked and cuddled her, sharing a closeness that thrilled the child. Dillon had never had a pet. She loved the kit; she had no notion that the kit was far more than anyone's pet.

These two, child and kit, had slept through all the excitement at the Pamillon house, slept curled together on the musty bunk in the cellar, so exhausted that even Harper's three shots to scare away the cougar had hardly waked them—only enough to sigh and roll over. Now Joe and Dulcie watched them tenderly.

But it was not until hours later, as evening fell and Harper's officers and most of his friends drifted away, that there was a truly quiet time again, for the cats and those they held dear.

As the line of cars wound away down the hills, Harper and Clyde and Charlie and Wilma moved inside to Harper's big kitchen table, to drink leftover coffee and to unwind. In the kitchen's bay window, the three cats snuggled together among the cushions, purring so loudly that Harper glanced at them, amused.

"Never heard them purr like that. They sound like a 747."

"Full of shrimp," Clyde said, "and crab salad and cold cuts."

To emphasize the truth of Clyde's remark, Joe belched loudly.

Harper stared at him and burst out laughing—the captain laughed until he had tears. Charlie began to laugh. Clyde and Wilma doubled over, convulsed with merriment. Joe had had no idea he was such a comedian.

"Nerves," Dulcie whispered, pretending to lick his ear. "Crazy with nerves, all four of them."

"Nerves? Or too much beer?"

The kit looked from one cat to the other, her eyes huge. Sometimes she didn't know what to make of humans.

"So," Charlie said to her aunt when they'd calmed, "are you going to tell me why you didn't answer your phone? Where were you the night Dillon and I sat out there in the van, with the phone ringing and ringing, and that thug firing at us?"

"I'm truly sorry. I wonder how it would have turned out if I'd been there?"

"Where were you?"

Wilma smoothed her gray hair, which she had wound into a chignon for the occasion of Harper's party. She was wearing a long flowered dress and sandals, one of the few times the cats had ever seen her in a dress. "That night—would you believe I'd unplugged the phone to get a good night's sleep?"

"No," Charlie said. "You only do that when Dulcie is safe in the house, when she's not out running the streets."

Dulcie gawked, but Joe nudged her.

Wilma shrugged. "I had dinner with Susan Brittain, at The Patio. During dessert, she felt faint. We thought I'd better drive her home. She refused to go to the hospital, said it was her medication, that she got like that sometimes. I spent the night on her couch, checking on her every little while—her daughter's out of town."

Joe and Dulcie looked at each other.

Charlie raised an eyebrow.

"It's the truth. You think, at my age, I'm off on some hot affair?"

"Why not? I wouldn't put it past you."

"Speaking of affairs . . ." Clyde said, looking at Charlie and Harper.

The cats came to sharp attention. Charlie blushed pink beneath her freckles. Harper looked embarrassed.

Clyde grinned. "Could I use your phone?"

Harper nodded uncomfortably. "You know where they are, take your choice."

Clyde moved down the hall and into Harper's study, unaware of Joe trotting along behind him; didn't see the tomcat slip under the desk, he was too busy dialing.

In the kitchen, Wilma rose to clean up the paper plates and rinse the silverware, leaving Harper and Charlie alone at the table. They hardly knew she'd left, there might be no one else in the room; they were completely engrossed in each other, their conversation ordinary but their looks so intimate that Dulcie turned her gaze away.

"What about this William Green?" Charlie was saying, looking deeply at Harper. "This witness who said—who lied that he saw you following the Marners?"

"He's in custody." Harper's hand on the table eased against hers. "He'll have to testify for the prosecution." His words were totally removed from the way he was looking at her.

"Green's testimony will be another nail in Crystal's coffin," Harper said, leaning closer. "If he cooperates with Gedding, he might get off with a fine for perjury and no time served."

Dulcie lay pretending sleep as Charlie and Harper discussed Baker's land scam, accomplished with Baker's carefully forged documents—and discussed Baker's victims, who were hot to prosecute and to get their money back. Soon Harper and Charlie moved out to the yard to pick up the last few paper plates, and fold up the tables and chairs. Clyde began to help Wilma, drying the silver and platters. He didn't mention his phone call. The cats moved to the back porch to wash their paws and enjoy the cool evening.

"Clyde spotted me under the desk," Joe said. "Told me to get lost. He can be so touchy. He and Kate seem to be an item."

"And Harper and Charlie, too." Dulcie glanced up as Wilma came out to sit on the steps beside them.

"I think both couples are cozy," Wilma said softly. "This might be promising, all around."

"Maybe," said Joe Grey, knowing how fickle Clyde could be.

"Maybe," said Dulcie uncertainly. Things had moved a bit fast, for her taste.

The kit, waking alone in the kitchen, leaped from the window seat and pushed out through the screen door, her yellow eyes so dreamy that Dulcie fixed on her uneasily. That faraway look meant trouble. "What are you thinking, now, Kit? Not of dark far places?"

"And not," Joe Grey said, "of petting lions!"

"Maybe not," said the kit, still half asleep. "Maybe I'm thinking of just *being*." She looked up innocently at them. "Don't humans know that? That no matter how ugly things get, it's lovely just to *be*?"

Wilma grinned and took the kit into her lap. "Sometimes humans don't remember that, Kit. Sometimes it takes a little cat to tell them."

Please turn the page
for an early look at
the next Joe Grey mystery

CAT LAUGHING LAST

by

Shirley Rousseau Murphy

Available in hardcover from
William Morrow and Company

2

"Like a colony of pack rats," Joe Grey said. "Such an appetite for other people's possessions, it's enough to make a possum laugh." He turned to look at Dulcie. "Humans are as bad as you, when you steal the neighbors' silk undies.

If a cat could blush, Dulcie's furry face would be red. She didn't like him to laugh at her. But it was true, she'd been driven by a longing for cashmere and silk, for soft, pretty garments since she was a kitten. Such a keen desire that she would slip out of the house in the small hours, and into her neighbors' homes, pressing in through a partially open window or swinging on the knob of a back door left unlocked. Slipping toward the bedroom, she would depart moments later dragging a silk teddy in her teeth or a sheer stocking, or a bright, soft sweater, taking each lovely item home to roll on, to sleep on, to rub her face against. And how else was she to have the lovely garments that she so coveted, except to borrow them? She was a cat. She couldn't indulge in shopping sprees in Lord and Taylor or

I. Magnin's. She only wanted to enjoy those lovely things for a little while before the neighbors came to retrieve them. Well, she had kept Wilma's good watch for over a year, hidden under the claw-footed bathtub.

As the sun rose beyond their leafy treetop, the crowded roofs of Molena Point caught gleams and flashes of light. Shingled roofs and red tile, sharp peaks and slanted were soon all aglow. The time was not yet seven. In the distance a dog barked, an insistent staccato against the soft pounding of the sea. The morning air smelled of pine, and iodine, and of multitudes of small, dead shell-creatures. Out over the Pacific, dawn reflected from the sea like burnished metal. But beyond lay black rain clouds—they might blow away north toward San Francisco or might creep in over the village and rain on the McLearys' sale.

Slow-moving traffic filled the narrow street as new arrivals tried to find parking places, so many eager shoppers that the lane was choked with vehicles. And the lawn was crowded with folks wandering among borrowed church tables piled with toys and clothes and baby garments, with bent silverware, outdated golf clubs, tarnished jewelry, with dented cook pots and old handbags and faded Christmas decorations. Between the tables stood scarred dressers, beds, breakfast tables and toy chests.

Watching folk argue over prices or haul away chairs and tables and broken toys, jamming their newly acquired treasures into cars and SUV's and pickups, watching all the little dramas, Joe and Dulcie, replete with a breakfast of wharf rat and young rabbit, were of much the same frame of mind as a human couple who, after a satisfying supper, had settled down in a front row at the theater to be entertained.

"The McLearys must have cleaned out not only their own attic," Dulcie said, "but the houses of all their cousins and uncles." Indeed, the Molena Point McLearys were a large clan. "An anthropological treasure-trove, an artifactual record of four generations of McLeary family history."

"Four generations of bad taste. A microcosm of useless human consumerism."

She stared at him.

He shrugged his sleek gray shoulders. "Look around you. Abandoned projects, thrown-away intentions, broken dreams, soured ambitions. Relics of human disenchantment."

Easing his position on the branch, he looked at her with tomcat superiority. "You don't see a cat going off on a dozen projects—golf, snooker, Chinese checkers, paint by numbers, needlework, photograph albums. You don't see a cat tossing away one craze after another. Look at the wasted time and effort, to say nothing of the wasted money. And then they have to get rid of it all. And their neighbors grab and snatch, until their own closets are bulging."

"You're in an ugly mood. What happened to live-and-let-live?"

Joe Grey shrugged.

"What you see down there," she told him, "is a lifetime of magnificent intentions. An incredible richness of human endeavor and imagination. You're looking at dreams down there—at the products of creative human energy. At happy, vital, and endlessly diverse moments in McLeary family history."

Joe Grey snorted, his ears and whiskers back in a derisive cat laugh.

She widened her green eyes, but kept her voice low. "I've never seen you so sour. Are things not good at home? What, Clyde's messed-up love life is making you cross? Or," she said, "is Clyde still thinking of selling the house? Is that what's eating you?"

"My mood has nothing to do with the house, or with Clyde's love life. I am not driven by Clyde Damen's vicissitudes. I am simply making an observation about the confusion of the human mind. You don't see a cat throwing out the living room furniture every year and buying all new stuff. Look around you. Why would . . ."

"Cats don't have living room furniture."

"I have an easy chair." His tone was so pompous that they both laughed. Joe's upholstered chair, that sat in the Damen living room by the front window, was so ragged and faded it resembled nothing as much as the hide of an ancient and molting pachyderm. "You don't see me tossing my good chair away at some yard sale."

"If that chair's a prototype of the quality of your life, that clawed-to-rags, fur matted, stained and smelly horror, then you, my dear tomcat, are in trouble."

Joe nudged her playfully; but soon they peered down again, fascinated by the bargain hunters. The locals were dressed in jeans and sweatshirts, some folks freshly scrubbed, some still uncombed as if they'd just rolled out of bed. The conviviality of neighbors brightened the morning with friendly talk and wisecracks. Here and there a weekender wandered, just as eager for a bargain, a tourist dressed in name-brand shorts, starched shirt and Gucci sandals, or golf or tennis attire. Some shoppers carried non-spill coffee mugs that they had brought from their cars. Two were munching on breakfast rolls wrapped in squares of waxed paper that they'd picked up at one of the bakeries on the way over. At events such as this, one saw a true cross section of the village. Besides the rich and comfortable, and the famous, who 'did' the yard sales for a lark, one saw clearly the Molena Point residents who lived on limited funds, people trying to stretch every dollar. The inveterate bargain hunters, rich or poor, showed up at every such event. The cats watched a portly, bleached blonde lady in walking shorts, a blue sweatshirt and red tennis shoes try to fit a six-foot wicker bookcase into a small Jaguar sports car. She had wrapped the bookcase carefully in blankets—whether to protect her ten dollar bargain or protect the hundred thousand dollar Jag wasn't clear.

Nearer to the cats' oak tree, two women stood arguing over a glass-topped patio table that both claimed to have spoken for first. And directly below, a huge-bellied man, stripped to the waist, carried a ruffled, flowered chaise lounge over his head, in the direction of a battered pickup truck. The cats watched a tiny little old lady precariously juggle a glass punch bowl of such proportions that she could have used it for a sitz bath. Maybe that was her plan. Fill it with champagne, and voila, just like the old Harlow movies. The sight of her prompted Dulcie to quote to herself, *When I am old, I will wear purple, and bathe in French champagne*. She caught her breath when the lady nearly dropped her gleaming treasure, and before she thought, Dulcie reached down a paw as if to offer assistance—she drew back quickly, glancing at Joe with embarrassment.

No one looked up to wonder what the cat was doing. No one had seen the two cats in the tree or, if they had seen them, would imagine their conversation, or dream of the thoughts churning through those sleek feline heads. Their human neighbors would never imagine that cats might discuss human frailties—though they might allow that cats didn't give a damn about human foolishness.

Of the residents of Molena Point, only four people knew that Joe Grey and Dulcie could speak, that the two cats read the Molena Point Gazette far more perceptively than some human subscribers, that they liked to frequent the village news racks, perusing the front page of the San Francisco Examiner, and that when there was nothing more interesting at hand, they watched prime time TV. Only four people knew that Joe Grey and Dulcie were not your ordinary, everyday kitties or that they had, during various criminal investigations by Molena Point PD, not only pointed a paw at their share of killers and thieves, supplying critical evidence to convict the miscreants, but that they had spied, as well, on any number of villagers, in the comfort of the villagers' own homes. No one knew that, posing as stray kitties, the two were adept at passing on sensitive information to police detectives. Not even Max Harper's own cops, nor Captain Harper himself, knew the identity of their best informants. Joe Grey and Dulcie were far too smooth to blow their own cover.

But the two cats had other human friends besides the four who shared their secrets. Peering down, they watched three of their favorite senior ladies making their yard sale selections with careful judgment—and with huge dreams. These three women weren't shopping for fun, they were searching out purchases to secure their own futures.

Mavity Flowers, small and sturdy in her threadbare maid's uniform, perused a display of china and crystal about which, through necessity, she had come to know quite a lot. Cora Lee French, a head taller than Mavity, a lovely, slim Creole woman with graying hair, slipped lithely among tables of needlework and linens, touching the stitching with gentle, experienced hands. And tall, blonde Gabrielle Row checked over the clothes that hung on long metal racks, looking not only for resaleable bargains, but for anything useful to the little theater costume department.

Gabrielle was still elegant, despite her nearly sixty-some years. Her short-clipped gray hair was skillfully colored to ash blonde, and the cut of her cream blazer was long and lean over her white slacks. Working full time as seamstress in her own shop, she had for many years been wardrobe director, as well, for Molena Point Little Theater. And now, frequenting the yard sales, she was not only hunting for costume material but was planning, too, for a time when she would be less active.

Five ladies made up the Senior Survival Club. Mavity, Cora Lee and Gabrielle. And Susan Brittain, who was not to be seen this morning, though Susan hardly ever missed a sale. Susan's garage was headquarters for wrapping and shipping the items the ladies sold on the Web. She handled, on her computer, all their eBay sales. The fifth member was Wilma Getz, Dulcie's housemate, retired parole officer, gray haired, in her late fifties. Wilma might be called a silent partner, agreeing with the women's plan, meaning to take part at some future time, but not totally committed.

The ladies were looking toward buying a communal dwelling that would accommodate them all plus a housekeeper and a caregiver when that time arrived. All of them had some savings, or home equity. And the cats were amazed at how much money they had set aside by hitting the yard sales and selling at auction. So far, it amounted to over ten thousand dollars.

Senior Survival's plan for mutual security and comfort, in a world of dwindling incomes, increasing taxes, and the possibility of deteriorating health, seemed to Dulcie infinitely courageous, a bold alternative to the ladies' separate interments in retirement or convalescent homes—a plan of mutual cooperation but individual responsibility. These ladies didn't like conventional institutions.

Slowly the sun slid higher above the hills, slashing through the oak leaves into the cat's faces, making them slit their eyes. Joe's white paws and chest, and the white triangle down his nose, gleamed like snow against his smooth gray fur. As Dulcie backed along the branch, her dark stripes cloaked in shadow, she resembled a small, dark tiger. Only her green eyes caught the light. A breeze fingered into the tree, to rattle the leaves, a chill breath that, by its scent and direction, promised not rain as the marine clouds implied, but a warm day to come. Perhaps only a cat would be aware of the message—how sad that humans, trying to assess the weather, had to read barometers and listen to the questionable advice of some book-educated meteorologist hamming his way through the morning news. Such dependence left one open to innumerable misjudgments in attire—to getting one's head and feet wet; while all a cat had to do was taste the wind and feel in every fiber of his body the changes in barometric pressure.

The sun was returning to stay, no doubt of that. No more tearing March storms with winds wild enough to jerk a cat right out of his own pawprints. Spring was settling in at last, the acacia trees exploding with brilliant yellow blooms that smelled like honey. All the early flowers were opening. Village cats rolled with abandon in the gardens, and the outdoor cafes were filled with locals and tourists—a perfect spring, in the loveliest of villages. Who needed to travel the shores of Britain and France, Dulcie thought, or trek through Spain and Africa. Molena Point was so beautiful this morning that Dulcie's purrs hummed through the branches like bumblebees.

But suddenly an unease touched the cats, a foreboding that made Dulcie stiffen and sent a chill twitching down Joe Grey's spine as sharp as an electrical shock.

They studied the crowd below, puzzled and alarmed, their ears flicking forward and back, every nerve on alert. They were crouched on the branch, wary and keenly predatory, when sirens sounded: a police car leaving the station, they could see beyond the treetops its red whirling beacon heading away through the village, in the same direction where, a quarter hour earlier, an ambulance had departed.

An ambulance, alone, was not uncommon. It could mean severe illness, a heart attack, the agony of a broken hip. A squad car alone could mean anything—a stray child, a driver ramming into a tree. But the two vehicles together, the law and the medics, was inclined to mean trouble.

The cats had crouched to leap away across the roofs to have a look when Joe saw, in the street below, the source of their unease. A growl rose in his throat as a petite young woman stepped out of her black Lincoln. The cats watched Vivi Traynor cross to the McLeary yard, trampling through a flower bed, shoving a child aside as she hurried to the sale tables. She was small and curvy, her black tights, plaid mini-skirt and black sweater clinging, her black hair teased into a bird's nest around her thin face, and held back with a red bow. She looked very out of place as she began to rifle through assemblages of household cast-offs.

The village locals, who had not, before, seen the author's wife at a yard sale, watched her with interest. A portly tourist whipped out a scrap of paper as if to ask for Vivi's autograph. Did the wife of an internationally famous novelist rate the status of autographs? Certainly Vivi always attracted attention. The couple had been in town barely three weeks, Elliott Traynor having come to oversee a little theater production of his only play, an experimental form that the Gazette called innovative and exciting.

Word had it that Elliott was fighting cancer, that this theatrical production was a project he longed to enjoy while he was still able. The play was set in this area of the California coast where Molena Point now stood, and the musical score had been written by a well known composer who made his home in the village. The cats watched Vivi wander the garden intently searching—for what? Perhaps looking for some stage prop for the play? Slipping between a stack of used windows and a flowered couch, she performed a theatrical little hip wiggle to ease past a rusty barbeque, then giggled shrilly as she shouldered aside a portly lady tourist. The sight of her made Joe's fur twitch.

Since their arrival, Elliott Traynor had kept largely to himself as he finished the last chapters of *Twilight Silver*, the third novel in his historical trilogy. But Vivi had made herself known around the village, and not pleasantly—as if she enjoyed being rude to shopkeepers, as if she took pleasure in being abrupt and demanding.

The Traynors had not wanted a staff for the cottage they had rented, but had hired the cleaning service provided by Wilma Getz's redheaded niece, Charlie. Charlie tended the Traynor house herself, early each morning, then left the couple to their privacy.

Molena Point's residents, numbering so many writers and artists, were not put off by Elliott's reclusive ways. They talked among themselves about his books and about the play, waved when occasionally they saw him on the streets or in the black Lincoln, as they headed to the theater; otherwise they left him to his own devices. The presence, alone, of the prestigious writer, seemed adequate enrichment to their well-appointed lives.

But no one warmed to Vivi.

Traynor's first wife had died three years before. Six months later, he married Vivi, a woman thirty years his junior. Besides her loud, rude ways, something else about her made the cats want to back away, hissing, a chill that perhaps only a cat would sense. Whatever reason she had for appearing this morning in the McLeary garden could only, in Joe Grey's opinion, mean trouble.